I0748321

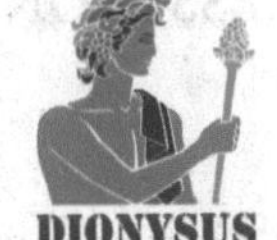

DIONYSUS

First published in 2024 by PRESS DIONYSUS LTD in the UK, 167, Portland Road, N15 4SZ, London.

www.pressdionysus.com

Paperback

ISBN: 978-1-913961-45-9

Windy City
Cafe Bellini

TULAY DUYGULU PIRLANT

DIONYSUS

ISBN- 978-1-913961-45-9

© Press Dionysus 2025

Translated by Melike Sarigül

Press Dionysus LTD, 167, Portland Road, N15 4SZ, London
• e-mail: info@pressdionysus.com
• web: www.pressdionysus.com

ABOUT THE AUTHOR

Tulay Duygulu Pırlant was born in Manisa, Türkiye.

She worked as an English teacher in several high schools. She has also published articles in newspapers and magazines.

She moved to the United States in 1985. Over the course of twenty-five years, she has witnessed many stories, met numerous people, and experienced real-life events that inspired her to write her books.

Her Published Books: *Windy City, (Rüzgarlı Şehir); You Must Be Born Again, (Yeniden Doğmalısın); Until We Meet Again, (Tekrar Buluşuncaya Kadar); Touching Time in the Light of Love, (Sevginin Işığında Zamana Dokunmak); New American Jokes; Anemon.*

Her Screenplays: *Anemon; Comrades of Hope, (Umut Yoldaşları).*

She is also a member of the International Association of Activist Artists.

Inspired by real life events *Windy City* novel draws upon a true story personally witnessed by the author.

The film adaptation of the book Windy City, starring Patrick Muldoon and Nehir Erdoğan, was produced in Hollywood and released as Broken Angel in the US and *Meleğin Sırları* in Türkiye.

She is living in Chicago and İzmir.

Lost Soul

It was an autumn day in the year nineteen ninety. Lake Park Tower was one of the most magnificent buildings on North Sheridan Street which was located on the shores of Lake Michigan. On the thirty-ninth floor of this tower, a young girl was standing like a statue in front of the window, watching the calm clouds before the storm. Lilac, gray and leaden-like clouds were gradually descending from the sky to the huge lake which had the size of the sea, the clouds and the waters were literally fighting each other, which was a movement that resembled a battlefield from a distance. It was a riot of colors. The darkening greyish color of the sky was gradually darkening the clear, beautiful blue of the lake.

The young girl was all alone in the middle of this twilight. She felt that she was slowly being dragged into this war, that her body and soul were slipping away into the cold and dark waters of the lake. Suddenly she came to her senses with startled, as if those icy waters had splashed her face. In fear, she turned her head away.

She began to watch downtown with skyscraper silhouettes that resembled a black-and-white photograph from a distance. The foggy mountains mentioned in the sad folk songs of her hometown were not visible here. Instead, there were skyscrapers, their tops shrouded in smoke. The lights at the ends of two tall poles, rising by piercing a gray cloud bank stuck on the top of the Sears Tower - the tallest building in America - were vaguely blinking. This dream city, which she had previously admired, used to turn into a paradise of light at night and used to take people to virtual worlds, and now it seemed like a nightmare to her.

She really liked the fact that Chicago was called the *Windy City*. Sailboats sailing on the lake on windy days, marine boats, cheeky seagulls on the beach, the willows on the shore of which the clusters would touch the water, giant plane trees with colorful birds perching on them, and skyscrapers symbolizing a rebellious freedom were some of the views she watched with admiration. Why did everything look different now?

Suddenly, a lightning flashed in the sky, followed by thunder. Angry clouds were pouring their electricity into the dark waters. It was as if the waves on the water were coming towards her as white horses of the sea. Could these waves wash away the burden of pain she carried like an invisible hump on her back? Would this deep and dark water take in her disappointments, her lost hopes, her pains, her tears?

Like a ghost, she moved away from the window and started walking towards the foyer. On an impulse, she reached for a jacket and handbag hanging on the coat rack. At that moment, she came across her own face in the mirror. She looked at this pale face, whose hair was messy and whose eyes were dull, as if she were looking at a stranger. Who was this tired young person? Where did she come from, in which direction was she headed?

The image seen in the mirror had neither past, nor future, nor present. This image was in a timeless dimension, unconscious and emotionless. Nothing could make her sad anymore, nothing could make her happy. She couldn't even see the anger that would connect her to life on that face in the mirror.

After putting on her jacket, she took her bag, and went out into the corridor, closing the door on her memories of this house where she had been staying for a while. The corridor seemed very long, dim and silent. Passing by a number of closed doors lined up just like hotel rooms, she somehow heard the sound of music coming from an apartment whose door was open. Without paying any attention, she continued walking and approached the elevator. At that moment, she heard someone shouting from behind:

"Hey, lady, come here!"

An old woman came out of the apartment with an open door that she had just seen, ran up to her and started pulling her arm. She intended to invite her.

"There's a party, there's a party at my place, please join us!"

Suddenly, without realizing what was going on, the young girl found herself in the old woman's house. The living room was decorated with balloons and colored papers. There was food and drinks on the table. There was no one else at the party except two old women, one sitting on a sofa and the other in a wheelchair. Still, the landlady implored her to stay:

"You are such a good girl; you took such good care of my beloved cat when I was in the hospital. I am grateful for your kindness. Please, join our party."

"I'm so sorry, thank you, but I have to go," said the young girl, barely letting herself out. She ran again and found the elevator button. Luckily, it arrived quickly. She was the only one going in there. She began to move her fingers down the elevator buttons. As the number thirteen had come to be known as unlucky, there was neither a floor nor a button with thirteen written on it. She pressed her finger on the button marked with the letter "L" and the elevator began to descend towards the lobby floor.

She was descending thirty-eight floors with her soul and body. When she arrived at the lobby, she encountered a snow-white woman carrying a black baby in her arms, waiting to get into the elevator. The woman said "Hello," to her with a smiling face, but she received no response, even though they had chat with her in the laundry room many times. The woman's husband was black. He would come to the laundry from time to time and help his wife. This cute black baby's blonde curly hair would always attract her focus of interest.

As she walked absent-mindedly through the lobby, she seemed to hear Valli, a Pakistani, seated at the information desk like a general in his burgundy uniform, saying "Assalamu'alaikum," with his usual affection. Valli always greeted her like this, knowing that she was the Muslim daughter of a sister country. However, this time even he could not get an answer, "Alaikumassalam." Without even looking at the familiar faces sitting in the waiting seats, she had already rushed through the revolving door and slipped out like a ghost.

The wind was about to turn into a storm. Suddenly, the coolness of the wind was felt all over her face. The American flag, with its tattered ends, hanging on the pole in front of the building, was blowing left and right as if it was about to be torn apart by the wind. She paused for a moment, looking at the taxi call button on the wall, then gave up. She went down the stairs and crossed North Sheridan Street, ignoring the wind that was chill to the bone. After walking along the sidewalks for a while, she turned right onto Bryn Mawr Street. She was walking among the dust flying in the air, the leaves that were about to dry were hitting her face, but she was walking without paying attention to anything.

Cheap clothing stores, markets, shabby bars, dirty restaurants, barber shops and vegetable shops were still open.

The drunks, vagrants, homeless people and poor people trying to shop on the sidewalks seemed to indicate that this street was a street of poverty. At this hour, walking all alone on this street, a vagrant could grab her bag and run away at any moment. She didn't care about anything anymore. Because she had nothing to lose.

Under the influence of the wind, the smells of alcohol and meat were spread from the restaurants to the streets, and the residents of the neighborhood, most of whom were Mexican, Puerto Rican, Filipino or black, were running around in this gray haze of the air, in a hurry to return home as soon as possible. At that time, a train passed over the upper bridge with screaming sounds. It was as if that train had made the heavens and the earth shake, despite that storm and darkness. Or so it seemed to her. When she first arrived here, she used to enjoy these two-decker trains traveling over the city was a matter of interest for her. However, tonight the trains were like monsters piercing through the night. The monster's voice echoed in her ears for a long time, then, suddenly became identified with her soul. She, too, wanted to scream along with the train. These were the last screams. As the train moved away, her voice became less and less. People rushing towards the stairs on the right side of the road to go to the train station above were bumping into her and apologizing from behind, but she didn't have any feelings. She continued on her way, even if she was stumbling, following the route her instincts took her.

After everything went on like this for a while, she stopped for a moment at the intersection of North Sheridan Street with North Broadway Street. Suddenly distracted and not knowingly what to do, she leaned against corner post, and started to think about getting herself together. The wind was shaking the *North Broadway* sign hanging on the pole with such a creaking sound that it almost fell on the girl's head. Meanwhile, the lightning and thunder evoked her instincts again, and leaving her memories behind step by step, she began walking towards the bus stop on Broadway Street.

When she arrived bus stop, she encountered a group of people. Some were standing, some were sitting on benches. This wretched-looking group showed a naked ugliness on display.

Old and young, women and men, everyone was so down the heels and incoherent that in the twilight they looked like creatures from another world. The fat black woman with curly-white and messy hair, sitting in the middle of the bench, was wearing a dirty jacket and torn trousers. She was waving her cane in the air and swearing at the people around her with a barely understandable black accent. The white man sitting next to her, hunched over, with a distorted face, wearing a cap, picked up a cigarette stub from the floor. The black woman took out a lighter and a few more cigarette stubs from her pocket and gave them to those around her. The old man with a scar on his face, who was standing, looking like a leper, could not light the cigarette stub in his hand because of the wind, so he was shouting and swearing like crazy. Behind this noisy crowd, a young blonde girl was standing against the wall. She looked neater, and although her body was not as deformed as the others, the exhausted and tired expression on her face made it clear that she belonged to the same group.

Whether it was the cold or another reason, an old and dirty sign appeared on the door next to the wall where the shivering young girl was leaning: *Rehabilitation Center*. For a moment, the two young girls made eye contact. At that moment, they were on the same line, perhaps at the same point, in life. At the very same moment, something desperate was being shared silently.

Meanwhile, it started to rain in large drops. The frozen tears of the Turkish girl, who was in the same place at the same time with these lost people, were mixing with the rain and flowing down her cheeks.

They all got on the old public bus that arrived a little later. The group of addicts piled into the back of the bus. There was a bad smell around. They continued to laugh loudly and swear. The fat black driver in the dark blue uniform was warning them through the microphone, saying, "Shut up." There were other passengers on the bus. The Turkish girl was huddled in the single seat in the front. As soon as she sat down, she heard the black driver scolding her in his loud voice: "Hey lady, you did not pay for the ticket. I'm telling you; don't you hear me?

After getting up from her seat and putting a dollar into the ticket box next to the driver, she looked at the people piled up at the back of the bus, defeated in this worldly life, and thought, "Where are we all traveling together?"

The driver was counting the stops one by one in her deep, booming voice: "Kedzie, Halsted, Belmont!" No one had gotten off until that moment. When she said, "North Clark," the only person who got off the bus was that Turkish girl.

It was completely dark, and the rain was getting faster. The streets were empty except for a few people darting around.

She was standing at the bus stop, looking at a restaurant on the opposite corner of the street. The restaurant sign with green and white neon lights read *Cafe Bellini Mediterranean Cousine*. She walked slowly towards that direction. When she arrived at the restaurant door, she looked through the window. The place looked quite crowded this evening.

A cheerful group was seated at a table in front, having their drinks and chatting. Three or four waiters were bringing a cake with birthday candles towards them. Then, an old woman blew out the candles. After they all sang "Happy Birthday" together, the waiters and all the other customers shouted and applauded the old woman.

A Turkish couple owned the place. Their names are Filiz and Metin. The young girl was familiar with them and loved them. Once upon a time, she used to wait at their place. She continued watching the inside but couldn't see the couple anywhere around.

Taking a couple of steps, she headed towards the entrance. She reached out to open the door, but two people inside were trying to get out and they inevitably pushed the Turkish girl aside. Raindrops were falling down her face and hair. The American customers apologized and hold the door for her. To enter or not to enter, the choice she would made now would determine her destiny. She paused for a moment. Instead of going inside, finding people she trusted, and asking them for help, she preferred to give up and walk away. While the pale lights of the skyscrapers spread indistinctly through the fog, she disappeared somewhere in the mysterious darkness of this city. Who would even care about a such small particle in a cosmic city?

Cafe Bellini

In the morning, I was looking out of the upstairs window of Cafe Bellini. It was sparkling out there. No trace left from the rain and storm of the day before. Such sudden weather changes in autumn here were extremely common. Putting on my sneakers and tracksuit, I was getting ready to take my usual walk by the lake.

There was a secret staircase leading from our apartment to the kitchen of the restaurant downstairs. When I came downstairs, Mexican chef Roberto Lopez appeared to have already started his work in the kitchen. As usual, he must have arrived early and must have started the necessary preparations for lunch.

"Good morning, Amigo!"

"Good morning," he replied slowly.

Roberto was a typical Mexican, short, dark-skinned, with a slightly puffy face, and extremely quiet.

"How's it going?"

"Good," he managed with only a few words of English. His nephew Jose Lopez was also working as a dishwasher here. For some reason, "Lopez" last name seems to be very common for Mexicans. Just like most Indians have the surname "Patel". Most Mexicans work illegally in this country. For this reason, they are shy and oppressed people who do all kinds of work cheaply. They cannot learn English properly either. That's why Spanish is a widely spoken language all over America.

"There's fresh coffee."

"Gracias," I thanked him, of course. Actually, we wouldn't mind speaking a few words of Spanish.

"Tea?" he asked in Turkish. (I taught him earlier.)

I said, "okay," and then left.

Even though it's been a year since I moved to the U.S., I still couldn't give up drinking tea instead of coffee for breakfast. I sat at a table by the window to drink my tea. At that moment, the scent of Turkish style tea that Roberto brewed spread like a fragrance and Roberto appeared with a glass of tea in his hand. Dishwasher Jose entered when I was having my tea and immediately started his work. Because I was the wife of the boss and the restaurant manager, they were afraid of me, and when they saw me, they would get into a panic.

Cafe Bellini was located on the bottom floor of a two-storey, old-style brick building on a corner of North Clark Street. My husband Metin and I lived in the apartment upstairs. Cafe Bellini was different from other typical Turkish restaurants in the U.S. Here, unlike the others, there were no carpets, saddlebags, swords, trays, pitchers, barbecues or large stone rosaries hanging on the walls.

The restaurant was on the first floor and consisted of three floor-to-ceiling sections, with the main entrance being the glassed-in section overlooking North Clark Street. Here, on the right side of the entrance, there was an American bar that was also visible from the outside. A striking, antique yellow brass cappuccino machine was placed above the bar. It was left over from the Italians who once owned this place and named it *Cafe Bellini*. My husband did not change the name *Bellini* because he felt a sympathy for the famous painter Bellini's painting of Sultan Mehmet the Conqueror.

There were French-style tables and chairs with white cloths at the front side of the bar. On the tables were small glass vases containing a white, red carnation and green branches, as well as orange candlesticks made of frosted glass. Candles were lit by the waiters immediately after the customers sat down at the table and the wine menu was given. In the right corner of the bar, there was a large flowerpot and an evergreen artificial tree inside. A funny fact about it is that I watered that tree every day for a month until one day waiter Ray told me that the tree was artificial. On the opposite wall, a Fairy Chimneys poster taken from the Turkish Consulate was hanging.

The second hall, being separated from the first part by mirrors, had a dimmer and more romantic atmosphere. There were sconces on the wall. Everywhere was decorated with ornaments specifically related to the sea. There were real or plastic starfish, lobsters and fish hanging from the ceiling on a fishing net stretched. On the walls were wooden carvings and reliefs of ships, captains, pirates and even a ship's wheel. The decorations adorning this section were the work of my husband, Metin. Although he used to say that he was a fisherman's child and came to the U.S. to not become a fisherman, these marine motifs that he placed everywhere with pleasure were like a reflection of his subconscious. From this part, a wide door led to the backyard. In the middle of this inner garden surrounded by walls, which they called *patio*, there was a small pool with a fountain, containing a statue of a child angel, and various colorful flowerpots were lined up around the pool. The pots had various flowers that were renewed every season. The place had a different atmosphere with the trees in front of the walls and the French-style streetlamps with long poles. There were white marbled tables and chairs made of white painted iron. If the weather was nice, this place would always be full. It was a corner that customers enjoyed very much. Because open-air restaurants and cafes are not common in the U.S., as in Mediterranean countries. So, I guess it seemed like an unusual place to them.

In this space consisting of three parts, the human landscapes I have witnessed for a year made me relive similar emotions, joys, pains, searches for hope and disappointments on the other side of the world, but in pretty different ways...

After the tea, I went out. I turned to the next street and started walking towards the lakeside. There was a slight breeze in the air. In five minutes, I was on the shores of Lake Michigan. Actually, I was not here to watch the lake, but the Chicago's gorgeous autumn. Rather than the lake, my eyes were on the riot of colors created by the colorful changes of the autumn trees. I sat on a bench under a weeping willow that was still green. Inhaling the wet soil and grass smell, I felt a light wind caressing my skin. Golden, copper and bronze colored leaves flew in the air and fell to the ground, forming a sun-coloured layer. The leaves of the large tree directly in front of me were a mixture of yellow, red and orange colors. The leaves of the one next to it were somewhere in between yellow and green, and the other one was completely covered in red clothes. The most mysterious one, however, was a very yellow tree next to me, crowned with ember-coloured leaves. It was as if I was in a color paradise created by yellows, reds, claret reds, greens and browns that no painter could capture on his canvas... Autumn's aura took me in. A black man on the beach was feeding the seagulls with the bread in his hand, as he usually did. He was throwing small pieces of bread into the air, and the seagulls were catching them in the air. He must have enjoyed doing this so much that I saw him here quite often.

Young girls, who immediately put on their shorts and t-shirts when the sun came up, were running cheerfully on the jogging path with their Walkmans in their ears, and the boys were riding bicycles around them. Some had preferred skating. As can be seen from his appearance, a middle-aged man from the Far East was doing yoga on the grass with slow movements, giving the place a mystical atmosphere.

Everyone found a way to enjoy this beautiful morning. Even though no one knew each other, they greeted each other and smiled, sharing the happiness of a common beauty.

Breathing in the fresh air, I noticed a red bird landing, without hesitation, behind the bench I was sitting on. I knew this bird. His name was Cardinal. Since it was a bird that mostly belonged to this region, there was always a picture of this crested red bird on the license plates of Illinois cars, as a symbol of the state. But what happened suddenly? The cardinal bird immediately ran away when a naughty squirrel climbing the tree scared it.

These colorful trees, and various people whose names I didn't know created such a beautiful harmony together. Wasn't this the harmony that was longed for on earth? People from all races, all religions, all cultures living together in peace...

Looking at the horizon where the sky and water merged and became one in color, I felt infinity. Wherever we are, we'd still be a part of this process called the universe. As a part of a whole, we exist with this universe forever. The important thing is to be happy during this process, right? Getting lost in such thoughts, a dry autumn leaf that had turned brown fell into my lap from the tree behind me, I took it in my hands and looked at it. It seemed to be emphasizing something in my hands that reminded me of reality. I came to my senses with a barking. An American guy was standing in front of me. A large, black-furred dog that he brought to the park for a walk accompanied him. He politely apologized to me for his dog and told me not to be afraid. He calmed his dog with a few words he used and asked my permission to sit at the other end of the bench.

Americans are generally extremely friendly, approachable and kind people.

"It's such a beautiful day, isn't it?" he began. And I, as always, said:

"Yes, it really is."

Pointing to the black dog wandering around us, he said:

"Buddy is angry today. Because I was late to take him out."

"A nice dog with a nice name."

"I agree. You have a different accent. Where are you from?"

"From Turkey."

"Oh... Interesting. I thought you'd be Polish or Russian."

"Why did you think so?"

"Because you are white and blonde. I always thought that Turks would have dark skin."

"Have you ever met a Turkish person before?"

"No but that is the way we always knew that."

"What else do you know about Turks?"

He talked about the harem, camels, etc. He asked whether we use the Arabic alphabet. I had replied all necessarily, but he suddenly interrupted me as if he remembered something important and said:

"I also saw the movie 'Midnight Express'. I watched the Turks there."

"The actors in that movie were not even Turkish. Apparently, you don't know anything about Türkiye. Please learn about countries and people by researching real facts, not from Hollywood movies, otherwise you will remain ignorant, as your wrong information on the existence of blonde people in Turkey. Good day. Bye bye, Buddy!"

I left there immediately. It was past nine o'clock. The restaurant staff should have arrived by this time. While walking at a trot, I hit the wheelbarrow of a homeless person. This miserable-looking man, with tangled hair and beard, who had filled garbage into the car he had stolen from a market, was drinking from a bottle of alcohol he had hidden in a paper bag. Who knows what kind of story he had? I thought to myself, "Hell in heaven!"

When I returned to the restaurant, our head chef, Ibrahim, aka Toni with his white apron, was trying to explain something to the Amigos in Spanish. Since he loved chattering, he immediately started talking when he saw me:

"Sis, I made pancakes, would you like to have one?"

"That would be great, I didn't have my breakfast anyway. I would appreciate it if you could also bring me an orange juice."

Soon, he ended up there with the pancakes and sat across me.

"What about my bro, Metin? Is he coming today or tomorrow?"

"He's coming this evening, is something wrong?"

"Yes, the building manager at Bryn Mawr called and said the roof leaked in yesterday's rain."

"Which side of the roof?"

"The Korean's clothing shop was under the leak. They put buckets everywhere. He said that unless you repair it immediately, he wouldn't pay the rent."

"How on earth did you understand the English of a Puerto Rican manager?"

"Same way he understood my Turkish English."

We laughed...

"Thankfully, it's not raining today. Metin will sort it out when he comes tomorrow. Without him, everything is very difficult. Whenever he is on a business trip, something always goes wrong. By the way, can you bring me the check from yesterday? I couldn't look at it because it was late."

Toni's face turned slightly sour. Before I arrived, Metin wasn't doing the restaurant's account checks seriously because he was busy with his other work. I guess he was balancing it the way he wanted. Apparently, he didn't like the fact that I was handling this. He brought all the receipts, cash and checks and put them in front of me. While I was doing the calculations, he was sipping his coffee reluctantly.

İbrahim was from Antalya. According to a memory he shared, five or six years ago, while he was doing his military service in Turkey, a military ship was going to New York. Due to his ignorance, he did not know why this ship was going there. He just heard that a folklore show was going to be held there. He managed to get himself on board by saying, "I can dance Silifke's Yoghurt very well, and I am also a very good cook." With his short stature, dark eyebrows, dark eyes and slightly bulging face, those who first see him would guess that he is Mexican. When I would tease him from time to time, "Show me how you dance Silifke's Yoghurt," he would immediately run to the kitchen, grab the wooden spoons and start dancing in front of us. He would entertain us too. Anyways, Private Ibrahim cooked delicious meals along the route, and when the ship arrived in New York, he performed Silifke's Yoghurt. Then, he found an opportunity to escape from the ship and meet up with a Turkish acquaintance he had arranged beforehand. After getting lost there and working as a cook in Turkish restaurants for a few years, he somehow ended up in Chicago. Here, he learned his job thoroughly by working in an Italian restaurant for years. If only it were a little cleaner, the food would be much better. Only a few people knew that he was a deserter. Metin used to say, "If they catch you, you might even be executed," which would make him pretty scared. On the other hand, he was longing for his hometown that he couldn't make a visit for years, by saying, "If they don't execute me, I am willing to do military service for two or even three years. As long as they allow me to enter Turkey, I can go to my village, see my mother, get married and have children..." He was obviously sorry.

After I was done with the calculations, I moved on to a topic that would attract his attention:

"Has Elizabeth arrived yet?"

"She might be here any minute."

"Well, Toni, I sense some sort of a relationship between you and this lady. Do I sense right?"

"No, sis, she is snuggling but I don't give myself in."

"As far as I know, you have known each other for three or four years, and you are the one who hired her. Well, she's not bad either, why don't you want to?

"I hired her here because she was such a good waiter. You see the way she works."

While having this conversation, Elizabeth entered through the door. She was a sympathetic woman with her light blonde, straight, short-cut hair, white skin, and plumpy body. She said, "Good morning," and took off her jacket. She was wearing his Cafe Bellini uniform, black trousers and a white shirt. She had never mentioned her age before. She looked like in between her thirties and forties. She had arrived from Poland ten years ago, now she was living alone in an apartment and earning her living as a waitress. As much as she was hard-working, she was also an extreme miser. Whether it was due to the influence of the regime in the country she came from, she would work tirelessly day and night and would not spend her money easily. Toni said she had over twenty thousand dollars in the bank. The other waiters didn't like her very much because they saw how she was trying to get more tables. Elizabeth would sometimes rattle for a dollar. I used to say to our lazy Turkish waiters, "Look how Elizabeth works; she straightens the chairs, washes the drinking glasses, creates a job for herself even when she is idle, look up to her." Give credit where credit is due. In any case, customers were happy with her.

Elizabeth, as usual, made herself a hot chocolate and came along us. Her skin seemed pinky. Apparently, she had made a visit to that tanning booth again. While she would prefer to wear the cheapest shoes on her feet, she would not hesitate to spend money for tanning. I guess she thought she was more beautiful with such tanned skin and could get a boyfriend. Her biggest problem was loneliness. Her entire family was in Poland. She never told us how or why she came here. I didn't even know if she had a green card or not. I never asked.

After telling me how nice the weather was while drinking her hot chocolate, she asked me the same question:

"When is your husband coming? It's been a while since he has been gone, right?"

For some reason, her face always turned red when she talked about Metin. I thought she was secretly in love with her boss. In reality, Elizabeth and Toni were not happy with my presence. They were trying to get along with me, thinking they had no other choice.

"He is coming tonight. I see that your face has brightened, is it because you have made a new friend?" They both looked at each other.

"No dear, I just went to the solarium…"

"You'd be more beautiful if you lost some weight," Toni added mischievously.

When I got up to go upstairs, Elizabeth began to replace the flowers in the vases with fresh ones. Toni also returned to the kitchen.

After taking a shower and writing a letter to a teacher friend of mine in Turkey, I went downstairs again. Only four or five tables were occupied. In general, lunch was not a meal from which one would expect much profit. Dinners with alcohol in the evenings would bring more money. Waiters also received more tips. The restaurant business is a truly profitable and enjoyable business if taken seriously. For us, this place was nothing more than a fun place where we slept upstairs, ate downstairs and become together with our friends and colleagues. Because Metin's main job here was real estate. For me, who spent years as a limited civil servant among students, this place was like an arena that opened new horizons in my thoughts.

When our other waiter, the Turkish boy Umut, saw me, he opened his book on the bar and said,

"Hello ma'am, could you please check these exercises? There is a homework assignment that needs to be completed for the course tonight."

He was the only person who called me "ma'am" here. No one was aware that I used to teach once.

"Let me see."

Umut was an eighteen-year-old young man who had just graduated from high school. He came here to pursue higher education with the help of a relative. Even though he came here, with a thousand dollars a month in school fees, five hundred dollars in rent, food, drink and transportation expenses, he won't be able to sort it out. For now, he's just trying to learn English in a free course he found. Of course, like many illegal Turks, he could only work in our restaurant. Even though it wasn't that long ago that he came to Chicago, he adapted quickly, but a university education seemed like a dream for him for now. He could only survive on average of two hundred dollars a week he earned from here.

"Ma'am, it's very nice out there. "If you wish, you can have a seat in the garden, and I'll bring your lunch there."

"Good idea, I'll have meatballs, bread and salad then."

On my way to the garden with my book, I saw the couple of Swedish origin, whom I had always admired, sitting in the corner. We knew the regulars here. Just like a family, we share feelings, sometimes we are happy and sometimes sad with them. This middle-aged, short-haired, woman with sports outfit and this bearded, intellectual-looking man of the same age would come several times a week, look into each other's eyes, hold each other's hands, and sip their wine while continuing an endless conversation.

I saluted them and asked how they were. It was also the usual thing to ask if everything was going well. They said they were happy with everything. Customers came here not only to eat, but also to be in a friendly, warm environment, to chat and to relax. Here, they could easily say what they did not like, and they knew that the necessary thing would be done immediately. There was only one person we could never please. Bearded Jew Sherven. Even though he had several conflicts with everyone, including me, he would not stop coming here again and again. He would get angry if the food was late, complain that it was not cooked well, criticize the tomatoes in the salad, so he would definitely find a reason to be upset. He would always, "ask for the manager," and I would promise that everything would be fixed the way he wanted. He often brought his friends along. After all, he was a good customer. He loved chatting with Metin. One day, I remember it like yesterday, he was shouting at the waiters again. I, as the manager, went next to him and asked what the problem was, he said, "The soup was too hot, my mouth burned, I will sue you!" I honestly gave up at that moment, this was the first time I heard something like this. "If you want cold soup, you can go and have it somewhere else!" I said. Oh my, he got so angry. He slammed his hand on the table and said, "I never liked you anyway. You don't know this business, I will tell Metin to fire you." I said, "I'm sorry, but he can't fire me because I'm his wife," and to this surprise, he left the restaurant immediately. When I told Metin that we had lost a good customer, he told me not to worry, that he would come back anyway after being upset for a while. And so, he did.

Umut brought me my sandwich prepared with a few large meatballs, chopped lettuce and tomatoes in a warm pita. He also made me a foamy, iced ayran to go with it. While I was drinking my ayran, the Swedish lady was curious about the white drink. I told her that it is called *ayran* in Turkish and is made from yoghurt. To satisfy their curiosity, I told Umut to offer them ayran too.

Soon, when ayran arrived, I asked them to try. I could tell from their faces that they didn't like it very much. Oh, if only those foreigners could learn the palatal delight of the Turkish people... Thank God, we managed to make them love meatballs, stuffed vine leaves, shish kebab, eggplant salad and baklava in this restaurant. They also drink Turkish coffee and Turkish raki occasionally. In addition to these, under the Mediterranean cuisine, there are Italian dishes worthy of the name, Mediterranean goulash, chicken cocotore, as well as Middle Eastern dishes such as hummus, baba ghanoush and falafel, as well as fish varieties, shrimp, frog legs, as being one of the most expensive dishes, are served on large plates for them. It was offered in abundance. Salad, soup, water and bread are offered free. People here don't get fed up easily. You would want to make them stuffed like a turkey so that they will come back.

You know what they say, "Speak of the devil and he is sure to appear." As I got up and went inside to smoke, who should I meet? Mr. Sherven! I passed by without even looking at him.

Umut was running a brush through his hair in the mirror. One of his most important characteristics was that he compared himself to Richard Gere. He would stick his hair back with gel and pose as Richard Gere in the mirror. I caught him again.

"Umut, haven't I asked you not to do this in front of customers before?"

"You're right," he said in a shy manner.

I said, "Come here, let me show you the mistakes in your homework," and then the phone rang.

"I'll answer, you please go to the garden and take care of that grumpy Sherven," I said. The caller was Ms. Özge from the Turkish Consulate.

"Hello, my dear Filiz, I am Özge."

"Hello, Ms. Özge, how are you? Did you call in for a reservation?

"No, no, we can't come this week. I called you about something else, thinking you might be able to help..."

"Sure, if there's anything I can do, I'll be happy to do it. What's it about?"

"Do you know someone named Ebru Erdem? I think she worked at your place for a while."

"Yes, of course I know her. She was a slim, pretty girl. And also, quite sensitive. So, what happened to her?"

"That's what we're trying to find about. The girl's family called from Turkey. They haven't been able to hear from her for three or four months. No letter, no phone call. They tried every way to reach her, but to no avail. Finally, they called us through the Consulate and asked if we could find her. I promised to investigate. They were very curious. Do you know where she might be now, or anything related to her address and etc.?

"I swear, I don't know where she is right now. It's been a long time since she left us."

"Alright, if you learn anything, please let me know. Her parents are devastated."

"Of course. I'll start researching immediately. I will ask the Turks who stop by here. If I get even the slightest information, I will definitely let you know. I hope she will be found."

Since I had witnessed similar situations before, I did not pay much attention to this incident at first. Metin was once one of those wanted by the consulate. When he first came, he was so caught up in work that he couldn't find a minute to call his family for three months. The second reason was that phone charges were expensive. He would sometimes say this jokingly.

How could I have known at that moment, while I was sitting in a corner enjoying a cigarette and coffee, what horrifying events I would witness!

Ebru

A week had passed. Even though I didn't take it seriously at first, Ebru Erdem was on my mind from time to time. I even asked the Turks who came to the restaurant during this period. Some said that they did not know her, others said that they remembered her beauty but did not know where she was. I felt like I needed to approach this job more seriously. Poor girl, like many others who would get caught up in the American dream, she set out with little belongings in her suitcase and many hopes in her heart. I hope nothing bad happened to her.

I remembered the day she first came to us last year. My kind friend Zeynep brought her here. It was an ordinary day at Cafe Bellini. My husband Metin and I were sitting at a table, drinking our tea and talking about the new building we were planning to buy. It was a boring afternoon. At that moment, the restaurant door had opened, and two women came in. One of them was none other than Zeynep, whom I have known since the first days I arrived. My friend Zeynep and I had a lot in common. She would come by here from time to time and we would chatter. However, we did not know the thin, pale-faced young girl next to her, and we had seen her for the first time. After saying "Welcome," we invited them to our table. Zeynep introduced this shy young girl to us as "Ebru". We kind of sensed that she was here to ask for a job. As soon as I asked how she was doing, Zeynep said that Ebru was a student, who currently was on a break from school due to financial reasons, and that she needed a job. The young girl resembled Mona Lisa with her middle-parted brunette hair reaching to her waist, sad eyes, clear white skin and slightly smiling figure. There was such an innocent, such an embarrassed expression on this face that it was impossible not to feel compassion for her.

"Where are you from?" I asked.

"I'm from Izmir," she said in a low voice.

"What a coincidence. I also came from Izmir. Where are you from in Izmir?" I wanted to make her talk a little.

"From Bornova. And you?"

"Karşıyaka, we are like fellow citizens. How long have you been here?"

"It's been a year."

This time, Metin jumped in:

"Where are you studying?"

"I finished ELS[1]."

When the girl did not say much, Zeynep tried to explain the situation in a nutshell:

"As you know, students from abroad have to pay tons of money for the F-1 visa to the school. Ebru graduated from this school with the help of her family. Now, she wants to go to college, both because she wants to make a career and to stay in America legally. But she has to work to pay for school. No one is hiring her because she doesn't have a green card. She will be very pleased if you give her a job as a waitress here."

"In truth, we don't need any waitress right now," Metin said bluntly.

I saw the tears that did not flow from the young girl's violet eyes. I felt sorry for her. Meanwhile, Umut had put Sezen Aksu's cassette on the tape recorder. "Don't you cry, I can't bear that, I can't bear your tears," Sezen was saying in her touching voice. As

---

1 A school that gives English lessons for foreigners.

Umut came towards us with a tea tray in his hand like an artist, after saying welcome, he turned to the young girl and said, "I'm Umut, remember me?" Ebru, slowly raising her head, said, "Yes, we met when I came to have a dinner with friends." Umut, who did not want to leave us, asked if we needed anything else. They said they were not hungry. Still, I asked Umut to bring some baklava. Umut, who was obviously fond of the girl, was circling around us like a rooster. After harsh looks of Metin, he headed straight to the kitchen. I said to Ebru, who was distracted by Sezen's song, staring into space, "My dear, you better fill out a form anyway. Umut will bring one. We will contact you when in need," and her eyes suddenly sparkled, making her innocent smile appear.

"Thank you."

"How can we reach you? Where do you live? Please write down your address and phone number." There was a moment of silence. Zeynep had to answer this question.

"She's staying with me for now. I can let her know."

Since she had no place to stay, the situation was even worse! After Umut brought the baklava and said:

"Metin, bro, there is a phone call for you."

Metin said, "See you later," to them and left the table. Taking this as an opportunity, Umut turned to Ebru and said:

"Do you like Sezen Aksu?"

"Yes, I love her" Ebru replied.

"Me too. This next song of her is also very nice, the one that is called 'Come back, come back.'" I reluctantly interrupted Umut's conversation and told him to bring a form. Umut was happy. As soon as he left us, I turned to Ebru and said,

"My dear, you better come here tomorrow morning at nine o'clock. We'll have a chat about the work in here. I'll arrange something for you for now. Many people leave here anyway. You can start learning now. Have you ever waitressed?"

"No, but I am a quick learner. "Thank you very much, I will not forget your kindness," she replied.

"Initially, you can just serve coffee or water. You can clean the tables. In time, you'll learn waitressing and perhaps, you'll even start preparing drinks. Other waiters will give you a training that'll last a week. If you can do the job well, you will make good money. We'll talk about wages and working hours."

I could see that Zeynep was very pleased with these words. At least I didn't disappoint her.

"Thank you, my dear Filiz. I had no doubt that you would do this favor. I'm busy tomorrow, but Ebru will hop on a bus and come."

Zeynep is a busy kind of person. Her genie-like black eyes are a symbol of her courage and initiative. She grew up in Adana and completed her higher education in Ankara, was extremely fluent in English. She would translate the official documents of most of the Turks here. Zeynep, who never gave up on working and was not yet over her twenties, was one of those struggling to survive here alone. One could say that there was no job in Chicago that she didn't work at. Currently, she is the manager of a limousine company that is owned by Turkish people. When necessary, you could see her wearing the uniform and even driving a limousine. You could spot her at all kinds of events. Once, she wore a mustache and dressed as a man in the folklore team she formed with Toni. Her biggest characteristic was that she helped others more than herself. We always criticized this aspect of her.

Common things such as the fact that we studied at the same school in Ankara, albeit at different times, brought us closer. I have always considered her an honest and reliable friend. Especially if you are in a foreign country, the value of such friendships cannot be measured by anything. Now, she was trying to help this girl found from who knows where. We would soon learn the story of Ebru, who did not even have a place to stay.

The street door reopened, and this time, a gaudily dressed Arab Girl and her boyfriend, a couple of our regular customers, entered. After waving at us, they sat at the most secluded table in the middle, as usual. The Arab Girl's clothes and jewelry emphasized her wealth. This time, she had her dark black hair tied up in a bun and was being flirtatious with the dark-haired young man with a black moustache and laughing in a sassy manner. Suddenly, Arabic music was heard. Ebru lamented:

"I wish he had continued playing Sezen Aksu."

I immediately called out to Umut. I asked him to continue with Sezen's cassette. Umut, who came to us with the form in his hand:

"Ma'am, what was is that you used to say to me? You know, the one about if an American comes, we would play English, if a Turk would come, it'd be Turkish, and for Greeks, we would play Greek music. Now the Arabs came, so I put Arab music." We all started laughing.

"Yes, I said that, but now you do as I say."

"Okay, ma'am. Will our friend work here? I can help her if you want."

I said, "We'll talk later," to send him away. Later, Zeynep said she had things to do and took Ebru with her. This is the memory of Ebru's visit to the restaurant that I remember like yesterday.

The next day, Ebru was at Cafe Bellini at the time I said. Despite Metin's objection, I initially started her working three days a week. Within a few weeks, with Umut's help, she had already learned to make cocktails and to carry three or four plates in her hands and arms, although not five or six at once like Elizabeth. Of course, Umut was the one who was most pleased with her arrival. In short, she worked for us for about three or four months. During this time, we got to know her better, loved her and worried about her. After all, like many adventurous young people we encountered here, she too had come and gone. Maybe we thought so, because now she was on the agenda again. The best thing to do seemed to me calling Zeynep, maybe she would know something. Hopefully she's in the Limo office right now. I was lucky. Zeynep was there. I briefly told her that Ebru Erdem's family was looking for her and if she knew where she was, she should tell them immediately. She said he didn't know where she was right now, but if she could stop by the restaurant sometime this evening, we could talk in detail. Talking to her for longer would be too optimistic for such a busy person. I was going to look forward to it this evening. She would definitely catch a clue that would lead us to Ebru.

It was Friday. We were usually full-on Friday, Saturday and even Sunday evenings because it was end of the week. Americans do not like to stay at home on weekends. Since their biggest pleasure is eating at good restaurants, restaurant owners attach great importance to weekends. Reservations are made in groups for celebrations. In addition to customers, we also have friends who come to Cafe Bellini to be with us. In fact, I know sometimes on nights when they outnumber other customers. That day, as usual, our best waiters, first, Ray, then Elizabeth, brother Cemil, Umut and their assistants were ready in full force in their black and white uniforms. They all had special customers. Regular customers, if they were satisfied with anyone, would always ask that person to serve them and leave a good tip. Because service is as important to Americans as good food. I noticed that Elizabeth once gave free champagne to her client as a favor. Other waiters also noticed and immediately informed me. Establishment treat is something that only the restaurant owners can give. I spoiled her badly that day. Even though she apologized, I felt like I could hear her swearing from inside.

Although it was only three o'clock in the afternoon, Peter had already taken his place in the mirrored corner, sipping his Remi Martin cognac as usual. The real name of Peter the Greek was Petro. He was a gentleman around forty or forty-five years old, with slicked-back hair and clean and quality clothing. Seeing him for the first time, one would think he is a wealthy and cultured businessman. You could have a chat with him about anything, and he would even give you good advice. If there is only one person he does not give advice to, it is himself. However, he has never accomplished anything other than producing words.

He hasn't even been able to get married and start a family so far. Supposedly, he is working as a traveling jeweler these days with a big bag in his hands. The rings and bracelets he sold as real gold and which I bought were all tarnished. When he is in financial trouble, he gets help from his two brothers, one of whom is a candle maker and the other is an antiquary. Since he is not listened to by his brothers, he hangs out here almost every day and finds people who will listen to him. He is one of Metin's best friends. As far as I can see, the people that Turks find closest to them are Greeks and Armenians. There is a Greek Taverna located just ahead of Cafe Bellini. We have been there a couple of times with our Greek friends. The dishes that felt pretty familiar, such as döner, kebab, music that we are familiar with, dances and friendly people made me feel like I was in Turkey. After drinking Ouzo raki, accompanied by dishes such as dolma, moussaka and baklava, which have similar or even identical names, although it is not clear whether the Turks learned them from the Greeks or the Greeks learned them from the Turks, we danced *halay*[2] together to the rhythm of *Aman Adanalı, canım Adanalı* played by the orchestra.

This must be one of those interesting aspects of America. The people living here from nations that were considered enemies in history do not adopt hostile attitudes towards each other, with a few exceptions only. A Palestinian and an Israeli, an Englishman and an Irishman, a Turk and a Greek can be very good friends. When such an issue would be brought up, the most common comment would be that hostilities are created by politicians and people love each other.

As for America, everyone who is successful and follows the rules of this country is welcomed here. Unlike in some European countries, there are no mass discriminations such as Turks are like third-class citizens. Individual evaluations always exist. For example, if you are a proven businessman, banks can give you

---

2 Halay is a traditional folk dance originating from Turkey and commonly performed in various regions of the country, especially in Eastern and Southeastern Anatolia.

millions of dollars in loans, regardless of your nationality. There is no need for an uncle to stand behind you.

I saw that Elizabeth was standing over Peter. Ready to bring a second glass of cognac. Because Peter was a well-mannered gentleman and tipped very well. Money-loving Elizabeth would not lose this client to anyone. I went over to them and asked Peter how he was doing. I noticed relief on his face when I told him that Metin had gone to the bank and would be back soon, because he was talking to Elizabeth as he could not find anyone else to listen to him. He would occasionally meet his girlfriend Adrianne here and have dinner. Speaking of which, I asked:

"How is Adrianne? Will she be visiting us today?

"Yes, I think she will come after work." He seemed to have a bit of a wry face as he said this. I couldn't help but ask:

"What is it? Is something bothering you?"

"It's become tasteless with Adrianne lately."

Adrianne was a lovely American lady of thirty-nine or forty years of age. From my one-on-one conversations with her, I understood that she was truly in love with Peter. Rather than getting married, her wish was to have a child with Peter.

"Sorry to hear that, I hope you can solve your problems."

"I don't think so, it's impossible for me to accept her wishes, I'm getting bored of this." In order not to bore him further, I changed the subject:

"How is your mom?"

His eighty-year-old mother was staying at his older brother Dimitri's house with his wife and children. Dimitri had a decent family life with his wife and children. His wife worked at the Greek Consulate. They often invited us to their place. His house, just like his shop, was full of antiques, including the old piano that Metin had given him, standing at a corner. They were raising their children according to Greek traditions. Since Dimitri's wife worked at the consulate, there were times when she would feel uneasy, even if she did not show it, because of her friendship with us. Once, according to the news, relations between Türkiye and Greece were really tense. At that time, the Dimitris were going to have an Easter party at their home. We were usually the only Turkish family invited to such parties. Since the atmosphere between the two countries was heavy, they probably did not want us to be there at that party, fearing that we would draw attention. He politely explained to us that it would not be appropriate as he would invite Greek diplomats.

Dimitris lived in a big house outside the city. One day, while visiting them, we met Peter's mother. She was happy to hear that we were from Turkey. Because, after all, there was a childhood and youth period that she spent in Turkey. She lived somewhere near Aydın. The places where a person spends her childhood have a very important place in her life, even her not being aware of it. This old lady would talk about the places she lived in Turkey, her Turkish friends, her neighbors, and like all old people, she would prefer to talk about the past, not the future. When she was telling her memories, her eyes would wander as if she were reliving those days. Aside from Turkish words she remembered, she would sing this folk song to us every time we made a visit: "*Sigaramın dumanı, yoktur yarin imanı...*"[3] When I asked her, "What should I bring you from Turkey?" she said, "I miss everything about there, but I miss the figs the most." I brought her a box of dried figs. Even though she mentioned in passing that it was the Turks who slaughtered her grandfather or her father, she said, "Everything happens in war," as she did not want to spoil her good memories. She would have been very pleased with our visits. I heard she has been a little ill lately.

"My mother is a little unwell," replied Peter, adding, "She is an old-timer, nothing will happen to her, she is just resting." I said jokingly, "That is right, after all, she lived in Turkish lands and is of course healthy." Just as I realized that he was preparing an answer to my words, Metin appeared at the door. He imme-

---

3 "The smoke of my cigarette, my beloved has no faith..."

diately sat at his dear friend's table. Peter was going to hold him captive for hours, as if a stork's life was to be spent in chatter. I found this annoying from time to time.

It was late afternoon; customers were slowly starting to fill the restaurant. Since this was not a fast-food restaurant, there would be people sitting for hours just drinking. I kept my eyes on the door, because I was looking forward to Zeynep's arrival. I had a feeling like we were going to find a clue. While I was thinking that I should go out to the backyard and smoke to pass the time, Cemil called me to the phone. I said, "I hope it's okay," and ran. The caller was Ms. Özge again from the consulate. After asking whether I learned anything about Ebru, she said in an urgent manner that Ebru Erdem's parents were going to come to Chicago next week to look for their daughter. She asked us to take care of them.

I told her that we would do our best. Then, I explained the situation to Metin and in an undertone and he said: "Man, they are making a big deal about this. Stuff like this happens all the time. She must have got a new boyfriend and moved away. It will come to light anyway, what's the point in making a fuss."

"Don't say that. It's been four months since they haven't heard from her. Can you imagine the situation of her parents?"

"When I first came here, I didn't contact my family for three months. In the same way, they also applied to the consulate. Ms. Özge will remember, she had found me right away."

"It's not the same thing. She is a girl. You remember Ebru, what an innocent and fragile young girl she was."

There was an absolute silence. As someone familiar with Chicago, Metin seemed to sense the gravity of the situation. Peter was dying to find out what we were talking about so passionately.

"Did something bad happen?"

I said, "Metin will tell you," and left. To be honest, I was not in the mood to listen to his long philosophical and sociological comments on this subject.

I went out to the backyard. A chaos there too! Umut was apologizing to a woman in a white dress at the table with a group of people. I thought to myself, "Oops!" Did he spill the hot coffee on her as happened before or what? Umut's accidents like this out of surprise were common when he'd get excited. Once, he spilled hot tea on the crotch of Dr. Yılmaz and once on the crotch of a singer lady who had come to give a concert in Chicago with İbrahim Tatlıses.[4] The poor lady had to go to her hotel and change. I examined the woman who had stood up, luckily there was no such trace. So, what was the reason for this argument? Umut, in Turkish, said:

"I was just about to call you. Apparently, that lady in the white dress is going to sue us."

"Oh, why is that?"

"She said that her white dress became dusty because of our dusty chairs."

Actually, we prefer not to speak any Turkish in front of customers. But we were surprised to encounter an absurd situation like this. When the woman heard that I was the manager, she started shouting at me. The part of her dress where she sat on chair was slightly dusty. Maybe, it could be even shaken off easily. But she kept saying that she would sue us because it served her purpose. An idea came to my mind to solve this problem as quickly as possible. I offered her the ten dollars for dry cleaning. She rejected the offer. Then I offered a twenty, and we had an agreement. I saw that the atmosphere was tense here too, so I decided to go upstairs and have some rest.

---

4 İbrahim Tatlıses is a famous Turkish singer, actor, and businessman, known for his powerful voice and contributions to Turkish arabesque and folk music.

Friends and Customers

After having rest for about an hour and tidying up a bit, I went downstairs again. The restaurant was full. Almost all of our friends were here this evening, as if by agreement.

Everybody was there! Our Turkish Jewish friend Moşe and his elegant wife Miranda, the successful Turkish doctor Mr. Yılmaz and his wife Mrs. Serap were sharing the same table. It was obvious that they were waiting for us. In another corner, elderly lawyer Bernie Freed and his wife, Joan, were trying to finish the huge salmon on their plate and clinking glasses of red wine. At the table in front were sitting the President of the Turkish American Association, Mr. Kemal and his American wife Karen. There were six other people with them. It was clear from their heated conversations that they had intensified the raki conversation considerably.

At the small table in front of the bar, Peter was talking loudly to his girlfriend, Adrianne. I think they were having some kind of an argument. It looked like it was going to break loose soon.

I was standing in front of the kitchen door, staring at the tables one by one. Among the crowd, at the bottom, in a dimly lit corner, Mrs. Hülya, whose husband passed away a few months ago, caught my attention with her American lawyer. They were drinking Turkish raki and chatting together. The young woman, who was said to have suffered a lot from her late husband, looked very happy and free with her stylish clothing and laughter. Next to them, gentleman Mark and his boyfriend William, one of our *gay* customers who would hang out here all the time, were having their cheerful conversation with a Bloody Mary, as usual.

There were also people of different nationalities at other tables. For a moment, I thought that food could not be the only factor that gathered these people from so many different backgrounds together under this roof. I thought for a moment. There are hundreds of restaurants in this city that serve much better food than us. Maybe there was a reason why they came from far away places to sit at these cramped tables of such a huge town, something that even they had never thought about. Whether customer or friend, almost everyone who came here knew each other. Especially on weekends, after working for a week, it must have been instinctual to choose to take shelter in a hole and be in a warm environment rather than getting lost in a sea.

Since we were considered the host, I was supposed to go from table to table and ask how everyone was doing. I couldn't decide where to start first.

I started with the ones closest to me, Bernie and Joan. Both of them were Metin's old friends. They got up and kissed me, with their usual close and sincere sentiments.

Bernie, of Jewish origin, was over eighty and was a well-known lawyer in Chicago. He was also doing real estate. Over time, his business relations with Metin turned into friendship. Although Metin was young, his friends were always over their forties or fifties. Hiding his inner child somewhere, he would get along well with them with a maturity not expected from his age. Because, in America, the age difference issue is not as important as in Turkey. Even if they are eighty years old, people are addressed only by their first names. As in Turkey, there is no need for qualifications such as father, brother, sister to address someone. When I said,

"Bernie, you look so good tonight, cheerful and healthy!" he asked,

"You look very pretty too. Where is Metin?"

"He must be around, he'll be here any minute now." Joan, who was much younger than him and also served as Bernie's secretary, with her short, cropped gray hair, always checked on

Bernie, taking care of him like a father. Bernie had already divorced his first wife for her. Joan asked me to sit next to her and said she would tell me about her recent trip to Israel. She took out a hand-painted bowl from her bag that she had bought for me in Jerusalem. She would bring small things from wherever she went.

As a husband and wife, they were both hard-working people who were equally devoted to life and lived it to the fullest. They didn't wait to sit in a corner and die because they were old, they wanted to live life to the fullest until to the the last moment.

Last year, on Bernie's eightieth birthday, they threw a big party at their house. Since the concept of family is quite valuable for them, at the party were his daughter, son-in-law, grandchildren from New York, his son and family from Seattle, and even relatives from Israel. Metin and I were the only Turkish people among the crowded guest list of the Bernie family, people with a good network in Chicago. Everything was organized by a party planner. In the living rooms and rooms of their large houses, round tables with white tablecloths, silver cutlery, candles, flowers and precious China plates were placed with great care and taste. Bernie Freed and his family were very wealthy. A wide variety of dishes, drinks, desserts and fruits were served. After Bernie blew out the candles on his eight-candle cake and cut the cake, songs were sung, and dances were performed to the accompaniment of Jewish music.

Bernie, who was playing with the white napkin tucked into his wife's collar to keep the food from spilling on herself, was very happy about this festivity. He took care of each guest individually. At one point, he came to us and said, his wrinkled, squinty eyes, still sparkling, "I want to live longer, I want to see what the world will be in the future, and I even want to study economics." Just as he loved every aspect of life, he also adored young and beautiful women. When he came to Cafe Bellini, he wanted the most beautiful waitresses to serve him. For a while, Ebru was his favorite. He didn't like Elizabeth. One day, he was gushing over Ebru again. He was telling her that she resembled

Mona Lisa a lot and that he would have a portrait of Ebru by a painter friend. His wife would never find him strange in this sense and would not get jealous at all. On the night of the party, all the rooms at their place were open. I felt a special kind of pleasure every time I visited their house, which looked like a museum of musical instruments. As a husband and wife, they both loved traveling. They had traveled many parts of the world many times. One of the places they liked the most was Istanbul, which they would visit every three or four years. Since it became a hobby to buy special musical instruments from every country they visited, they would show us the saz and qanun they bought in Istanbul, displayed on a console, every time visited their place. They would ask us to play these instruments a little, but unfortunately, we did not know how. Moreover, they could not stop praising the opera and ballet they watched every time they went to Istanbul. Even though they met us later, they were true Turkish friends and admirers.

Bernie suddenly asked, as if he felt it in his bones, "When will that beautiful young girl, Abby (Ebru), arrive?"

I never mentioned her disappearance so as not to spoil their joy. I just said I didn't know. Then I asked for permission and left.

Meanwhile, Metin, went next to Dr. Yılmaz and Moşe's table and was talking to them. As I greeted the other customers with a smile and moved towards their table, I noticed Hittitology Professor Mr. Sinan sitting at one of the back tables. Next to him was a young girl named Gaye, whom he had introduced to us before. I said hello from afar and said I would stop by later.

When I came to Metin, I realized that he was talking about Ebru. While sitting on the chair that Umut brought, Metin said that the girl's family would come to Chicago to look for her. The doctor and his wife, Serap, were joking and laughing, making comments in their own way. Dr. Yılmaz was a good surgeon who made a name for himself in this region. Another important he had was that he was one of those who made an effort to properly introduce Turkey in America. Wherever he saw an article or publication against Turkey, he would immediately send a letter, condemning them and asking them to correct their mistakes. He also carried out significant work in the Armenian cause. He would also contribute to the campaigns of American senators who promised to support Turkey. In his usual humorous way:

"What shall the girl do? She is tired of living under pressure in Turkey. She must be living here as she pleases. Well done. Even though I was a man, I could not live my youth in Turkey. I couldn't sit hand in hand with girls in pastry shops because of poverty, studying, and being shy around people. Was there anything else than coffee houses where men sat together in Turkey? Let the girl live her life and do whatever she wants."

There was laughter. The doctor's wife Serap intervened and said:

"At one point, we heard that she got married. Then, we heard that she broke up or something like that. She probably found someone else and ran away."

Doctor Yılmaz, flirtatiously:

"Would they leave such a beautiful girl alone? Someone must have stolen her heart," he replied.

Mrs. Serap, who was bored with these words, pointed to Professor Sinan, who was sitting aside, as if she wanted to change the subject, and asked who the girl next to him was. Even though I told her that she was a friend of him, she was not satisfied.

Moşe, a man of the world, with his white-haired appearance, was listening to the conversations carefully, taking the issue more seriously and explaining the situation to his French wife, Miranda, in English.

Miranda, in her usual classiness and elegance, said with a worried expression:

"That beautiful waitress Turkish girl is missing! What was her name? Abby? Ebru? It was something like that. Poor girl. I hope nothing bad happened to her. Let's notify the police immediately."

I told her that this kind of decision could only be made after her family arrived from Turkey. I thought Miranda, who was an extremely emotional person, and Moşe, who was a complete gentleman, were very suitable for each other. The woman was in her fifties and Moşe was fifty-eight. It was the second marriage for both of them. Strangely enough, in America, once-married couples, whether Turkish or foreign, were rare.

While Umut was putting the shish kebabs on the table, Dr. Yılmaz:

"Umut, you couldn't steal Ebru's heart all this time, and look, now the girl is missing." Umut shook his head as if he didn't know what to do and walked away silently. Metin, to break the silence:

"You're right, the girl ignored this brilliant boy and went after that scruffy guy. And then she disappeared. If this is what it means to live free..."

I wanted to clarify the issue by saying: "Metin is telling the truth. That girl was so pure and fragile that she did not seem to have a character that could live independently. Only a person who can take care of herself when she is in a difficult situation can live freely. I'm worried about her!"

Later, while having coffee, Dr. Yılmaz started talking about the books he had recently read and the letter he wrote to Aziz Nesin. For a moment, he turned to Moşe and said:

"Me and Filiz are from generation of the sixty-eight. Once upon a time we were protesting against the Sixth Fleet. Now we live with the Yankees. This is a long different story to be told." And then I said:

"The development of nations, to me, is similar to human life. One will experience what needs to be experienced when the time comes. The events that coincided with our youth were events that Turkey needed to experience. The price of every experience is paid by an individual. Unfortunately, at that time, the prices were really heavy. Those years are like a wound inside us that will not heal..." Metin, interrupting:

"I swear, we were leftists too when we were young. But Abraham Lincoln has a quote that I like: *You can't help the poor by destroying the rich*. If you take down the one who pays the wages, the one who takes the wages will also be in trouble, right?"

Moşe, trying to change the subject a little, said:

"I don't know any left or right. I was not in Turkey at that time. If there's one thing I know, the country where I was born and raised, Turkey, has always been a beautiful country for me. I did my military service for four years, peeling potatoes, but despite that, I love Turkey and visit it every year. Turkey is a country that welcomed my ancestors with open arms. My siblings and relatives still live there. The only thing I regret is that Turks do not appreciate their country. They don't work hard and try to improve their economy. They're always looking for someone to blame."

Mrs. Serap was bored with these conversations, as usual. Looking at the table where the professor and the young girl were, and at the table of the beautiful Hülya and her American lover, she wanted to go and talk to them and was dying to understand what was going on. Meanwhile, she couldn't help but asked:

"Filiz, my dear, look at Hülya! How long has it been since her husband died? She came here with her lawyer without any hesitation. The other day, they saw them leaving a hotel. Do they come here a lot?"

She was obviously fishing me for information. There was the one and only issue on which Turks could be united in Chicago; that was gossip. The news would spread instantly via telephone chain. And of course, by adding something to the story. Because it was a ritual to talk on the phones for too long. Long distances would cause longer conversations. I have never heard so many rumors in Turkey. Hülya, who has two children, needed a lawyer regarding real estate issues after her the death of her husband. Then, apparently, they liked each other, which, eventually, brought them together. Hülya was enjoying life as if she was born again. Of course, I had heard a lot about them, but I had no intention of sharing them with Serap.

"Sometimes they do come. Private lives of our customers are none of our concern. If you want, go ahead, talk to her. You know Hülya too."

"Oh, you're right. Let me go and talk to them for a bit." When saying these things, her face seemed like she admired them.

On her way to Hülya's table, she did not forget to greet the Hittitology professor. Thereupon, Professor Sinan stood up and headed towards the table we were sitting. His girlfriend Gaye followed him. Mr. Sinan, eyes filled with tears under the influence of Turkish music and raki a moment ago, now came to us with a very cheerful attitude:

"I've been watching you, and I envied your conversation and laughter. May I join you for a while?" He introduced the drunk Gaye, who could barely stand, to Dr. Yılmaz and Moşe. "I'm glad we have this Cafe Bellini; we can disperse all our thoughts and relieve our stress here. This young friend of mine also has some problems, we are in support of each other," he said.

Dr. Yilmaz said: "It is obvious that you support each other! What's wrong with this girl? She is young, beautiful and has a friend like you." Upon these words, the girl suddenly started using bad words:

"Who gives any fuck about youth or beauty? Fuck all the problems..."

Everyone was in shock. It was unbelievable that such bad words came out of the mouth of a young and beautiful girl like her. I wasn't surprised because I had seen this side of her before. Because I've heard her story before. I guess, this was her method of stress relief. After a short moment of surprise, everyone started laughing. Dr. Yilmaz encouraged her in his usual fatherly manner:

"Good for you, curse it. Damn everything. Speak as you feel. You'll get it off your chest."

The conversations and laughter continued like this.

Professor Sinan had been teaching at the University of Illinois on "Hittites", on which he was an expert, for a year. He had books published on this subject in three languages. He gave us an English version as a gift. He would occasionally go to other cities to give conferences. He even came here from Germany. His wife and two children lived in Germany. Probably because he was lonely, he was walking around with this girl who had suddenly appearing next to him lately.

There was another person from afar who envied the lively and cheerful atmosphere at our table. Mr. Kemal, President of the Turkish American Association, could not resist and came to us.

"Good evening, everyone, I wouldn't want to interrupt your joy. I just came to ask if you bought your Republic Ball tickets. There is very little time left. Get it now or it will be sold out. We prepared a very nice program."

We all said that we would definitely attend the prom.

Metin, nudging me: "Look at the door, look who's coming!"

"Oh, Lou Wolf and his wife Debby!"

Leaving our cheerful table behind, we went to the door to welcome our new friends.

Although Lou Wolf was a small man of sixty-something with blue, beady eyes, he was known as the real estate mogul of Chicago. Just as New York had Donald Trump, Chicago had Lou (we called him Lui) Wolf. He owned more real estate than he knew. The rows of bazaars, theater buildings, nightclubs and office buildings that he owned could sometimes cover a large part of a street. Last week, he appeared on the cover of a magazine as Chicago's biggest real estate investor. He had two children with his wife, who was thirty years younger than him. He said Debby was a hippie when she was a young girl. She was now a very attractive and wealthy woman, around the age of thirty or thirty-five.

Metin bought this two-storey Cafe Bellini building from Lou, and that's how they met. Even though Metin was young, Lou sensed his courage, determination and talent for this real estate business. Initially, they bought a joint building or two together, but Metin later chose to invest on his own. But their friendship always continued, and my husband learned a lot about business from him. With his Turkish manners, Metin never failed to respect him. As for Lou, Metin was like a son, too. Debby said she wanted to be somewhere secluded tonight. We preferred to talk to Dr. Yılmaz and other friends casually and we all went to the table on the side we showed them. Debby brought a different atmosphere to the restaurant late at night as she walked swaying with her long blonde hair, blue eyes, newly plastic breasts and white dress with a deep slit on the side. The smoky heads and long eyes suddenly turned towards this tall woman like a cypress next to an old man.

Right after taking our seats, Metin and Lou started talking about real estate. Although always admiring each other, there was a vague rivalry between them. Metin was not yet at a level where he could compete with him, but when he told how he bought his twelve-store building on Broadway at a cheap price, Lou could not help but be amazed and envy the way he managed to do this. When one thinks of a real estate agent in Turkey, what comes to mind is real estate brokerage, usually done by retired civil servants in a small shop. Real estate in America is not such a simple job. The branch of business called "Real Estate" is one of the most important jobs done in a very professional way. Real estate brokers must be graduate and have a degree, and they must also pass state exams and know the laws regarding this matter. Like Lou, Freed, and Kenny, Metin's business was real estate investing, not brokerage. Our dear friend Ken Goldberg, the real estate agent who worked with us, was always pleased with the hundreds of thousands of dollars in commission he received from us. Ken and his esteemed wife, Harline, were among those absent tonight.

Lou, Freed, Kenny, Ken were all Americans of Jewish descent. Another issue that caught our attention with Metin was that many of the successful businessmen in America were generally of Jewish origin. Indeed, all the Jews we knew were hardworking and knowledgeable. For example, Lou's mother was once a poor florist. Maybe they are so hard-working and calculating because of difficult conditions they had in earlier periods of life. Despite all his wealth, Lou was an extremely economic and even further, stingy man. However, his young wife was squandering his fortune in the best way possible. The last thing she bought herself was a jet plane. In fact, she took pilot training and flew her own plane. Because she was bored with all the real estate talk, she told me where she was going on her plane. She said that she often went to the Netherlands and Mexico with her young friends. She said that it was more comfortable there in every way. Considering that she used to be a hippie, we suspected that she occasionally attended parties there, perhaps where drugs were used. Lou wouldn't bother her too much, as that was Debby's character. Even if she was married, she had to be free. I thought that she definitely had a boyfriend.

"Filiz, if you'd like, I can take you and Serap to Mexico on my plane. I'm going next week. We'll leave and return in a few hours. Don't have any doubts about my piloting. I use it very well. But for long distances, such as Europe, I hire private pilots," she said.

God forbid, I get on her plane! Serap would not either. I managed to get away from her by thanking her and saying I had things to do at the Immigration Office next week.

Later in the night, when the wine and raki continued and the humorous conversations deepened, the missing Ebru Erdem, whose whereabouts were unknown now, had already disappeared from everyone's minds. Zeynep, from whom I thought I could get information and was waiting for her, did not come here at all tonight.

Windy City

The date is October 20, 1990. I started this day by writing in my diary my impressions of the city of Chicago, which I have been wanting to write about for a long time. Since the day I arrived, I have seen, learned and heard many things that impressed and intrigued me in this mysterious city. Chicago was like a summary of everything beautiful and ugly in America. But, as I got to know Chicago and Chicagoans a little more, I realized there was more to this place than meets the eye. Things that amaze you, make you think, and are sometimes enviable and hard to believe... After what I will tell you now, I think anyone in my shoes would believe that this city has a unique spirit and character.

I believe the nickname "Windy City" was given to Chicago by the Native Americans. However, the name "Chicago" was taken from the Indians and it means "Wild Onion Plant". The name of the indigenous tribe living in this region was "Potawatomi". Unfortunately, as in many parts of America, the Potawatoms were not able to continue their happy lives for a long after being invaded by non-natives. Even though they were the real owners, they had to leave this beautiful town settled along the lake and river by the dances of war. It is impossible to understand the reason that there is no place for Native Americans, the original people of Chicago, in Chicago, which hosts seventy-two nationalities today. Especially, I was quite surprised to learn that Abraham Lincoln, who was known as *noble soul, patriotic heart, a martyr of rights loyal to rights* and the pride of Illinois in which Chicago is located, who was a lawyer at the time and would end slavery in the 1860s, had a role in the "Battle of Bad Axe" in 1832, in which many Native American men, women and children were massacred. Under the pressure of the American Army and government, in 1835, as the last Potawatomis left Chicago, they threw the axes and spears in their hands around the streets they passed and performed their final dance with terrifying screams, leaving behind names to be given to the famous streets and squares... And now they are remembered only for the annual canoe races on the Des Plains River. Also, with a memorial totem erected on the lakeshore and equestrian Indian statues in a few certain places around the city.

The first foreigner to settle in Chicago in 1779, other than the Indians, was a black, fur trader named Jean Babtiste. He built his first wooden hut on the river bank and started his trade. From that date until today, the immigrants who came and settled here have accomplished such incredible things that they have made Chicago one of the youngest and largest cities in the world. Even though they have a short history, they obviously aimed to be the first and most important in almost every subject. This is the most important character of *Windy City*. It always wants to be number one and does so at all costs. One of the best examples is that it has become the city with the tallest building in the world -before the Kuala Lumpur twin buildings were built in Malaysia- with the one hundred and ten-storey Sears Tower in the city center, which has a unique architecture. The world's first open heart surgery was performed by a black doctor named Daniel Hale Williams in 1913. This is also where the first blood bank was opened. In 1850, it had the largest railway terminal in the world. George Pullman invented the pullman here in 1857. This has been the region with the fastest developing industry. Of course, the first workers' uprising took place here in 1886. The airport is the busiest airport in the world. McDonald's hamburgers, which surround the world today, first started in Chicago in 1955. The first McDonald's building was turned into a museum in Des Plains, a suburb of Chicago.

Well then, where does this strength, this determination, this belief come from? I think that the difficult feats accomplished one after another since the first people who settled here have been a source of inspiration for every new generation. I feel that this city still has the same spirit since those times and even the new arrivals are caught up in this magic. As early as the 1850s, the people of Chicago showed an example of perseverance that no one could have imagined. In those years, while the town's lake port was showing itself as an industrial center, it encountered a major mud problem. Streets, houses and buildings were flooded with mud. So much so that, according to a rumor, a man whose only head and shoulders were visible in the mud was walking with difficulty in the middle of the street. Someone standing a little further away asked, "Can I help you?"

"No, thank you, I have a fine horse under me," replied the other. Jokes aside, after trying many methods to get rid of this mud, the Pipe and Canal Commission gathered and put aside the useless methods and prepared a brand-new plan. According to this plan, Chicago would be raised fourteen feet! Well, but how? The answer is ready: with jack! No joke, really, big buildings, houses, hotels were raised by hundreds of people using large jacks and their bottoms were filled or lifted and taken to another place. In fact, while the hotel called Briggs House on Randolph Street was being removed and upgraded, the people inside were continuing their daily lives. Historians say there could be no better example of the energy and determination of those who built Chicago.

The more I learned, the more amazed I became. I believe that the people who come here are really crazy, but real go-getters. Now look at what a mayor did: In 1861, while Long John, who was super tall, was drinking like every other day, he suddenly got angry and fired the entire police force. After a while, they noticed that the crime rate considerably decreased on its own.

I can say that the fact that the people of Chicago have to faced unfortunate disasters from time to time has never discouraged them, on the contrary, it has accelerated their determination. In the famous Great Chicago Fire of 1871, almost the entire city was burned to ashes. Hundreds of people lost their lives, hundreds of thousands became homeless, and large buildings turned into ruins. After this great disaster, this lentous city would of course be reborn from its ashes with a new spirit, like a phoenix. And so, it did. It was achieved with a brand new and perfect city plan, and eventually received the title of the best planned city.

For Chicagoans, who have acquired a special talent for always finding a solution to every problem, "Solutions are endless!" would be the most appropriate saying. Another jaw-dropping event occurred in 1900. The opposing force says that even if the solutions never end, neither will the problems. This time, there is a problem caused by the river passing through the city. Germs and dirt mix with drinking water, resulting in cholera and many other epidemic diseases. There is actually an easy solution, but it is a very difficult and long-term task, which is to reverse the flow of the river. At the end of the day, they did it. Of course, they became number one again with their engineering skills in this field. Damn people!

I wonder if these people, who are not afraid of anything, would have made these efforts with such ambition and dedication if they had stayed in their own countries? I don't think so. Because a person's homeland is like his own home. A person likes to be comfortable and lazy in his own home, the house gives him confidence. If one has gone to another country, the one will have to fight tirelessly against all the difficulties encountered in order to exist there, otherwise one will perish and no one will even pity.

One of the things Chicagoans love to talk about is basketball. They are proud of the top professional basketball team, the Chicago Bulls, and their famous gravity-defying player, Michael Jordan, whose statue has been created.

One thing people don't like to talk about is that they were once considered number one in terms of gangsterism! All I knew about Chicago before coming here was that it was the second largest city in United States and was once the most important mafia center, along with the famous Al Capone. Whether it is the effect of the movies I've seen or something, sometimes when I see a Cadillac while passing through those labyrinth-like underground roads, I feel like armed men wearing fedora hats, striped suits or overcoats are about to come out of it, and I get chills. When I asked a few Chicagoans about this mafia issue, they explained, "Since alcohol production was banned at that time, this industry went underground, and that's how it turned out." And when I reminded them that the mafia was a part of American history, that in those years the mafia gave orders to the police, the judge, the governor, and all the politicians in Congress, they changed the word and tried to explain with a humorous story or two that the worst politicians came from Illinois, and that such things were in the past now. But they did not forget to add that they had many colorful faces to boast about. The point that interested me the most was that when Alphonse Capone was caught, he was sentenced to eleven years in prison, not for the massacres or illegal acts he committed or commissioned, but for his $182,000 tax debt. It is clear from here what Uncle Sam cares about most... Among the people they are proud of are the famous writer Ernest Hemingway, the famous saxophonist Louis Armstrong, who also lived here, and the world-famous *The Blues*. There are many famous artists, architects and businessmen from Springfield, from Abraham Lincoln to the most recent talk show host, Oprah Winfrey.

Today, important names such as Mc Cormick, Marshall Field, George Pullman, Potter Palmer and William Wrigley are among the businessmen who gave their names to many buildings, streets and squares, and who had the biggest share in Chicago's rise to its current level. The most interesting of these to me is William Wrigley, the chewing gum king, who gave his name to the magnificent Wrigley building, which resembles a cathedral in the city center. This is the most striking example showing that people come to Chicago to make money. William Wrigley, Jr., a third-grade middle school dropout, started working in Chicago selling soap with $35 in his pocket. He gave baking soda as a gift to those who would have bought extra soap. He realized that there was more demand for soda, so he started selling soda. This time, he gave a gift of chewing gum to those who would have bought a lot of soda. Then, realizing that chewing gum was more in demand, he shifted his business in this direction. And thus, the chewing gum empire has been established. When he died in 1932, his real estate was worth $200 million. Many of the people passing by this building, which is still used as the headquarters of the chewing gum company, point at each other and tell this story by repeating the words of the chewing gum king: "Listen to your customers, they may be right!"

It doesn't stop there. This ambitious city had to be one of the best in the world in the field of culture and art. Founded in 1879, *The Art Institute of Chicago* offers a collection full of artworks by famous painters such as El Grew, J.F. Millet, and Marc Chagall. However, these were not enough for them. They had to put more interesting creations over the visible parts of the city. Each generation was supposed to add something new, and each innovation was supposed to be more assertive than the other. In the 1900s, a commission gathered again and selected Architect William E. Hartman and gave him the task. Taking various gifts and a check for one hundred thousand dollars, William, with various gifts and a check for a hundred thousand dollars, went to Southern France and knocked on the door of the famous painter and sculptor Pablo Picasso. Picasso's modern-style works were to be erected in several important places in the city, especially in front of Federal Plaza. Picasso sent the models even though he never even saw Chicago. When he finished his creation and the Mayor unveiled the gigantic work in front of Federal Plaza, while the crowd were looking at the statue with curious eyes, not knowing whether it was the head of an Afghan dog, of a woman, or Picasso's second wife, the mayor said: "In order to become familiar tomorrow with what seems strange today..." As for me, whenever I go to the city center and look at this work of Picasso, I think that he, like us, came here from another country and remained in the situation of a mysterious stranger, an enigma.

Of course, for insatiable Chicagoans, this would fall short. There had to be something magnificent in the Grand Park in the heart of the city that would attract tourists, so that they would compete with the culture and art of Europe dating back thousands of years. They thought on it and made a decision. Why wouldn't the same famous fountain pool in the garden of Louis the Fourteenth's Versailles Palace in France be also located here? In 1927, they built the magnificent pool called Buckingham Fountain, which was twice the size of the original! It is now one of the corners that tourists find most romantic, with its illuminated and musical water shows held in summer.

Even though I didn't want to write more about this strange city in my notebook, I thought I would be doing Chicago an injustice if I didn't mention the Playboy Empire. Because Hugh Hefner, who claimed to have made America's sex revolution by printing Marilyn Monroe's nude picture in the first Playboy magazine in 1953, is considered one of the hundred most important people in Chicago. Hefner, famous for the parties he frequently threw with his bunny girls and guests, in his forty-eight-room mansion on State Street, wearing either pajamas or a dressing gown, expressed his revolution as follows: "Purity is unhealthy. My naked girls have become the symbol of disobedience, the triumph of sexuality and the end of purity." Despite the intense criticism it has been subjected to by religious, feminist and some political groups, Playboy magazines have been sold with great enthusiasm all over the world. The Palmolive building on Michigan Avenue, where the magazine was located, has been named the Playboy building ever since. They later moved to the Lincoln Park neighborhood and then to California.

While I was going to talk a little about the Chicago Symphony Orchestra, ballet, theaters and universities, I noticed someone standing over me: Metin.

"What are you working on so hard?"

"I am just writing down some information about Chicago and my thoughts on it."

"What kind of information or thoughts?"

"I am writing about how ambitious, determined and hard-working Chicagoans are. Just like you..."

"How so?"

"So much so that the charm of this city has passed on to you too. A middle-class fisherman's boy like you, comes here from Turkey, starts everything from scratch, or even from below zero, and returns home ten years later as a shipowner with ships sailing around the Mediterranean. This, for me, is kind of a miracle."

"If a person wants, he can create the miracle himself. I have done everything I set my mind to and I will continue to do so."

"Perhaps, this is one of the reasons I admire you..."

"Anyway, let's stop talking and get down to business. We have a lot of work to do at this time of the morning. I'm going to tour a few buildings, are you coming?"

"Gosh, that'd be good. Actually, I was feeling like getting tight, I've been trying to distract myself since the morning."

"What's the problem?"

"I was thinking about that girl, and her family coming to look for her."

"This issue has gone too far. I've seen many like that. As I said, she must have found a new 'boyfriend' for herself. Soon, the girl will appear. They come here looking for adventure, not to work as I do. Come on, get ready, we're going.

A Mysterious Person Died

As Metin and I were heading towards Downtown, I was thinking about Ebru's parents who were going to arrive by tomorrow. I wonder how we could help these people. There is a hotel called Days Inn across from our restaurant. If they'd stay there, Cafe Bellini would be at walking distance for them to have lunch. Anyone who would be interested or have acquired any information about the issue could come here and inform us.

Metin broke the silence with the following words: "First, we'll stop by the lawyer on State Street."

"Isn't the office closed on Sundays?"

"I'll get a piece of paper from an officer there and come back quickly. If you'd like, you could wait in the car."

While I was waiting at a central place in Downtown, my heart felt a bit heavy among the buildings rising above me. A sky the size of a handkerchief was visible from the car window. Young people and tourists in shorts with cameras in their hands were wandering around the streets, looking with great admiration. Anyway, Metin arrived without too much delay.

"I'm bored," I said.

"I see. Alright then, there is a very nice coffee shop over there, they serve all kinds of coffee, let me take you there, you will be refreshed. But smoking is not allowed there, just so you know."

"It's fine, I'm used to it. In a way, it is for our own good, even by force."

When we arrived at the cafe, Metin understood that I was going to talk about the missing girl.

While having our French Vanilla coffee, he said:

"Well then, tell me, where should we get started?"

"Do you remember the first time Ebru came to our restaurant? Last year, we had so many Turkish students who came to ask for a job. You didn't want this girl because you preferred male waiters. We hired her at my insistence."

"We have gone through quite a lot of trouble because of this mercy of yours. Free food for the hungry, free place to sleep, goods, and money for those living on the streets... The way things are going, it looks like the restaurant will turn into a public soup kitchen, and we will turn into a Humanitarian Association. I went through so many difficulties to reach this level, without asking any help. Those who are self-confident should come to America. Every tom, dick, and harry comes, and then they become wretched here."

"You talk like this, but I know best how many Turkish people you have helped. Whether they appreciate it or not, that's a different matter. Let it be. A favor is most valuable when it is for free."

"Let alone returning the favor, people won't even bother saying hello when you stop providing some help. I don't need their greetings!"

"Anyway, let's leave that alone now. Was hiring Ebru a bad thing to do? She was, after all, a Turkish girl in distress. Besides, she was working well."

"Yes, we listened to you and our place became full of illegal workers. After that, we got raided by the Immigration Police and they all ended up at the police station..."

I remember that day very well. I was very worried too. Everything was going so well actually. The restaurant was pretty full. Delicious kebabs were coming and going, the waiters were carrying wines, beers and coffees to the tables, and Julio Iglesias was singing *Nathali* from the tape recorder with his romantic voice. Conversations were being had and laughter were spread around. We were having dinner with our friends Moshe and Miranda. It was a happy evening. Suddenly, two undercover policemen came and said that there was a tip-off and that they would check whether there were any illegal workers. Turkish waiters and Mexican workers, sensing the situation, began to scurry around. While some were trying to hide in the garden, some in the basement, and some in the garbage bin, Ebru went upstairs to our flat. Then, of course, they were all caught one by one. Ebru's image never leaves my mind. The girl was shaking all over. When the police asked her if she had a green card, she replied "I'm a student," in a very shaky voice. The blood had drained from her face. I tried to comfort her by hugging, but Erkut and Ebru were taken to the police station along with the Mexicans. Umut was lucky. Because he was taking his English course that night. As for us, they gave us a warning and a fine for this incident. The sad thing was that the police said that the report was made by the Turks. Why wouldn't the Turks here support each other? Why does everyone try to undermine each other instead of solidarity? What is up with all the jealousy, the envy! As Metin said: "A scorpion wouldn't do to another scorpion what the Turks here do to the other Turks..."

After finishing our coffee, we got back into the car. To change the subject, Metin:

"Here's a thought. While we're on State Street, let me show you Hugh Hefner's mansion, as I promised, you've been asking it for a while."

"Is that the famous house of the owner of Playboy?" I asked.

"Let's see the house of the guy who got rich by showing off naked female body in erotic magazines and clubs."

"Don't say it like that. If the women who do this do it out of desire and are happy with their lives, who cares? Besides, let me tell you a thing I read somewhere: 'The real message is not eroticism, it is an escape, an escape from the harsh realities of life.'"

"Say so then, he created a message of his own."

"I'm not finished yet: 'Life must be something more, something more than a sea of tears. So have fun and live the American dream!'"

"But, as beautiful as the American dream is, its nightmare could be just as scary."

"You're right, I'm just joking, by the way, we couldn't find the house anyway."

"Never mind, we might as well not see the house of the man in the dressing gown."

"Now, we're heading straight to Bryn Mawr. To get rent from Peter Johnson."

"Didn't he send the rent again?"

"This makes two, he's escaping me, but this time I'm going to corner him."

"That's right, it's Sunday, they have ceremony."

We owned a few old buildings on Bryn Mawr Street.

These buildings ended up being classified as historical ones. One of them was a large two-story structure, the exterior of which was made of red brick. The ground floor used to be a movie theater. Since it was now empty and dim, only large mice were making a film inside. A large part of the upper floor was converted into a church by some black people from Nigeria. Some empty rooms existed in one section, where homeless Turks were staying. The other building, which is the continuation of this one, has fifteen apartments, a bar on the ground floor, a Gyros restaurant which sells doner kebab and a shoe store. Except for the Turks, everyone else pays rent every month. Most residents here were Puerto Rican, Korean, Filipino or Mexican. Collecting the rent was a big issue here because most of the tenants either don't have much money or are not legal residents.

One day, I'll never forget, taking my pen and paper with me, I went to the building to find out who was staying in which apartment. They were so mixed up with each other that Suarez, who was in flat ten, was coming out of flat sixteen. It's kind of like commune life. When I entered the apartment, I knocked on the first door I came across. A few Far Easterners were coming down the stairs. They've never seen me before. When the door opened, a dark-skinned young man in a cherry-brown tank top appeared. I told him, "Hello, I'm from Chicago Management Company. I'd like to ask your names, phone numbers and amount of rent you pay, what would your name be?" As soon as I finished my words, the man started yelling: "Immigration!" Those three men coming down the stairs said something in their own language and went back up. The man in the tank top shut the door in my face. A running, a shouting in the building... People jumping from the back balconies and windows and running away... I realized that blonde lady with a notebook and a pen in her hand, glasses on her eyes, and speaking English scared them, and made them run away, thinking that I came from the Immigration Office. Within five minutes, all the doors were closed, and there was an absolute silence in the building. It means that they didn't even know proper English. I left there helplessly.

As Metin and I were climbing the creaking, moisture wooden stairs to the second floor, we heard a strange music coming from the hall used as a church. It was such rhythmic and playful music that when I looked through the open door, I was not surprised to see black people dancing like crazy. It looked like a disco; the hall was covered with a red carpet. In the front, on a high stage, an orchestra-like group playing the organ and a few other musical instruments, wearing white turbans on their heads and white nightgown-like dresses, were playing with great enthusiasm and singing a questionably religious song at the top of their lungs. Both the people in the hall and the group dancing like crazy were all dressed in white. Black women looked very fancy in their elegant white toilets and white turbans. They looked like they were in a festive mood with their big earrings and dark make-up. When Father Johnson saw us at the door, he got a little upset and stopped dancing and came to us.

He was a young man. I think those gathered here were of

Nigerian origin. Because they had a little darker skin color and their religious rituals were a little different than other black communities. *Father Johnson* had already found an excuse not to pay the rent again. He started complaining about the Turks staying in the building. He said they were disrespectful and dirty. He explained that they used the church's toilet and left it dirty, and as if this was not enough, they pasted mosque posters in the corridor leading to the church hall. Metin stated that he would talk to the Turks, but this could not be a reason for not paying the rent and said:

"You don't even keep your word, what kind of a priest does that make you? This is the third time in two months you've been faking me. But this time I won't be understanding, if you don't pay, then you're free to leave the apartment. How am I supposed to pay my taxes?" Realizing that he was in a tight spot, Father Johnson made a half-hearted attempt to his check book in his pocket and filled it out reluctantly. While leaving there, Metin knocked on the door of Cemal, the former cook who had been living in a room we had given him free of charge for years, and was muttering to himself: "Cemal, brother, this one will cost you, find a place for yourself. You live here for free, the least you could do would be not giving any harm to anyone. I will fire you now. Who knows who you may have gathered in your room without my permission!"

"Don't do it, pity him! Where will he go at this age! I'd better wait for you in the car."

The man we call Cemal was a poor man who came to Chicago twenty-five years ago and spent his life working in doner kebab industry as a cook but could never go back to Turkey and never called his family after the first few years. When he came here, his wife was pregnant with their second child. Even though he later learned that he had a son, he never had the chance to see him in person. Like many poor Turkish people who came here to work but feel helpless in the face of the difficulties here, he found himself in a predicament. If he came back, they would make fun of him, saying, "Look, he couldn't make it, he came back." He didn't have a good job in his hometown, and if he had, he wouldn't have come here anyway. As for staying here, life must have seemed like an iron chickpea to be chewed, which, eventually, would make him lose all teeth left in his mouth. While you're trying to chew it, you realize you have no teeth left in your mouth. Brother Cemal chose the second path and after more than twenty years in difficult conditions, both of his legs became weak and he had surgery on his legs, using the poverty fund. But, despite the surgery, he shouldn't be on his feet for long even now. That's why he can't work. He gets free food with food coupons given by the government to the poor. He occasionally helps the Greek doner shop downstairs and thus tries to meet his cigarette and other small needs. But in this case, it is not possible for him to pay any rent. That's why we let him stay there. One day I asked him why he did not return to Turkey. He replied, "How come will I go back? I haven't called or sent a penny for twenty years. How could I look at my children's faces? Besides, after all these years, can one return there empty-handed?"

As Metin heard, last year his twenty-four-year-old son in Turkey decided to look for his father, whose face he had never seen. Of course, he called the Turkish Consulate and described his father. After doing a lot of research on this subject, the helpful Ms. Özge called Metin and asked if an old man named *Cemalettin* was staying in one of his buildings. Metin, who learned at that moment that the real name of the old man we know as *Cemal* was Cemalettin, said that he would find out whether he was the same person. Ms. Özge said, "His son is calling, asking for his address, and says, 'No matter what, tell him to come, we will forgive him.'"

When Metin told this to Cemal, and the old man, whose eyes filled with tears, said, "I am a man with pride, please do not give him my address, I can't go back anymore, I will die here somewhere." We still try to persuade him to return to Turkey when we encounter him. We are even ready to buy his plane ticket. But he doesn't want to go back as a waste. It made me think of *Homeless Rasim*, a man who died a few months ago. I didn't know his story exactly, but he was probably one of those in the worst situation possible. We would occasionally come across him on the streets. He wasn't very old, maybe around thirty or thirty-five. But this poor man, whose hair and beard were tangled, and who was swaying in the dirt with his old and dirty clothes, and who was obviously always drunk, looked older and more like a shadow of himself. Every time we saw him, he would ask us for money. We would give him money, knowing that he would buy drinks with that. Where he lived and how he lived was unknown. In fact, Mr. Cemal allowed him to stay in his room secretly from us, but when he couldn't deal with an alcoholic drifter, he kicked him out. One day, the hospital authorities found this man, whose death in a garbage dump or park is still a mystery, realized that he had no one, but somehow, they succeeded in finding Mr. Cemal. However, Cemal is another poor man like him, what could he do? He told Metin. After Metin went to the hospital and performed the necessary procedures, they provided a place to bury him. They took Chicago's newly appointed young imam with them and decided to bury the poor man according to religious obligations. After Mr. Cemal, Metin and the young imam got permission from the hospital authorities, they started to wash the dead body, under difficult conditions, without being able to properly look at this poor body, which was only skin and bones, and it was not even clear why he died. Moreover, since the young imam had never done this job before, with a book in one hand and a water bowl in the other, after reading a line from the book and learning where and how to pour the water, he still did not know which prayers to recite, so he was putting the water bowl in Metin's hands and turning the pages of the book. Then, all of a sudden, he'd say, "Hah, I found it," and try to perform his duty with clumsy movements. As if this were not enough, the so called Imam the Preacher, who came to the cemetery without studying his lesson, and who was not unable to find the necessary page even though he had the book in his hand, could not decide in which direction to put his feet and his head, so he waved his prayer beads in his hand from side to side and said, "The prayer beads indicate that the qibla is on this side, let's put his head on this side."

"It shows, let's put its head on this side," he said. When the funeral ceremony of three people was completed and they were leaving the place, all three had an expression on their faces that was hard to define, between laughing and pity. When I remembered this incident, I couldn't help but think how it will end up with brother Cemal. A little later, when Metin returned to the car, I said,

"Did you end up chasing him or what?"

"What chase are you talking about, I ended up paying twenty dollars on top of everything!"

We walked away with a heavy heart.

Umut

I went downstairs thinking about what I would say about Ebru to Ebru's parents, who were coming to Chicago today. Mexican waitress Margarita, standing at the bar, was looking outside with a saucy smile on her face. As soon as she saw me, she started arranging the glasses in her hand on the shelves. Umut would also be here today. But he was not around yet. There was no one in the restaurant yet, except for two American guys sitting at the table by the window. They were drinking wine and chatting sweetly, looking into each other's eyes. This duo was none other than the romantic and gentleman Mark and William. This couple, one of the regulars of this place, was one of the homosexuals called "gay" here. They were extremely polite and romantic. Some evenings, in a dimly lit corner, under the candlelight, they would sing along to the melody and have their happy moments together.

Metin said that they were actors in a chamber theater on Halsted Street. It is impossible for me to forget how helpful they were to us once.

It is a tradition around here, from time to time, a few people from Chicago's local magazines and newspapers visit the restaurants and write down their impressions. Since one of the greatest pleasures of people in Chicago is to taste different dishes in different restaurants, people always read that column of the newspapers which talks about *Where and what to eat* with curiosity. Critics go to the restaurants they choose without any invitation. One day, we invited them to our restaurant. Metin explained to the cook, the waiters and me one by one how to host them. They were supposed to eat and drink as they liked and not pay anything. They wouldn't bother paying anyway...

That day, two middle-aged, well-dressed gentlemen, who said they were from the newspaper, introduced themselves to us, and we welcomed them with special attention and invited them to the table in the corner of the mirrored partition we had prepared in advance. The best wines were put in ice buckets, the most delicious appetizers and meals prepared carefully were served hot and with care. At the end of the meal, after baklava and coffee service, the remaining food on the table was put into packages and given to them. Umut, being one of our waiters, never left the table upon the boss's instructions. After all this service, I thought that we earned our right to read a complimentary article about Cafe Bellini. The following week, I saw that the article about Cafe Bellini, which we had been eagerly waiting for, had been published. There were nice compliments, except for Umut not being able to open the bottle of wine and some of the packed meals being missing.

Curious customers who read these compliments about our restaurant had already formed a queue in front of the restaurant on Sunday morning. To be honest, I was surprised by how effective this advertisement was in such a short time. Our restaurant did not have the capacity to accommodate so many people and provide equally good service to everyone. Seeing this crowd, all our staff were in a tizzle. There were neither enough waiters nor cooks. There was a great chaos. When this young male couple who were there that day noticed the situation, they immediately started to help, cleaning the tables on one hand, and running around on the other hand to bring coffee orders to the tables. But no matter what they did, it was futile. There was such a surge of crowd that our job was very difficult. The result was a complete fiasco. Some customers, tired of waiting, had only salad and left. Some started shouting and hitting plates with forks. We could not provide food for all of our customers. I finally ran upstairs out of shame. Metin realized that it was beyond our reach, so he turned away those still waiting in the queue, politely stating that there was no room left inside. Then he came upstairs like I did, put a moving cassette on the tape recorder and started dancing with me. It took me by surprise how Metin didn't worry about anything at all. It was as if nothing had happened. Whenever I see William and Mark this incident will come to my mind. Still feeling the embarrassment of that day, after saying "Hello" to them and asking how they were doing, I went out to get some air.

The sun was shining through the clouds and there was a warm breeze outside. Meanwhile, I saw Toni, our cook, wandering around as if he was looking for something. What was he doing outside in his white apron and cook hat?

"Hey Toni, what's up?"

"I'm tracking."

"Tracking what?"

"Auntie, do you see this?" He continued to talk by pointing to the dog poop in front of the door:

"I'm tired of cleaning in front of the door every day. Now, I will track down this dog's owner and his place by following these droppings."

"What then?"

"Then I will find out his address and take this man to court. Because this is a restaurant and people come here to eat. This filth will only make you sick to your stomach. If people can sue us over a dusty chair or a spilled coffee, why shouldn't we? We will get a lot of money, auntie, a lot of money!"

"Jeepers creepers! Get in quickly! Also, Metin told you not to walk around in this business outfit outside or in front of customers, did he not? Your job is to cook in the kitchen. Tell Roberto to clean that up." We were about to go inside, when a black limousine suddenly stopped in front of us.

A shiver went down my spine. I knew who was inside the limo. Zeynep, the limousine driver, got out of the car first, wearing a white shirt, black trousers, burgundy vest and bow tie. She hurriedly opened the back doors. A confused and tired-looking middle-aged couple got out after her. Meanwhile, Zeynep was taking out their suitcases and pointing the restaurant to them. I greeted them right away and invited them inside: "Welcome, please come in." Toni, who was gawking at them, took the suitcases from Zeynep's hand and entered. Zeynep, obviously in a hurry, turned to me and introduced us:

"My dear Filiz, here's Ebru's mother, Mrs. Şermin, and her father, Mr. Zeki," Then to them:

"I'm sorry, I have to get back to work immediately. Filiz will take care of you. They will take you to your hotel. Goodbye for now." Both of them, with a touching expression:

"Thank you. Thank you very much." They were looking desperate, as if they did not know what to do. Then turning to us, Mrs. Şermin said,

"I hope we aren't bothering you!" She looked like she wanted to say some things but did not know what. I wanted to give them some relief, so I pointed a table inside and said:

"You're welcome. This way please, get some rest first." As soon as I turned that way, Umut appeared in front of me.

"Umut... Let me introduce Mrs. Şermin and Mr. Zeki. Ebru's mother and father."

Although Umut knew that they would come today, he was surprised when he suddenly met them. After welcoming them, he sat them down at the table I showed and asked how their trip was. After Mrs. Şermin put her handbag on the table and timidly sat down in a pretty shy manner, she suddenly turned to me and asked,

"Is there any news from Ebru? I suppose she must have heard we were coming."

Her eyes were shining, as if she was sure to receive good news. Two big blue eyes were looking into my eyes, assuming I knew the answer to that question. At that moment, I felt as if it was Ebru sitting across me and it was her eyes staring at me. There was only one difference, her eyes were misty.

"There is not any definitive information yet. Why don't you have a rest and make yourself comfortable? We will talk everything, and investigate the issue, I hope that we will come to a conclusion soon. You must be hungry. Umut will bring something for you."

Toni, placing the suitcases somewhere, came back and asked how the guests were doing:

"I am the cook here. We loved Ebru very much. I couldn't believe when she got lost. I hope she'll be found soon." After his foolish remarks, he finally returned to his kitchen.

Mr. Zeki had not spoken a single word yet. While Umut took the coat from the tired man's hand and took it to the hanger, the man called out to him lightly and said,

"Thank you, son," and continued to sit timidly. He was wearing a brown suit. With his dignified demeanor, he gave the impression of a middle-class gentleman.

"How was your trip?" I was trying to create a speaking environment.

"The journey was comfortable, it was us who were not, Mrs. Filiz. That's why this journey felt like it would never end. We would have liked to come here under different circumstances." One could sense sadness in Mr. Zeki's brown eyes under the bushy eyebrows.

"I see. Shall I offer you some tea first, or would you like to have your food right away?"

"Believe me, we are not hungry at all. Maybe, just a cup of tea," said Mrs. Şermin, taking out a pack of *Maltepe* cigarettes and a ginger-colored lighter from her bag, which matched her two-piece suit. Without asking if smoking was allowed here, she handed the package towards me and asked, "Would you care to join me? It's Turkish cigarette..."

Mr. Zeki was watching his wife with a little embarrassment.

"Thank you. Let me offer you some of mine. An extremely light cigarette." I took out a pack of Virginia Slims Ultra-Light from my pocket.

When she insisted, "No, no, let's smoke one of mine this time," I had to keep her company.

"I couldn't light up one on the plane either. I don't actually smoke much, but my heart sinks big time these days."

People who just met sometimes can't figure out what to talk about at first. One may say things thay may seem absurd or even funny later. For example, even though Mr. Zeki knew that the hotel was right in front of us -Zeynep must have mentioned it to him on the way- he wanted to come up with something and asked,

"I wonder if the hotel we will stay in is close to here?"

"Sure, it is. Very close, right across the street. It's a walking distance. After you're done eating, we'll take you to the hotel."

While Umut was serving our tea on the table, Metin appeared. He had realized who the guests were, he just came to us. After introducing himself, he listed the most cliché American sayings with a kind smile,

"Don't bother please, relax, everything will be fine." After these comforting words, the uneasiness of the husband and wife seemed to lessen. Mrs. Şermin loosened the flowered beige scarf she had wrapped tightly around her neck. While having their tea, they were listening carefully every word Metin said, hoping to hear something about their daughter.

"What do you have today, chicken or vegetable soup?" he asked.

"Chicken soup."

"Let's have it right away then, and warm the pitas, please. We'll think about what to have afterwards."

They liked Metin's fatherly attitude. They couldn't even say, "We don't have the mood to eat anything." During the meal, Metin made Mr. Zeki talk mostly, we learned that he was a manager at a bank branch in Bornova, Izmir, and that they had a seventeen-year-old son besides Ebru. Mrs. Şermin, who stated that she did not have any work life, reminded me of the housewives who went to Alsancak to play cooncan by ferry from Karşıyaka, with her short-cut, highlighted hair, well-groomed nails, stylish rings and an extremely polite attitude. After a while, in the friendly atmosphere created by Metin, Mr. Zeki suddenly opened up about the subject that we could not approach and that they were eagerly waiting for:

"Mr. Metin, how will we find Ebru? We don't know these places. We need your help. Thank God, Mrs. Zeynep is a very good person, she welcomed us and put our mind at ease with her talks on the road. She said she'd discuss it with us in more detail later. Please tell us what you know. If anyone has any information, let us know. We'll do anything to find her. As long as we know where she is."

This request, coming from the heart of a desperate father, was like a begging.

Metin, who had not been very interested in Ebru's life and did not know the details about this girl, was suddenly confused about what to say, but continued to give them morale:

"Don't worry. We will track her down by collecting information from everyone who knew her. Maybe she doesn't even know that you have been looking for her. There will definitely be someone who knows or sees her. These things happen all the time here."

Meanwhile, a group of four or five men entered. It was obvious from their speech that they were Turks. They sat at a table in the front. While Margarita was taking orders, Umut immediately put the cassette of İbrahim Tatlıses on the tape recorder. They would ask for it anyway. Hearing Turkish being spoken next door, Mrs. Şermin suddenly asked:

"Oh, Turks! I wonder if they knew Ebru? What if we ask?"

"No, they don't know her. These are people from a different environment," said Metin bluntly.

"Then, please explain. According to what she wrote in her letter to me,she worked with you here for a while and even mentioned that she loved you very much. You helped her out a lot."

"Yes, we loved her too. She worked here for three or four months. She was extremely gentle, quiet and emotional. If she felt like it, she would sometimes talk and describe her feelings, thoughts, and impressions of America. We would have nice conversations. She was a little pessimistic when she first came, but later she had good days here. She and her husband came several times. Though she hasn't appeared lately."

After listening to me carefully, Mr. Zeki suddenly started speaking as if he were bursting with emotion:

"I did not approve of that marriage from the very beginning. It seemed like a hasty decision to me. We never wanted her to marry a person we had never seen or known. But she didn't listen to us. She kept telling us that Hakan was a very good person and that she could stay in America legally if she married him. There wasn't much we could do from miles away. Then she told us that they got married and she was happy. She sent photos of herself with her husband. They seemed to be happy photographs taken at home and other places. After a while, the letters and phone calls started to become less frequent. We started wondering, sensing that something was not going well. Not only did she not open up to us, she did not tell us what kind of problems she had. We couldn't always reach her on the phone number she gave us. Or, in short, she would tell us that she was fine and not to worry about her. Would we ever leave her around if she told us what her problem was? Even if she didn't come, I would come and get her."

While telling these, the tremor in Mr. Zeki's voice, the distressing expression on his face, and the tears gathering in his eyes were as if he were subconsciously expressing a confession that blamed himself. After taking a sip of water, he continued:

"Later, we received no answers to our calls or letters. It didn't take us long to realize that the address and phone number she had given no longer belonged to her. After waiting for a while more, we realized that we had no choice but to apply to the consulate. In a few conversations with Ms. Özge, we learned that we could not get any information about Ebru and that we had no chance of reaching her husband. According to the information we obtained, she said that they had not been together recently and that the man might even have gone to another city. Damn him! I wonder what he did to my daughter. No matter what, we will embrace her. As long as she is in good health."

As he said his last words, the tears in his eyes began to flow down his cheeks. Unfortunately, a father's love for his daughter, which he could not show openly for many years, was revealed in such a bad incident. These tears were a kind of expression of what he couldn't say, as well as what he said. After wiping his tears with his hand:

"We will definitely solve this riddle, definitely! Anyone who harms her will be punished!" He expressed his ambition and determination in a sharp language.

Faced with this sight, Mrs. Şermin could not hold herself back and started to sob. Mr. Zeki put aside his dignified attitude and turned to his wife:

"What are you crying for? These things happen to us because of you. You were the one who wanted to send her here. What was it? To say out loud that our daughter is studying in America!"

Mrs. Şermin did not want to spoil the ladylike attitude she had displayed since her arrival. She gathered herself together and said:

"Zeki, is it time for this now? We are here to find our daughter, not to have an argument. There are hundreds of young Turkish people like Ebru who came to America. With God's permission, we will find Ebru, for sure. In my opinion, Ebru feels ashamed of us because she made a marriage that we did not approve of and finally realized that she was wrong. My girl respects us very much.' She must be ashamed. But how can we ever have heart to harm her in any way? No matter what her mistake is, she is our daughter, our life, our heart. That's why I came here anyway. Somehow it will come to her ears that we are not angry with her, and she will come out. Oh, if you only knew how much we missed her."

After taking a deep breath, she continued:

"I think all we need to do is let her know that we are here, that we are not angry with her, that we love her and miss her very much."

By expressing her feelings and thoughts at once, Mrs. Şermin prevented the conversation from drifting in an undesirable direction and demonstrated the practical intelligence of the Turkish women that are skillful in every matter. But there was something she forgot. This was not Turkey.

Mr. Zeki put the final point to Mrs. Şermin's words:

"As soon as I find her, I will take her to Turkey. I would never leave her here, not even for a day..."

They were pouring out their hearts, and we could do nothing but listen. Umut, who was secretly listening to our words, approached the table. He asked if they would have a Turkish coffee or an American one. When he didn't get any answer from them, and said,

"I suppose you would like to have a Turkish coffee, I'll have it done right away," I understood from his looks that he wanted to participate and that he thought he might have the opportunity to express his deep feelings of love for Ebru, which had not been taken seriously until now.

"How would you like to take your coffees? Medium or plain?

Mr. Zeki stated that his sugar level was high and asked for his coffee to be plain.

When Umut went to bring it, Metin spilled the beans:

"I can say that Umut was Ebru's good friend, or rather her fan. But your daughter always considered him as a friend, a brother. If you'd like, we can call him, and he can tell us what he knows. Maybe we'll get a clue."

"That would be great," said Mrs. Şermin.

Meanwhile, as İbrahim Tatlıses's gazelle was heard around, the Turkish group, who were saddened, started talking loudly and swearing. A little later, when Umut brought the coffee, Metin, who did not like this noise of the Turks, said:

"Umut, go change that tape, put on some light dinner music, and then come over, the guests want to talk to you." While Umut was gone to change the cassette, I said:

"He is a good kid. He has been working for us for a long time. Also, he is studying as much as he can."

"You can see from his face that he is a good boy," said Mrs. Şermin.

Realizing that the music had changed, the Turkish group got a little upset. After saying something to Margarita, they asked for the bill. Just as Umut was approaching us, the Swedish couple appeared at the door. Umut:

"Metin, brother, the customer has arrived."

"Let Margarita take care, and have a sit, please."

"She is also taking care of Mark and William. This was my turn, but okay."

From where I was, I could see Mark and William sitting quietly in a corner. I was glad that Mrs. Şermin and Mr. Zeki could not see them, who were obviously *gay* from every perspective. It might not have been pleasant for them to encounter such things upon their arrival. Also, Mark and William, who were already disturbed by the looks and noise of that Turkish group, did not seem very pleased.

Umut pulled out a chair and sat next to Metin in a very shy manner. Mr. Zeki started to talk:

"Where are you from, son?"

"Istanbul, sir."

"Is your family here?"

"No. They are in Istanbul. I came to visit a relative of mine here. Then my uncle's son found me this job. Now I have enrolled in courses to improve my English."

"Mrs. Filiz said that she knew Ebru well. Can't you give me

any idea of where she might be? It would be best of you if you could tell us everything you know, my son."

Umut was very excited. He didn't know where and how to start explaining:

"We met Ebru last year when she came to the restaurant... She was a very nice girl. We became good friends when we started working here. I was teaching her to be a waitress. Sometimes we would go to the movies together or do other things."

"What happened next? How did she marry that guy called Hakan? Who is that man?"

Mr. Zeki was trying impatiently to learn something from Umut. Umut let his initial hesitation go and opened up a little bit:

"I swear uncle, l warned her, but she didn't listen. Everyone knew that Hakan was an unreliable person. He would occasionally come to Cafe Bellini to have lunch or so. As soon as he saw Ebru, he set his eyes on her and started coming more often. He tried every way to pick her up and succeeded. Before that everything was great. While Ebru was studying at the language school in Oak Park before coming here, she has had some difficult times lately, both financially and spiritually. She wanted to pursue higher education here but could not because of the high fees. She was hesitant to ask you for more money. She would say, "They spent a lot of money on me." There was no opportunity to find a job. She was very happy when hired by Mrs. Filiz. One day, I asked her, "The language school is finished, why don't you go back to Turkey?" and she had said, 'I have bad memories there, I'm running away from them.' She was talking about the betrayal of a close friend of her or something. Another reason was that most of her friends had passed the university exam, she was upset that she could not pass. She was hoping that maybe she would find an opportunity to study here. Like every young person who came here for this purpose, she too would find a way for herself after all the struggles. She thought she was stronger, but she wasn't. She was too sensitive, too fragile, too innocent. She believed and trusted everyone and did not look for ulterior motives in anything. She thought everyone was like her. It was as if she had come down to earth from the world of angels. The place is full of demons, yet..."

Umut was in flow just as water, adding a poetic tone to his voice. I knew that he wrote poems for Ebru but could not win her heart. His face was slowly turning pink as he explained.

"I may also be immature yet, but I still tried to protect her. Hakan was a cool guy. He came from New York two years ago. He was previously married to an American, probably to get a green card. He was dealing in carpet business. He had a nicely furnished apartment, a luxury car, etc. He was hanging around with American girls. However, after getting to know Ebru, he only brought her flowers, gave her expensive gifts and took her around in his luxury car. He deceived her with such things. Because Hakan is a man who does not know what true love is. He was not of a nature that could understand Ebru's delicate soul, her unconditional dedication to her loved ones, and her emotionality. He was looking to spend his time with a beautiful and naive girl. One day, while I was having a heart-to-heart talk with Ebru, I took a good look at her face. Her eyes, colored according to the color of the place she was in and the color of the dress she was wearing, were the green of dry leaves that day. She was sad because Hakan did not come to the restaurant that day. I knew right away that she was in love with him. She confessed to me that day that she was interested in him. I tried to explain that Hakan was not suitable for her, I even begged her, but she did not listen. Sometimes I say, if this man had not appeared before her, maybe in time she would consider me as a... Anyway... But please, when you find her, do not mention what I told you. I'm telling you these in case I can help. Where were we? So, I just couldn't talk her out of it. Ebru and I would go for walks by the lake from time to time. The blue of the lake and the sky would hit her eyes, and they would turn cyan. When I told her these things, she would laugh in surprise. We would go to the fishermen, warm up by the fire they lit some nights, and talk to them. Sometimes we would go to the French Café, and sit at the tables outside, even if it was cold, because it reminded us of Turkey, and drink different kinds of coffee every time we went. We would usually talk about our lives in Turkey, things we saw in America that seemed strange to us. I would read poems to her." While saying these words, Umut unknowingly made a Richard Gere pose. He pushed his hair back with his hand, then gathered himself and continued:

"Everything changed after the raid by the immigration police. She was very scared when the police caught her. When she was taken to the police station, she called Hakan and informed him. I was at school that day, so I didn't get caught. I learned about it later. Hakan took advantage of this opportunity, paid two thousand dollars bail for Ebru and released her and told her that she could pay her debt later. He took Ebru, who was extremely frightened, home to console her. At that time, Ebru was staying at the house of Mrs. Zeynep, who brought you here. From that day on, she started to stay at Hakan's place. A week later, at Cafe Bellini, she said that Hakan wanted to marry her. This way, she would avoid staying here illegally. Moreover, she was looking for a place to take shelter, both spiritually and physically. She thought this shelter was Hakan. Everything seemed fine until there, but I always had doubts. I honestly didn't believe he could make Ebru happy. I didn't go further on Ebru in case I could be wrong. I wish I was wrong. Anyway, the man did what he said and had an American wedding with her. For some reason, after they got married, he didn't want Ebru to work in this restaurant. I thought he was probably jealous of me. After Ebru left work and moved to his place, they came to dinner together two or three times. Then we couldn't see her at all. I was actually very curious. I wholeheartedly wanted her happiness. At the same time, because I understood her very well, because I knew how easily she could get hurt, I always had doubts. My worst fears came true. Months later, one day, she called me. She said she wanted to talk. Her husband went on a business trip. She didn't want to meet here. We met at another restaurant. She looked miserable and was crying. She didn't tell me much. She just said that she made a mistake by marrying Hakan and that I was right. Even though I insisted, "Come and stay with us if you want, or Mrs. Filiz will find you a temporary place," I couldn't convince her, I don't know if it was because she was afraid of Hakan. Even though I pushed her to explain her troubles, she said, "Good days are behind me. When the light on Hakan faded away, I realized there was only dirt inside." After that conversation, she never called me again. As for me, I never had the courage to call her, thinking that her husband would answer the phone and maybe he would cause trouble because I called. A month or two later, I heard from Mrs. Zeynep that Hakan left her and went to Los Angeles. I also learned that she had to leave the apartment that they were staying in because she could not pay the rent, and that she did not go to Mrs. Zeynep because she had just gotten married. After a long search, I found her at the American bar, where Mrs. Zeynep first met Ebru. She had an American girlfriend named Elvira who worked there. We used to go to that bar together to visit Elvira before, who was a friend she knew from school times. Ebru had stayed at her house for a while before. Actually, I didn't think she would go there, but when there was no other place to look for, so, I went to that bar one night. She was behind the counter, preparing drinks for customers. I realized she was working there. She was both happy and a little annoyed when she saw me.

"Ebru, how are you?"

"I'm trying to be okay."

"What are you doing here? You could work at Cafe Bellini again. We'll talk to Mrs. Filiz, she'll hire you again." She didn't make any sound.

"Where are you staying?"

"At Elvira's place. You know, I've been there before."

"I know, but how do you get along with this American girl? Drop it. Come on, come with me. Let me take you to us and we can talk in detail there."

"Thank you very much, but no. You're already living in a small studio apartment. I can't come and bother you. Elvira's apartment has two rooms, she gave me a room. I also pay part of the rent by working here."

"You look very sad. Come with me, at least let us have a talk somewhere else. If you tell me, we can try to solve everything together."

"Thanks, Umut. You are a very good friend. I'm not even worthy of your friendship. You better try to save yourself. Move on with your education. I'm sure you'll be successful. You deserve every kind of happiness too. It's too late for me now."

"Don't talk like that, you're breaking my heart. You know how I care about you. I'm sorry to see you like this. You used to be a cheerful, lively girl. We used to hang around and have fun together. Your eyes were a source of peace for others. I miss those days. Even the color of your eyes has become smoky in this dark place."

"Don't make me upset even more by talking like this. Customers are waiting. I won't be able to talk any more. You'd better not come here again. I'll call you."

"I am not leaving without asking you something. Where is Hakan? Did you break up? Does he give you money?"

"Could you leave, please? You see, I'm busy." It went exactly like this between us. I remember it like it was yesterday. As I was leaving there in distress, I looked around to see if I might see Elvira and talk to her, but she was nowhere to be seen.

This was our last conversation. I waited for days for her to call me. Unfortunately, she did not. One night, after two weeks, I couldn't resist and went to that bar again. She wasn't there. Elvira said that Ebru left both home and work a few days ago and she didn't know where she was going.

Mr. Zeki interrupted Umut:

"When was the last time you went?"

"About three months ago."

"It means that she was there when she stopped communicating with us. I wish she would call and tell us everything. Umut, dear boy, haven't you ever thought of calling us and letting us know?"

"Of course, how can I not think about it! She never gave me your address and phone number because she predicted I would do such a thing. Then again, how could I have known that things would reach this point?"

This time Mrs. Şermin thought she had a good idea and said excitedly:

"Well, if we find that girl called Elvira and get her to talk, we could definitely find a clue that would lead us to Ebru."

I reluctantly answered:

"We met with Elvira before you came. She doesn't know anything, because Ebru left suddenly without notice. One day, when Elvira came home from work, she couldn't see her. She noticed that her suitcase and some of her belongings were there in the cabinet. After a couple of days, seeing that she did not come back home, she realized that she was gone for good. She said that it could be her husband that called her, and she might have gone to him. She also said that she was very upset with Ebru because she left without even leaving her a note.

Mr. Zeki, after some consideration:

"We have to do whatever we can to find this man called Hakan. If necessary, I will also go to Los Angeles."

I had to intervene again:

"Yes, Hakan's Los Angeles address and phone number information turned out to be fake. There was no such person at that address. They say that he might have gone to another city."

Mr. Zeki, after sighing:

"Ugh, all the doors are closing one by one. How will we find this girl?"

Metin couldn't stand anymore and finally put forward the idea he wanted to say all along:

"The best thing would be to go to the police. We will report that she is lost. They'll find both Ebru and Hakan. Let's not flog a dead horse. What do you say?"

When they heard the word police, the husband and wife were startled. They obviously didn't want this issue to reach this level.

The *police* evoked possibilities they never wanted to consider.

Mrs. Şermin opened her tired eyes and said:

"No, no, Mr. Metin. Can you imagine how scared Ebru will be when she sees the police in front of her? You just told us how afraid she was of those immigration officers. Then again, she'd get angry at us for why we informed the police. We don't want to upset her even more. We just came here today. If she hears that we're here in a few days, she'll definitely show up. The important thing is to let her know that we are looking for her."

Mr. Zeki was undecided on this issue.

"First, let's find all the people who knew her and talk to them. If nothing comes of it, our last resort would be to contact the police."

Since it was now midnight in Turkey, it was time to send the guests, who were sleepy and tired, back to the hotel. Metin:

"You are very tired. Let Umut take you to your hotel, have a good rest. Tomorrow's another day. We will be waiting for you for breakfast."

They both thanked us very much and left the restaurant with Umut. Umut, carrying their suitcases, and the unfortunate parents, carrying the hope of finding their daughter, walked away towards the hotel.

Zeynep and Elvira

The next morning, I knew they would come early, so I got up at eight o'clock and went down to the restaurant. There was no one there yet. I sat at a table by the window, looking outside. People were in a hurry, moving left and right with quick steps. Some were walking toward me. When I saw people passing by with their coat collars turned up and their hands in their pockets, I realized that the weather was a little colder than yesterday. After all, it was the last week of October—winter was slowly approaching Chicago. A garbage collector was sweeping up dry leaves. Across the street, shops were opening one by one. The signs on the glass doors were being flipped one by one to the side that said, "We're Open."

Breaking this routine, the two hurried people finally appeared on the sidewalk across the street. They were standing across the street, looking around to make sure where our restaurant was. In a foreign country, even the easiest things are difficult. And if you don't know the language at all, woe to you, you'll feel even more distressed. I'll go right outside the door and I waved to them. When they saw me, they crossed the street cautiously and came to me. Mrs. Şermin, wearing loose black trousers and a black jacket, said:

"Good morning. Are we here early?"

"No, I was already waiting for you. Newcomers from Turkey wake up a few days early. Because their brains are still set to Turkey time. It is a matter of biological rhythm," I replied.

Mr. Zeki, wearing a thick jacket, said with a smile:

"Good morning Mrs. Filiz. You are right, we haven't slept much. With thousands of questions on our minds."

"I can understand. Let's all have breakfast together," I said.

After seating them at a table by the window, I went into the kitchen to get butter, cheese, olives, tomatoes and toast and I prepared a Turkish breakfast. I also brewed some Turkish tea that I had saved earlier.

At first I preferred to make small talk so that they wouldn't get upset in the morning.

"It's pretty cold today." I said.

"Yes, it's colder than yesterday," Ms. Şermin said while drinking her hot tea and continued her speech: "I feel sorry that we are inconveniencing you."

"You're welcome, what a thing to say. I think it is our duty to help each other in a foreign country." I replied.

While we were having breakfast, they asked me how long I had been here, why and how I had come here.

I tried to explain to them that I had come to America as a tourist for a few months to visit a relative, but during this time I had met Metin and we had gotten married in a short time, and that as an example of how life is full of surprising coincidences, it is difficult to explain how two people who have never met each other in Turkey, meet at a certain time and in a certain place in the world as if arranged by an unknown power and unite their lives, and therefore it is defined with the word "fate" and is passed over; on the other hand, I tried to explain the argument that people make their own fate, we always have a choice, and the important thing is to be able to choose the right one.

At this time, Metin came downstairs and tried to cheer them up again. Then he left us saying that he had work to do, that's why he had to go, and that they would meet again when he came back. A few minutes later, the phone was ringing. It was Zeynep.

She said she would be here in a minute. She had about an hour. When I told this news to the mother and father, their eyes shone with a ray of hope again.

Ms. Şermin, as if praying opened his hands to the sides: "I hope she brings good news!"

Half an hour later Toni and Roberta went to work in the kitchen. Then Zeynep appeared at the door. This time she wasn't wearing her work uniform. She was wearing blue jeans and a coat-like thing.

She sat down next to us with her usual smiling face. After a quick snack, she got to the main topic and started telling us what she knew: "Let me tell you how I know Ebru from the beginning. There is a bar on Halsted Street where the kids who drive limousines for our company sometimes go. Don't mind me saying kids, most of them are young people studying at university. That's what I call them. One day they told me that they had seen a Turkish girl named Ebru there. I think our boys were a bit obsessed with her. Ebru kept them at arm's length.

She was not working there; she was just sitting there. When the young people realized that she was a Turkish girl, they didn't want to disturb her anymore. They asked me to go and talk to her because she looked very strange. But first let me tell you that what I am about to tell you may seem strange to you, but these things are considered normal here. Who knows if they say to my mom, 'Your daughter was sitting in the bar,' I cannot imagine what she would have thought? The bars here are where everyone goes, men and women. There are no bakeries like in Turkey. The next evening, out of curiosity, I stopped by that bar. When I walked in, a girl with an innocent face, who I knew intuitively was Turkish, was sadly sitting on a stool. an American young man standing, drinking his beer and trying to talk to her.

I approached her, both to meet her and to save her from this unwanted loneliness: 'Hello! You must be Ebru. I'm Zeynep.' She looked up and said in a low voice, 'Hello'. I sat down next to her saying, 'Can we talk for a bit?' I said I would like to get to know her, and I could help her if there was a problem. At first, she was hesitant, but after a while, realizing that I was friendly to her, she told me about herself with sincerity. She said that she had successfully completed his English course and received his certificate, and that she was staying at Elvira's house for now because she had no other place to stay. I asked her what she planned to do next. She was looking for a job and a place to stay. She looked sluggish and tired. She said that she didn't know any Turkish people, that when she first started school she had a close friend from Turkey, but unfortunately her friend now lives in Boston."

Ms. Şermin interrupted Zeynep: "You are talking about Aslı. Sorry for interrupting you but the story of coming to America was thanks to Aslı. She was Ebru's friend from Turkey. She came here first to learn English. She was chatting with my daughter. Aslı encouraged her and helped her with the registration and so on."

Mr. Zeki couldn't stand: "Yes, this girl is the one who put the idea in her head. I won't lie, I never wanted it because Ebru is not that talented, I mean, she is not talkative, but I couldn't get her mother to listen."

Ms. Şermin got a little angry, "I supported her because I thought about her future, her well-being. As women, we think about some things more delicately. Ebru was very upset because she did not pass the university exam. As a young girl, she also had problems among her friends because of some emotional issues. As a mother, I didn't want her to get depressed, so I wanted her to take this opportunity. Anyway, go ahead Zeynep."

"Yes, what was I saying, she needed a job and a place to stay. I promised her that I would look for a job and accommodation and then I left her. She said she felt lucky to know me and thanked me. A few days later, I took her to Cafe Bellini." I was sure that Filiz would help her. Indeed, they hired her. Also, since I didn't find it very appropriate for Elvira to stay with her, I suggested that she stay at my house for a while. Thus, beautiful days had begun for her once again. Since both of us were working, we couldn't be together very often. She was very pleased with her job at the restaurant and the people she met there. In fact, some of our friends and people she met here became her admirers. However, she said, "I've had my share of disappointments in this area, so I don't want to start dating for a while." One day, she shared that she came from Turkey with a broken heart and that he had an American friend named Kevin while she was at school—apparently, he was a teacher at the school he attended—and ultimately, she experienced a great disappointment. I don't know if you are aware of any of this. We must lay everything out clearly to uncover the truth.

Mr. Zeki said, "Oh My God, every time we listen, new people keep emerging. Just when we were talking about Elvira, now Kevin has come up. This situation is getting increasingly complicated."

Zeynep continued: "I want to explain one more thing: A few days before you arrived, I did some research. Eventually, I was able to reach Kevin. I explained the situation regarding Ebru to him over the phone. I asked if he had any information. He remembered Ebru. He said she was a very sweet and very nice girl, but he hadn't seen her since school ended, that is, after June. In fact, he felt hurt that she never called him. When he learned that she had been trying to reach him, he became worried too. He took my phone number. If he hears anything, he will let me know."

There was a moment of silence. None of us knew how to comment. Zeynep broke this silence: "Now let's move on to the second act. After Hakan left the house and Ebru, for some reason, the poor girl who had to leave the house seemed to hesitate to disturb us again, and without informing any of us, she went back to Elvira's. We later learned that she had started working there. I was worried about her and went to that bar once more to see her. She was very different from the old shy Ebru. It was as if she had adapted to that environment. She was joking with the customers, humming songs, and even when people made gestures at her, she didn't react, and she was saying things that didn't suit her at all. After watching her for a while that night, I really didn't like the change I saw in her. It was as if the innocent Ebru had gone. Now, in front of me, there was a young girl who seemed to be someone else entirely. She gathered herself a bit when she saw me. "I wasn't expecting to find you here again!" I said, somewhat scolding her. "Go work at Cafe Bellini, get out of this filthy place!" I told her. "I can't go back there anymore, I would be ashamed," she replied. She said something else that touched my heart. "You are all very good people, I don't deserve this kindness. For now, I want to stay here. Don't worry about me. Thank you all. You've already done everything you could for me," she said. "We would do it again," I replied. No matter what I said, I couldn't change her mind. I left there feeling helpless. Mrs. Şermin, with a new hope, said, "I think if we talk to that girl named Elvira again in more detail, we might learn something. How can we find her, I wonder?"

"Well, I was just about to say that. I met Elvira in the evening. I explained that you all came from Turkey to find Ebru. She said she would be happy to help if she could. She will be here short-ly to share everything she knows." Thus, Zeynep answered Mrs. Şermin›s question.

Suddenly, the door opened. We all looked in that direction. It was none other than Umut. He had arrived earlier than usual that morning. After inquiring about Mr. Zeki and Mrs. Şermin, he spoke with Zeynep, hoping to receive some news. When he learned that there was nothing new apart from Elvira's visit, he began checking the salt and pepper shakers on the tables and filling the empty ones. Fifteen minutes later, when the restaurant door opened and a strangely looking young girl walked in, we all realized she was the American "bartender" named Elvira. The first thing that caught our attention was her reddish hair, which was sharply extended towards one cheek, and the ivory-shaped earring that dangled to her shoulder on the shaved side of her head. The area around her blue eyes was framed with black paint. She approached us wearing chunky-heeled boots with a rounded toe beneath her mini skirt. She looked to be about twenty-five years old. Ms. Şermin and Mr. Zeki looked at each other in astonishment. What caught my attention the most was the small suitcase she was holding. After the introductions were over, we told her to take a seat. However, she didn't want to sit down right away. She told Zeynep that she wanted to discuss something private with her in the other room. They went to the other room together. Elvira was still carrying the suitcase in her hand. Ms. Şermin, who was staring at this strange woman, looked at me with curiosity as if to say, "What's happening?"

"I'm sure she will say something special. We'll learn soon, don't worry," I said. A few minutes later, when Zeynep called me too, Şermin and Zeki became even more curious. When I went to there, I saw that Elvira was taking something out of her suitcase. As I got closer, I realized that these were Ebru's belongings. They were clothes like a sweater, socks, a scarf, and a belt. A notebook resembling a diary also came out of the bag. Elvira showed the items and asked, "Should we show these to mom and dad? Would they be upset?" We couldn't decide right away. I wanted to see the notebook. When I flipped through it, I found writings in Turkish that I believed were written by Ebru. Zeynep and I were puzzled about what to do. Should we give this notebook to her family or not? I thought that this notebook was very special and might contain things that her family wouldn't want to know, so I suggested that we at least not give it to them for now. Zeynep and Elvira agreed with my idea. I went upstairs with the notebook. I hid the notebook in a place where Metin wouldn't be able to see it. I thought I would read it myself at an appropriate time. Hoping to find a clue...

When I returned to them, Ebru's belongings had been brought out. Mrs. Şermin was crying, pressing the sweater in her hands to her chest. Mr. Zeki's eyes were also filled with tears. Elvira had mentioned that she found this suitcase in Ebru's closet some time after she left the house. Ebru had either forgotten these belongings or had intentionally left them behind. Elvira couldn't give them to her because she would never see her again.

When the American girl saw the sad state of the mother and father, she said, "Is there anything I can do?" We told her that if she told us everything she knew about Ebru in detail, she could help us in this way. And Elvira began to explain: "I met Abby (Ebru) thanks to Kevin. Kevin has been my friend for a long time. He was Abby's English teacher at the language school in Oak Park. He mentioned that there was a very cute Turkish girl among his students. One day, they came to the bar where I work together. That's how we met. The young girl was quite shy. She drank a beer reluctantly. Then they started coming together more often. I realized that they had a closeness that went beyond friendship. Kevin was showing her around Chicago, taking her to the cinema, theater, and dinners. Abby was staying in a student house close to the school at that time. I also saw her at Kevin's friend parties a few times. Abby was probably in love with him. Kevin actually liked her too."

Zeynep and I preferred not to mention some details while translating what Elvira was saying into Turkish. Elvira continued to explain: "Kevin is quite a bit older and more experienced than Abby. To him, this girl was nothing more than a cute child. He enjoyed spending time with her and teaching her things. While he was helping her improve her English, he was also preparing her for social life. Abby seemed very happy in those days. Everything was going well until Kevin's ex-girlfriend returned from Texas. Kevin could no longer spend as much time with Abby as before. He believed that Abby needed to fly with her own wings now. After all, Abby had graduated from school around that time. We thought she might be going back to her country. But it didn't turn out that way. One day, Kevin brought her to me. 'Abby is not returning to Turkey; she has decided to stay here. Can you help her?' he said. I suggested that she stay at my home until she found a job and a place to stay. She accepted my offer and came to my house with her suitcases the next day. My apartment is a two-room flat, and I gave her one of the rooms. She didn't go outside at all for three days. She was writing something in Turkish in a notebook. I felt sorry for her. It was obvious that she was in love with Kevin. I tried to comfort her. She was very young; there were so many loves and adventures ahead of her. She had spent pleasant times with Kevin and gained experience; wasn't that enough? "Finally, one night I managed to convince her to go to the bar. I thought it would be good for her to meet different people and continue with her life. However, she just sat in a corner, not looking at anyone's face. I wanted to teach her bartending. She was afraid that no one would hire her because she didn't have a Green Card. I didn't know how to help her. One night, when those Turkish young men came to the bar, I told them that Abby was Turkish. She didn't trust them, but for some reason, the person she trusted was Zeynep. Then, as you know, she moved in with her and started working at that restaurant. Occasionally, she would drop by and we would catch up. She was happy with her life. One day she came and announced that she was going to get married. I was very happy for her. Abby was beautiful, she was a good person, and she deserved to be happy. But sometimes, things don't turn out as one hopes. These are all life experiences. One shouldn't be crushed by misfortunes. Abby was very fragile. After her husband left her, she fell into depression. I encouraged her a lot to seek her rights legally. She was scared. This is America; there is law. There is no point in giving up on life. You must fight for what you want. Or you must leave everything behind and start a new life. Life is short; it's not worth being sad about anything. I gave her encouragement in this direction. I took her to fun places. She had to leave her home because she couldn't pay her rent. Since Zeynep got married, she had no other place to go. I opened my door to her again, but she didn't want to go back to Cafe Bellini. I arranged a job for her at the bar where I worked. She was laughing and having fun. I thought everything was going well. One night when I came home, she wasn't there. I looked, and her things were gone too. I couldn't understand why she left so suddenly. I waited, thinking she would come back or call within a few days. She didn't call. With friends, we thought that she had been saying a lot recently, 'I need to get my life in order.' She was talking about wanting to study again and build a career. So, we always thought positively. Another possibility was that she had gone back to her husband or returned to her country. We believed that she would inform us sooner or later. We are still waiting. I miss her very much. Please let me know as soon as you hear anything." Turning to Ebru's parents, she said, "Don't worry, everything will be fine. For now, good luck, bye-bye!" and left. After she left, we all tried to connect what Elvira had told us with our own knowledge. No matter how we organized the events, we couldn't reach a tangible conclusion. As we gained new information about Ebru and her life, our concerns only grew. Mr. Zeki said, "So she was last at this girl's house, and after that, it's unknown. According to what she said, this girl helped Ebru a lot, but still, I didn't like her much. What was she doing with this hippie? Oh, my foolish girl!"

Ms. Şermin completed Mr. Zeki's words: "I wish she had returned to Turkey then." Ah, my beautiful child. She never showed us that she was in such trouble; that she was broke and homeless. She had only written that she might go to Aslı's place for a while. Who knows why she changed her mind?" Well, didn't you ever ask Aslı?" Zeynep asked. "How could we not ask, my dear?" We talked on the phone before coming here. She last spoke with Ebru two or three months ago. She also does not remember the exact time. She told her that she was not happy with her husband. Later, Aslı called her a few times, but Ebru didn't answer her phone. She was very curious. She didn't say anything else. She is also waiting for news from us. From Ms. Şermin›s statement, it was clear that unfortunate Ebru had not received any closeness from Aslı, whom she called her close friend, at a time when she needed it the most. "Anyway, let's leave those aside for now. Although Elvira didn't give a specific date, since she said the beginning of September, it has been a little over a month and a half since Ebru left her house." So, if we are going to track her down, we need to find anyone who has seen her or heard anything about her in the last one and a half months. Up to this point, those who know her closely; namely, Zeynep, Umut, Aslı, Kevin, and Elvira, if we do not know what Ebru has been doing and who she has been with in the last one and a half months, two options arise. Since it is certain that she did not return to Turkey, in my opinion, Ebru is either with Hakan or with other people we do not know. In that case, first, we should broaden the scope of our investigation. Secondly, we must find Hakan. "I put forward such a strategy, even if it was clumsy." Mr. Zeki said, "You are right, Ms. Filiz."

How will we implement these two suggestions of yours? That's
the problem." he said."

"Of course, we will find a way."

"We need to think," I replied. Listening to all this conversation while standing, Umut said, "I just remembered something,"
pulled up a chair, and sat down next to us. All eyes were curiously turned towards him. It was as if we suddenly had a feeling that
we would find a clue in what Umut was about to tell us. And he
started to narrate: "Honestly, was it two and a half months ago?
I can't remember the exact time, but one day Ebru showed up
here. I was very happy to see her. "Umut, you hadn't mentioned
Ebru's last visit to the restaurant before, why?"

"I couldn't help but ask."

"Honestly, she was in a very miserable state during her last
visit." I hadn't told them to avoid upsetting her family, but now
that I think about it, it would be better to explain everything." Ms.
Şermin, 'Now I'm really curious. "Quickly tell me, son," she said.
Umut continued: "It was a quiet day." Ebru suddenly showed up.
Filiz Sister and Metin Brother had gone on vacation to Florida.
When she found out they weren't there, she decided to sit for a
while. Her clothes were very shabby. Her face was pale. I convinced her to eat something. Despite not being fond of drinking,
she surprised me that day by asking for Turkish raki. She drank
a lot with white cheese, tomatoes and fried potatoes. When the
customers decreased, I sat next to her for a while. She seemed to
be out of her mind. He told me, even though it was not his style,
to play İbrahim Tatlıses's song "Yalnızım Dostlarım." I put on the
cassette. She was both drinking and humming the song:

> 'O eski halimden eser yok şimdi
>
> Istırap içinde yorgunum şimdi
>
> Tutun kollarımdan düşerim şimdi
>
> Yalnızım dostlarım, yorgunum yorgun.'[5]

---

5 "There's no trace of my old self now. I'm weary, in agony now. Hold
my arms, I might fall now. I'm alone, my friends, I'm tired, so tired."

"That day, she wanted to be Ebru, the Turkish girl, not Abby." I told her that I was her friend and that she should tell me everything. She kept telling me that I was a very good person and that she didn't want to upset me. She drank and cried; seeing her like this, I hated that traitor, that scoundrel Hakan even more. If I knew where he was, I would have put him in his place. She told me she didn't know where he was. She couldn't bring himself to call him either. Ms. Şermin was shaking her head from side to side, saying, "Ah! Ah!" but couldn't finish her sentence. Mr. Zeki asked, "Well, who is this man?" "Is there anyone else here who knows him?" he asked. The one who could best answer this question was Zeynep. Because this man had also scammed Zeynep's husband. When I looked at Zeynep, she had to explain: "According to what we heard, this man came from New York to Chicago three years ago." She said he was in the carpet business. We didn't hear that he had any relatives or very close acquaintances here. He was a bit of a mystery. He was a wealthy-looking, attractive man. However, as my husband got to know him, he began to see his true character. We have not seen him do anything else other than bringing four or five Turkish carpets to a shop that sells Turkish goods. He ran away without paying the last two thousand dollars he borrowed. "At that moment, a work-related issue regarding Hakan also came to my mind."

"There had been a business relationship with Hakan as well." Actually, Metin didn't like Hakan very much. He was only being tolerant for Ebru's sake because he was her husband. In fact, when they got married, we even held a small party at the restaurant in their honor. They would come here for dinner from time to time. One evening, while sitting together, Hakan mentioned a project to Metin. A friend of his who works in the marble business in Turkey wants to export marble to America. "Metin Abi, there's a lot of money in this business; but we need some capital." Let's do this business together. "I'll take care of everything, you just put in the capital," he was saying. After discussing in detail, he managed to convince Metin to get involved. Ebru said, "I will take care of it too, I'm tired of sitting around doing nothing." "I want to be useful," she said, and partly out of consideration for her, it was decided to bring marble from Turkey and market it here. Metin suggested conducting preliminary research on where we could sell the marble. Hakan stated that we first needed to pay a twenty-thousand-dollar deposit. In the following days, everyone had started their research. I will never forget, it was a cold day. Ebru entered through the door, her face flushed from the cold. Her boots were covered in mud. "You're cold, sit down and have something warm," we said, but he excitedly and breathlessly started to explain. She was holding something wrapped in paper, like a package.

"I found it! I found where we can sell the marble!" she said.

"What's going on! Where are you coming from?" I asked.

'From the cemetery! Don't even think about asking what I'm doing there in this weather.' I wanted to contribute to this as well. An idea came to my mind; I walked to the cemetery over there. 'What does it have to do with it?' we looked at his face curiously. He continued: "I spoke with the cemetery director there. "In the meantime, he was opening the package in his hand. Something like a marble vase came out of it.

"They put the ashes of the deceased into these marble containers, according to their will." There is one made of clay, but the one made of marble is more valuable. The man said, "If necessary, we will buy it." I did a good job, didn't I? I haven't even told Hakan yet. "I came to inform you immediately," she said. Metin and I tried hard not to laugh at the dead dust container on the table and Ebru's condition. Metin, not to dampen her enthusiasm, said,

"I wish you hadn't gone all the way there in this rainy and cold weather." Let the men work, you take care of your comfort. "We'll think about this matter thoroughly later," he said.

"Months went by." There was neither marble nor money around. After a while, Hakan informed us that this job would not happen due to some complications, and he paid us back the money we had given him in two installments of ten thousand dollars each. Later, we suspected that he might have used this money elsewhere.

Mr. Zeki suddenly: "May God curse this guy!" This scoundrel thinks my daughter is naive. "The fault is mine, I should have come and done research on this man.

Zeynep jumped out: "My father is an officer. He had the MIT in Turkey investigate the man I was going to marry." Ms. Şermin explained why they did not need to investigate: "My daughter praised this man so much; the letters, the phone calls, the happy photos, we believed it. We decided to come with Zeki at one point. We missed Ebru very much and we wanted to meet her husband. But she told us not to come, that she and her husband were planning to come because she missed Turkey very much, but unfortunately, they didn't come." By this time, we had forgotten about Umut. Maybe he remembered something important that would be useful. I turned to him: "So Umut, you were telling me. You were telling me that she drank raki with İbrahim Tatlıses' song that day, that she was very sad, and then what happened?"

"Oh, yes. What was I saying? That day, Ebru was the Turkish girl, not the Abby she was trying to be. She was very touched. She was saying a lot of things I couldn't make sense of. The last words I remember were: 'I am a sinful person, I can't even face my family anymore.' I don't know what she meant. Despite all my insistence, she didn't open up to me much. She absolutely refused my suggestion to inform her family. Seeing her like that, my heart felt like it was in pieces. I think she was depressed. I told her to go and rest, suggested that we talk about everything again the next day with a clear head, and tried to explain to her that pessimism was not the answer. After she left, I couldn't clear my mind for a long time. I waited for her the next day, and she didn't come. She never called again. I asked around, but I couldn't find any trace of her. Since that day, every time the door opens, I keep waiting as if she will come.

"There was silence; we all had tears in our eyes. I broke the silence and tried to make a comment: "From what she told me, she must have been in psychological depression. She needed spiritual support beyond friends. She had lost her self-respect spiritually. Couldn't she have gone to a psychiatrist, maybe with someone's help?" Zeynep jumped in: "Yes, yes! Why not? I'll search all the hospitals with my children. Even Dr. Yilmaz can help us with this." Thus, as our research shifted to a new area, there was one thing that kept haunting me: Ebru's notebook. I had to go upstairs as soon as possible, read it, and learn the truth from her own pen. I was sure that what I would read would lead us to her.

Abby - Ebru's Diary

That evening, we sent the Erdem family to the hotel early. While Metin was sitting in the restaurant with his colleagues, I took the notebook out of its hiding place and started reading it with great curiosity. I was alone with Ebru's diary or rather, with Ebru herself.

In her memoirs, which she wrote from the first day she arrived in the New World full of beautiful dreams, I was heartbroken to see how a young girl's feelings, loves, and expectations for the future, the foundation of her life, were transformed into universal pain in a foreign storm.

From the diary:

September 5, Chicago

I arrived in America exactly five days ago. The first reason this was exciting was that it was my first time on a plane, and the second was that it was my first time abroad. I was happy to leave everything behind and start a new life. But I would be lying if I said I didn't feel a little fear inside. What if Aslı doesn't come to meet me? What will I do in a foreign country? I don't know the way, and I don't speak the language properly. I am sure she will come. Then I thought, what if they ask me something when I go through customs and I can't understand or answer—won't they let me into America? I had my passport and student visa all ready. I immediately convinced myself that I didn't need to worry.

What a big plane it was! So much food and so many drinks came and went. We also watched two movies between naps. I couldn't sleep much because of the excitement. I took a nap for a while. I couldn't talk to the passengers next to me, except for a few words.

It felt like there was no night at all. It was like a time warp. When I looked out the plane window, the sun never set over the clouds, which looked like a white cotton field. This view of the endless sky made me feel lonely. I was going from one side of the world to the other. I wondered what was waiting for me there. This change would be one of the milestones of my life: a new country, new people, a new life…

After the plane flew over the Great Lakes, the captain announced that we would land in Chicago in a few minutes. We were already watching on the TV screens in front of us as the plane flew over the map. When the plane descended, I looked out the window and saw very neat settlements, green fields, as if drawn with a ruler. Then very tall buildings began to appear. It was a tremendous view. I was amazed by the bird's-eye view of Chicago from the airplane.

My fears were realized. My visa procedures were completed quickly. My luggage was not searched. At the exit, I found Aslı waiting for me with a boyfriend. What an exciting, extraordinary day it was. Aslı and I embraced with joy. She had a classmate named Enrike with her. He had come from Brazil. Aslı had come here last year and made many friends. After traveling for about an hour by taxi, I arrived at the house where I was going to stay in a place called Oak Park. I couldn't believe that I was in America. The dream I had been dreaming of for a year had come true.

The landlady was a middle-aged, blonde woman. She had no husband. She lived with her eighteen-year-old son. She greeted us at the door with a smiling face. She showed us my room. There was nothing but a bed, a built-in closet, a small table, and a chair. Another student who lived next door in this house was a chubby Japanese girl. After she said "Welcome" to me, she mumbled something, but I didn't understand anything. After Enrike left,

Aslı helped me settle in. After informing me about the procedures here, she made sure to tell me to call the host woman "host mother". The word sounded funny to me, and I laughed. I was only given breakfast and dinner at home, but I was to have lunch at school. Sandwiches, burgers, stuff like that. Six hundred dollars a month for rent for the house and six hundred dollars for school. We have already paid part of it in advance. I hope I learn English well so that my father's money won't be wasted. I have to be worthy of them. When I return to Turkey, I will pass the university exams and become an English teacher. I can also show off that I learned English in America. It was hard to leave my mom, dad, and brother, but they will be proud of me in the future. We will endure the separation for a while.

In the evening, I was tired and sleepy, so I went to bed without eating anything. Aslı was going to pick me up the next morning and take me to the language school. It was already a ten-minute walk from home to the school. Let's hope for the best! Welcome to your new life, Ebru!...

September 20

Dear Diary, I had planned to write to you every day, but fifteen days have passed and I haven't written anything. Everything is so new to me, so exciting, that I would rather live than write. I will write longer in the future.

We have a class of twenty. How nice! All kinds of people from different countries: Chinese, Mexicans, Puerto Ricans, Iranians, Poles. There are no Turks except me. It's better for me. If I don't speak Turkish, I will learn English faster. Our teachers are also very nice. Especially, there is a grammar teacher; his name is Kevin, a very attractive man. He is also very friendly. When Aslı and I eat sandwiches in the cafeteria during lunch break, sometimes he comes to our table and drinks coffee. He makes a lot of jokes and makes us laugh. He is both handsome and kind. I study grammar a lot to win his favor. I spend my evenings doing homework. Aslı helps me sometimes because she knows English better than I do. She's preparing for what they call the "TOEFL" exam. When she gets it, she'll go to a college in Boston to get in. She's rich, of course. She can do her higher education wherever she wants. She has a friend waiting for her in Boston. "Maybe you can come next year," she tells me. I know that won't be possible, but even if I finish here and get my certificate, that's enough for me.I'm a bit cold at home. Aslı gave me a blanket. Also, I don't get enough to eat in this house. The host mother only gives me cereal and milk for breakfast. Where are those delicious Turkish breakfasts? Toasted bread with butter, olives, cheese, tomatoes, and boiled eggs. Anyway, American grocery stores don't have the kind of olives and cheese we can eat. What to do? We'll make do. Recently, I got very angry with this host mother. She only gave Akimo and me instant soup for dinner. She herself cooked meat with her son and ate it. I didn't speak enough English, so I couldn't say anything to her. But one day, I will definitely put her in her place. I don't eat much at school to save money. I think I'm going to lose weight.

October 10

How quickly the days go by. It's already been over a month. Everything is going very well. I'm learning a lot of English; six hours a day is not too little. I don't write to my parents very often, but they call me once in a while to satisfy their curiosity. I tell them that I am working hard, that I am doing very well, and they are pleased. I don't know how I'll repay them. Maybe in the future, I'll get a part-time job and take some money with me. If I have time, I can work in the school library. Let's see what happens.

We became good friends with an Iranian boy in our class; his name is Habib. Only two of us are Muslims in this class. When he sees me, he says, "Assalamu alaikum," and when I say, "Wa alaikum as-salam," he is very pleased. He likes me, but I don't feel anything more than friendship for him. What I like the most is that Kevin has nicknamed me "Abby." He takes a lot of interest in me in class and in the cafeteria. Aslı is going to Boston next month. I'm very sad. What am I going to do among all these strange people? But I have to be strong. I have to face life alone.

November 2

I saw Aslı off in tears. She promised to phone me, to write me a letter. Last night, I felt as if I was all alone on an island in the middle of the ocean. I missed my mother, my father, my brother, even Izmir. I cried all night. Fortunately, Kevin comforted me today. "Don't worry, I'm here. I will take care of you," he said. It made me feel better. I had stupid thoughts. What is a big American teacher doing with me?

November 15

A very nice thing happened the other day. Mr. Kevin Davis asked me to visit Chicago with him this weekend. I was very happy and excited. I had been to the city center twice before with Aslı and Habib together. We went to an Iranian restaurant called "Reza's Restaurant". The food was delicious, just like Turkish food, but the portions were huge.

On Saturday morning, Kevin picked me up in his car from the house where I was staying. Half an hour later, we were in Downtown. On the way, he was telling me a lot about the city, but I couldn't understand it all. Sometimes, I pretended to understand so as not to be rude. There is a Cafe Restaurant on one of the top floors of the Hancock Tower, the second tallest building in Chicago. We went up there. The view was great. The cars and people below looked tiny. He had a beer, and I had a coke while we had dinner at our table by the window. During dinner, I told him about Turkey and my family as much as I could. I think I did well, although I was a little shy. He kept correcting my mistakes and said, "Very good, you should keep talking like this and practicing. This is your biggest shortcoming, talking. I will help you with that," he said. I was very happy.

In the afternoon, he showed me Picasso's works in certain parts of the city. One of them really caught my attention. Something that looked like a woman's head, how lonely and foreign it looked...

When he drove me home in the evening, he said, "I still have many more places to show you. Be ready next week, sweet Abby..." I blushed and thanked him. I didn't sleep much that night with mixed feelings.

December 10

I'm so happy. I phoned Aslı right away. I told her everything, about my friendship with Kevin, even my feelings for him. She was very happy for me. She told me to go on, to relax, not to feel any guilt or regret. That's what I'm trying to do. Kevin and I meet every weekend now. One time, we took a cruise on Lake Michigan, and the view of the city from the lake was so beautiful. During the tour, the tour guide was telling the history of every place and every building we passed. We had romantic moments. He also took me to Chinatown. We ate Chinese food together, bought various Chinese teas. He always paid for it. When he realized that I was embarrassed, he patted my hand and said, "Don't worry, there will come a day when you will pay."

The most exciting moments were when I was visiting the botanical garden. After watching the white polar bear at the zoo from a place like an aquarium, we found ourselves in the botanical garden in a large greenhouse nearby. As we were walking among the huge tropical plants and flowers, our eyes met for a moment. Suddenly, he kissed me on the lips. There was no one around. The smells of flowers and plants mingled in the misty air. "No one saw us," he said slowly. I felt completely different. He had kissed me on my forehead and cheek before, but this time it was completely different.

That night, I couldn't sleep again. I had beautiful dreams. "He must love me too. Who knows, maybe in the future we'll marry," I even thought. I wonder what our children will be like, blond and blue-eyed like him, or brown-haired like me? And what will their religion be, Muslim or Christian? Oh my, I'm already thinking so much. What can I do? There is no limit to dreaming! There is no prohibition...

December 15

Everywhere, streets, trees, houses, shops were decorated with colorful lights. The allure of red and green colors everywhere... Preparations for Christmas began a few weeks ago. The host mother put one of the pine trees with shiny balls, snow, angels, soldiers, trumpets, red bows, and bells on it in our house. Small gift packages were lined up underneath. Maybe she will give Akimo and me something too. The snowfalls and freezing temperatures were very much in the spirit of Christmas, which they call "Christmas". The smiling faces of the volunteers in red and white Santa Claus outfits, in front of the big markets, ringing bells and collecting money from shoppers for charity organizations, and the "Christmas Carols" and "Jingle Bells" songs playing in the shops, regardless of the freezing temperatures, have a religious effect on people. Among all the various decorations inside the market, the Santa Claus carriage pulled by six reindeer was my favorite. Parents lined up to take pictures of their little children with the live Santa Claus. Santa was giving them little gifts. Americans live all holidays to their fullest. All the people who live here share these beautiful feelings and love together, and aside from religious differences, it is as if they have an invisible spiritual bond uniting them. Just like Kevin and me. It seems to me that we will deepen our love that has developed in this sacred atmosphere with the gifts we will give to each other on Christmas Day, December 25th.

December 20

I'm going through such intense emotions that I don't have time to write. I've even stopped writing letters to my parents. When we talk on the phone sometimes, I tell them I'm happy with my life, that everything is going well, but never mention Kevin. It's still early.

I get along better with Kevin now that my English has improved. We are teachers and students in the class, although some of my classmates seemed to sense the situation. I even accepted an invitation from Khabib, an Iranian, so he wouldn't find out. One Sunday, he took me to the Baha'i Temple. It was an enormous building with a high dome, a mixture of a mosque and a church. Habib told me that it doesn't matter what religion you are; it brings all religions together at a common point. It has millions of members from all over the world who help each other financially and spiritually. Then we went to Taco Bell together and ate the famous Mexican taco (ground meat and lettuce salad in a cornmeal phyllo). "You are my friend, my brother," I said to Habib. Although he had other expectations, he was pleased by this closeness. I told Kevin all this, and he was not jealous. I guess that's what a civilized American looks like.

Kevin was not a very religious man. He didn't go to church every Sunday at noon. Say it was an important day. One Friday, he asked me to go with him. I wanted to see and learn everything while I was in America. I went with him. Unlike our simple mosques, the church was very ornate. Even though it was Friday, the schools were closed. It turned out that day was Good Friday. Gosh, Fridays are considered holy in our country too, but we don't call one of the Fridays "Good Friday". I didn't really care why they called it that. What mattered to me was being with Kevin, no matter where we were. Everyone was immaculate and very well dressed. Men and women, children, were in a single file line. At the entrance, they were lighting big candles with a long stick. We lit one each, and I made a wish. In Turkey, we sometimes light candles at the tombs and wish for something, I thought it was something like that. Then, when the queue moved towards the inner part, I saw something even stranger. A priest wearing a long, loose dress, white lace garment, and a skullcap on his head was touching everyone's head lightly with something like a ladle in his hand. I got my share of the scoop too, and I could hardly stop myself from laughing. It was not over yet. We came across a table covered with white lace. On the table was a large book with one page opened. When I looked carefully, I saw a picture of the Virgin Mary on one page and a picture of Jesus Christ on the other, with their holy halos around their heads. One by one, everyone kissed these pictures and then bowed and passed under the table. It was too much for me. I didn't do that. Kevin said to me, "There's a belief that if you go under the table, your wishes will come true." My dreams have already come true; I'm a brand new person. I'm "Abby", the free and happy girl!

December 24

Tonight, the American people celebrate Christmas, the birth of Jesus Christ. Everything is closed, the streets are empty. Everyone is at home with their families. Food is eaten, gifts are given. Family members who haven't seen each other in a long time are catching up. Kevin went to Minnesota to be with his family. He didn't talk much about his family. His father was a real estate agent. His mother worked in a library. He had a sister who lived in New York. I've seen photos. They were all having a reunion in Minnesota. Kevin left with presents for all of them. Before he left, he gave me a little package. Inside was a necklace with a pink alexandrite stone. This pink alexandrite stone was my birthstone. He bought me this crystal necklace because I was born in June. It's an interesting gift. I was able to buy him a wool scarf. He loved it. On December 31st, he promised us he would spend New Year's Eve alone at his house. I miss him already.

January 2

I entered the New Year as a completely different person. A woman, I would say. On the evening of December 31st, when I walked into Kevin's house, it was just like in the movies. Red roses, red candles, glasses, and champagne on a table set for two. Soft romantic music completed this dimly lit ambiance of love. Deciding what to wear for that evening was hard for me. I wanted to be a little sexy, but I didn't have anything like that. In the end, I settled on a white silk blouse with a flounce and black tight pants. I didn't forget to wear the pink necklace he gave me. I left my hair straight, the way he liked it. A little blush, mascara, light lipstick, and I was ready. Just as I was leaving, I realized I had forgotten to put on perfume. I took care of that on the way out and set off.

Kevin greeted me with a kiss. He was wearing a red sweater. When I saw the preparations he had made for me, I thought, "What kind and romantic men there are in the world." Recently, my mother told me on the phone that Tolga, my former fiancé, and my good friend Ayşen were getting married. Ayşen can go to hell for him. Now I understand better what a rude bastard he is.

That night, Kevin brought to the table a steak, pasta, and salad that he had cooked with his own hands. "Don't do anything tonight," he said, not asking for my help. Before we started dinner, we toasted to a happy, successful year, and as our meal of salad and tortillas continued, he made jokes and made me laugh. A man who tells humor in moderation always attracts women. We were laughing and trying different wines, and later that night, as we danced to romantic music, he whispered in my ear how much he liked my eyes and hair. On the best night I've ever had, give myself to him.I was. Actually, I was saving myself for Tolga. Anyway, he's the one and got married. There was no point in keeping my virginity that I had brought from Turkey.

"I was surprised, I didn't know you were a virgin," Kevin said when he woke up in the morning. "It's amazing that you've stayed that way until this age!" he continued. I couldn't quite make out what he meant by that. "In my country, most young girls are like that," she said, "but I'm not a virgin, Ebru, anymore, I'm your Abby," and he was very pleased. "Sure, sweet girl, you are my darling Abby," he said. He was listing many more beautiful words. Except for one; he never said "I love you".

February 3

The days go by so fast, and I live so fast. It seems like there is no place I haven't traveled to. Kevin and I continue our touristic trips on the weekends. At the Field Museum, I saw the remains of the Indians, Egyptian mummies, an enormous dinosaur skeleton. At the art museums, I saw original paintings by famous artists. The thing I was most impressed by was the nine different jars I saw in the Museum of Industry and Science, showing the nine-month process of a baby in the womb. I got goosebumps looking at these fetuses, which I did not know whether they were real or not, in nine jars filled with liquid. I thought, "I'm glad I'm taking precautions not to get pregnant."

Kevin often takes me to see his fellow countryman Elvira, who works in a bar. There we drink beer and chat. The girl, Elvira, despite her strange appearance, is a very sincere, friendly, and cheerful person. She is very warm. Sometimes his other friends join us; we go to discos and nightclubs together; we have fun. Sometimes we gather in our houses and have parties.

There is drinking, music, jokes, friendly behavior. Even though I don't understand some of the jokes and don't understand some of the actions, I try to fit in with this cheerful group. To tell you the truth, I haven't seen too many bad things. I am never bored; I actually have a lot of fun. But what is it that suddenly makes me feel a pang inside even in the moments when I am having the most fun?

February 15

Recently, I attended a funeral for the first time in America. Out of curiosity, I decided to go with Kevin to the funeral of the father of a close friend of his. We arrived at a place called the "Funeral Home." The place was spotlessly clean and filled with flowers. Everyone, men, women, children, boys, and girls, were dressed very elegantly, usually in dark clothes. The coffin, decorated with satin fabrics, was lying on a table in the center. In it, a man dressed in a black suit and made-up to look as if alive was lying. On the front of the coffin was a large framed photograph. Robert, the dead man's son, was greeting people at the door in a dark suit, white shirt, and tie. He shook hands with me, hugged Kevin, but he wasn't crying. Then we sat down in the chairs that were lined up. With these immaculate people who had come here not to lament the dead, but to show their love and respect for him and to say goodbye, with the smell of fresh flowers in the air and the org music, with arias or hymns sung by a young and elegant black woman in a black suit and tie, it was not at all like our houses of the dead.

There was a small dais next to the coffin. After the song was over, some members of the family, whom I assumed were family members, would come up one by one and share their memories of the deceased, pointing out his good qualities. They were usually funny stories. Everyone was smiling, of course. No one said anything sad. It was time to say goodbye to the deceased. Everyone lined up in a single file. Each person who came in front of the coffin took a rose from the pile of roses there, put it in the coffin, said "Goodbye," and kissed the dead. It was our turn. I was a little scared when I saw the dead. Of course, we didn't kiss him because we were not close. But as I put the flower into the coffin, I recited a Fatiha for the soul of the deceased without letting anyone know.

The ceremony didn't end there. There was a gathering later at Robert's house. It's like a party after the death; food and drink were served, and good things were said about him. That's exactly what happened. I don't know why I'm writing all this; is it because I've really lived it? Because it seems strange to me? Because I can't decide whether our customs are better or their customs are better? I don't know...

February 18

February 14th was St. Valentine's Day. I had never heard of such a day in Turkey. Kevin gave me a teddy bear (the symbol of the day), red roses, and a box of chocolates. In my life, no one has ever given me anything like this. There is human value here. People know so many ways to express their love for each other. How lucky I am. I love and I am loved.

March 5

Everything is going well. I have broken my taboos, my prohibitions; I live as freely as I want. But why does that ache that comes from deep inside me when I don't want it bother me? I look at the people around me, how comfortable they are, they don't worry about anything. If someone breaks up with his girlfriend, his sadness lasts for a week at most. He is immediately advised to find a new lover. Someone's relative has died, they accept it with such calmness. I have adapted to this environment quite well. Have I not forgotten the people and events that upset me in the past? Or have I forgotten other things I shouldn't have forgotten while trying to forget them? If I can explain to myself what it is that makes my heart ache from time to time, maybe I will find the answer. "Am I the real stranger among these strangers?" Why am I asking myself these questions, can I not ask them? Speaking of questions reminds me. Recently, I couldn't resist asking Kevin the question that I had never been able to ask him (not even on Valentine's Day): "Do you really love me?" "Of course I do, I wouldn't be with you if I didn't! You are my sweet Abby, you know that." Why wasn't I satisfied with this answer? Forget it! "Enjoy your life, Abby!" Enjoy your life...

April 1

I'm doing very well in my studies. I'm getting high grades. School is almost over. I will take the TOEFL exam. If I win, why not, I will enroll in a college here. I will have a career. And I won't go back to Turkey. I will live here. I will bring my parents and my brother. As soon as I finish school, I should look for a job. Kevin will help me anyway.

Only, I've been feeling a little bit down recently. Maybe unnecessarily. Kevin's girlfriend came in from Texas. She used to teach at this school. According to Elvira, she was Kevin's girlfriend at the time. Her name is Mimi, what a strange name. I wonder why she came back. She's a tall, thin, yellow-haired girl, like a worm. I think she's going to stay with Kevin for a while.

Well, they're Americans. I guess it's normal for her to stay temporarily at an old friend's house. Am I jealous? He's not jealous of me at all. Or do I still think that when I love someone, they're my property? Or do I feel like I'm his property now? I have to get rid of these doubts. Kevin loves me, or else would he have introduced me to that Mimi girl? I hope I'm not deceiving myself on this April Fool's Day.

April 8

I got a job in the school library. Now that there are fewer classes, I work in the library three days a week, in the afternoons. At five dollars an hour, that's twenty-five dollars a day. Seventy-five dollars a week is not bad for now. My father doesn't have to send extra money...

I've only met Kevin once in the last week, and we went to the movies together. He seemed a little down. Mimi is still staying at his house, so we can't meet at Kevin's house anymore. Occasionally, I see them together in the corridors of the school, in the café. Mimi speaks to me very cordially wherever she sees me. Kevin told her about me. Like a civilized person, I decided to make them a gesture. I had heard from Aslı that there was a Turkish restaurant in Chicago called "Cafe Bellini". I invited them there next Friday night, and they accepted.

April 15

We were in Kevin's car on Friday night to go to Cafe Bellini. I had called ahead and made a reservation. I had some money anyway, and I was glad I was paying for the first time. They sat in front of the car, and I sat alone in the back. I was bored the whole time until we got to North Clark Street.

It was because of me that Kevin and Mimi came to a Turkish restaurant for the first time. It was actually my first time here too. It was quite crowded inside. I couldn't see any decor from Turkey, except for the poster of the Fairy Chimneys on the wall. The waiter, a young man, greeted us at the door and asked if we had a reservation. Since I realized he was Turkish, I answered in Turkish with a smile. He said his name was Umut. When he found out that I had brought my teachers, he promised to pay special attention and showed us to our table. It was a candlelit, with carnations, and Kevin and Mimi liked the dim lights and the soft music. As for me, I felt an indescribable pleasure there. Shish kebabs, meatballs, eggplant salad, stuffed leaves, hummus, everything was delicious. How much I missed Turkish food; Umut brought us *Kavaklidere* Turkish wine. I told them a lot about Turkey with praise. There were Turks at a crowded table up ahead. "Play Bülent Ersoy," they insisted. Umut could not break them. Bülent Ersoy was singing a song with her loud voice, crying and crying. I was so touched, my eyes filled with tears, and Mimi said, "Is this singer crying or singing?" and they both laughed.

The food, the music, the people speaking Turkish; for a moment, I felt like I was back in my homeland. I was thrilled to be there. Especially when I ate the baklava Umut offered with Turkish coffee at the restaurant, my joy was complete. I was certain that Kevin and Mimi did not share my feelings at that moment.

When we left the restaurant, I wasn't sure if it was just courtesy, but they said they enjoyed everything. Kevin wanted to cover the bill, but I insisted on paying. It had become a matter of honor for me. A hundred dollars was a significant amount for me, yet I paid it willingly. Kevin, following his custom, said, "At least let me leave the tip," and handed Umut a twenty-dollar bill. Umut, beaming, said to me as we left, "Let's meet again; come by as soon as you can." He's a lovely guy. Kevin and Mimi thanked me profusely before they left me at home and vanished into the night. As they drove away, I missed Kevin stroking my hair.

April 30

Fifteen days had passed since that night. Each day, I waited in vain for Kevin to come and tell me that Mimi had left. Nothing changed. Finally, he invited me to dinner. He was taking me to a Greek restaurant. "I have something to discuss with you," he said. I was overjoyed. I thought my patience would finally pay off. After all, I had less than a month and a half left of school; we had important decisions to make.

On the way, I confessed that I had missed him terribly; I couldn't help it. He admitted he missed me too. However, at dinner, he shared the kindest yet most painful news. In essence, he and Mimi had resolved their issues and decided to reunite. He said he would never forget the good times with me, always remembering "sweet Abby." He reminded me that I was young with a bright future ahead, promising many more loves. "Don't worry about anything, make new friends, plan your future, be happy," he advised. I was speechless, overwhelmed by emotions. He probably thought, like many in America, that I would take such news in stride, perhaps saying, "We had good times, I learned a lot from you," and move on to another relationship the following week.

"I understand," I said, allowing my tears to flow quietly. On the way home, I couldn't contain my tears; I felt utterly helpless. He stroked my hand and my hair, hugged me tenderly, and asked me to promise not to be sad. If I needed anything, he would be happy to help me. Mimi even felt sorry for me. Both of them said they would help in any way they could. I was in shock; I couldn't think of anything, and I still can't. My head is like a mixed-up suitcase; I can't find anything I'm looking for... I can't write any-more...

May 15

I have not been myself for fifteen days. I live as if I am a ghost in another world. My body goes in and out of classes, works in the library, but it's as if my soul is not in it. School will be over in a month, and I don't know what to do. Kevin doesn't teach our classes anymore. He's been replaced by another teacher. Occa-sionally, when we meet at school, he says, "How are you, Abby? You look beautiful today," or "It's beautiful outside, go and walk around with your friends; I've taught you everywhere," in that American way. Every time I see him, it's like a hole in my heart. Especially when I see him and Mimi together, I feel very bad.

I must get away from here as soon as possible, but where? I stopped by Elvira's recently. I told her everything. She already knew. "These things happen in life; it's not the end of the world. Throw your sorrows behind you, start a new life, enjoy life like me," she said, offering me a beer. After I drank the beer, when she saw that I was feeling better, she said, "Come here when you're bored, we'll go for a ride together." What a nice girl.

May 20

As I was thinking I should pull myself together and make a plan, Aslı came to my mind. I have some money saved up. I could go to Boston with her. I believe she will help me. I will enroll in a college there. I've learned English now anyway. Aslı must have made a network there by this time. I think she can find me a job. In our last phone call, I told her that Kevin and I were over. "Don't be sad, you've had some good times, right? With the experience you've gained, you can have even better days in the future. You're young, you're beautiful, you have a long future ahead of you," she said.

Oh my God, everyone is saying the same thing. Aslı thinks just like Kevin, just like Elvira. I wonder if something is wrong with me.

May 23

Today I decided to call Aslı and talk to her about my plans for Boston. She was at home anyway. I excitedly told her my thoughts. Unfortunately, her answer was nothing but a big disappointment. She said exactly this: "Ebru dear, it would be very nice for you to come here, but my current situation is not suitable to accept you. You know Selçuk, whom I told you about recently, who is doing his master's degree in engineering here, and now we live together in my house. The apartment is very small. I wouldn't be able to find a job for you here right away; it's not as easy as you think. And you know, everything is more expensive in Boston than in Chicago. I think the best thing for you to do is to go back to Turkey. Don't get me wrong, you know how much I love you. You're a sensitive person; I don't want you to get lost here. You can come to visit me in the future, okay honey? Don't worry about anything. Choose what's best for you. Kiss you. See you again, bye..."

I decided not to call Aslı again. She doesn't understand that I don't want to go back to Turkey. I am no longer that innocent Turkish girl Ebru; I am no longer Abby. Who can I offer my broken and shattered heart to? I have to find a way. I have to stand on my own two feet without depending on anyone. Yes, a way...

June 15

I am now at Elvira's house. On June 10th, I successfully finished the language course and received my certificate. That day, Kevin came up to me in the cafeteria and congratulated me. We had coffee together. If they had touched me, I would have cried, but I talked to him as a friend without showing my feelings. It's very difficult, almost impossible, to stay friends with someone you're in love with. As for him, he was happy with Mimi. They haven't talked about marriage yet. Time will tell.

He asked me about my plan. He thought I was going back to Turkey. I told him that I was not going back, that I would find a job and work. He knew I had nowhere to stay. "If you want, stay at Elvira's for a while, I'll phone her and ask her to help you. Besides, she is very helpful; she will be able to find you a job. You know she loves you very much," he said. Desperate, I agreed.

The next day, I packed my bags and left Oak Park, saying goodbye to the sullen "host-mother" and Akimo, who spoke English like Japanese and with whom I could not get along. Kevin did me "one last favor" and drove me to Elvira's house. Mimi wished me success and happiness in my new life before I left the school. "I'd love to hear your good news, call me if you have any problems, take care sweet Abby," Kevin said, kissing me on the forehead as he used to when he said goodbye.

I knew I never wanted to see Kevin or Oak Park again. I had closed another door on my past. I unlocked the door with the key under the doormat and went inside. After I closed the door behind Kevin, I couldn't contain myself and burst into tears.

I didn't leave the house that day; I was feeling very tired. I sat down and wrote a letter to my parents. They had asked me when I was going back to Turkey in our last telephone conversation. I explained in proper language that I would not be returning for the time being. I wrote that there were opportunities to find work in a few places and that I wanted to earn some money and do research to complete my higher education. I told them that I was staying with a girlfriend, not to worry, and that I would write in more detail as soon as possible. I did not give the phone number of Elvira's house. I do not intend to stay here for long anyway. After finishing the letter, I looked at the photos of my mother, father, and brother that I had taken out of my suitcase. I'd even forgotten. My eyes filled with tears. When I was unpacking my suitcase, a few novels I had brought from Turkey caught my eye. I had never had a chance to read them. I opened one and started reading it, Orhan Pamuk's "The Black Book."

June 18

Last night, Elvira took me to the bar where she worked, against my will. I was sitting in a corner thinking. I was at such a crossroads that there was no way out... I rejected Elvira's offer to teach me how to be a bartender because I didn't feel ready for anything yet. I don't have a green card anyway. Even though she convinced the boss and told me I could work illegally, I honestly didn't want to work there.

With the money I saved, I bought food for the house, cooked meatballs, soup, and pasta. Elvira was happy about it. She is very close to me, too close. She hugs, kisses, and caresses me every now and then to console me. Sometimes I get bored with this intimacy.

While I was sitting on the stool in my corner drinking beer

and smoking, Elvira brought me a shot, a drink whose name I didn't know. "What's this?" I asked, and she said, "Danny's buying for you," pointing to a young man on the other side. The man raised his drink in the air and greeted me. I thought I was working in a pavilion in Turkey. I wanted to refuse, but Elvira said it was rude, thanked him, and told me to drink. I reluctantly did as she said. Ten minutes later, another shot came. So... ...it was too much for me. Even though my helpful girlfriend told me, "People who come here alone usually leave in pairs. You are a nice and pretty girl, you need someone too," I said, "I'm leaving," and left.

I need to find a job and a place to stay in a few days, but how? In the meantime, I thought of that Turkish restaurant. "Cafe Bellini", what a name. If I go there, what was the name of that cute guy, Umut, I think it was, and he puts me in touch with the boss, I wonder if they will give me a job as a waiter or something. I have a feeling that I am ashamed of meeting Turks. I feel like everything is written on my forehead; they will read me, make fun of me, humiliate me. That night, Umut had already seen Kevin and everything. I wonder if he understood our relationship. I'd better think about it for a few more days. Or like Scarlett in the movie "Gone with the Wind": "Tomorrow is another day," and not think about anything for now.

June 21

I spend my days crying at home. The tears I never show to anyone drip on my diary and on "The Black Book." "I will read my diary to you when I come back," I wrote to my friends in Turkey. I thought it would always be full of beautiful and interesting things. Everybody who comes here starts writing a diary at first and then stops for some reason. Let's see when I'll stop. Everything is getting harder and harder for me. I have no job, I'm running out of money, my purpose is unclear. I am in a state of uncertainty. I've started to dislike myself. I can't find the strength to fight. I need a miracle. I'm waiting, not knowing what I'm waiting for.

Tonight, bored, I went to the bar again. Elvira introduced me to some young Turkish guys who came there. What was the point? Some were studying, some were working as limousine drivers. They were looking at my face and smiling wickedly. Who knows what they thought I was when they saw me at the bar. They immediately asked for my phone number and said things like, "Let's meet and have fun together." I was so embarrassed. I never want to see these drunks again.

June 23

Tomorrow, which was another day, turned out to be today. I walked straight through the day and passed by Cafe Bellini. I looked in the window. Only a few tables were occupied, there were two waitresses. I couldn't see Umut. If I had seen him, I would have gone in and talked to him. I said I would come back another day and walked away. But there are some coincidences that fate, perhaps destiny, somehow brings people to the same point.

I couldn't resist Elvira's insistence and went to the bar again tonight. While she was praying that no Turkish kids would come, a lady with an angelic face, Zeynep, came in. She had been told about me by some young Turkish boys who worked in the same workplace as her, and she was curious. After talking to her for a while, she immediately realized that I was unemployed and in trouble. She told me that she could help me with everything and even find me a job in a Turkish restaurant. The restaurant she was talking about was Cafe Bellini. She said that she knew the owners and that she would call me tomorrow after meeting with them to let me know. I couldn't tell her that I had wandered around there during the day. I think I'm getting a little lucky. Last night I slept well for the first time.

June 24

Sister Zeynep took me to Cafe Bellini. I met Mr. Metin and

Ms. Filiz, very nice people. I wish I had met them before. Umut was there too. He was very happy to see me. I will start work in four days. I am very happy and excited. Moreover, Zeynep Abla said I could stay with her. She will get married in two months and move into her husband's apartment. After she leaves, if a suitable roommate is found, I can stay there, sharing the rent. Thank God everything is going well.

June 28

Today, in the morning, I excitedly went to my new workplace and was greeted with smiling faces. I will serve water and coffee until I learn how to be a waiter and how to prepare drinks. And then there is the cleaning of the tables. So it's like being an assistant waiter for now. Umut, the cook Ibrahim, whom they call Toni, and Cemil Abi helped me a lot. They started teaching me everything from the first day. But I didn't like that Polish waitress named Elizabeth. She didn't give me much attention. That's okay, it doesn't matter. Tomorrow, Zeynep Abla will take me to her house, and the first thing I will do as soon as I get settled is write letters to my parents and give them good news.

July 20

Thank God, everything is slowly getting better. Zeynep Abla's apartment is very comfortable, and I have a separate room, albeit small. We don't see each other much because we both work, but we have good conversations when we are together. She encourages me to go to college. We also talk to Filiz Abla and Metin Abi from time to time. They give me advice on everything. Metin Abi says, "Open your eyes, reach whatever your goal is."

Toni taught me to laugh and cheer up again with his jokes. They are all very nice people. As for Umut, he never takes his eyes off me. What a kind-hearted child. There is no evil in him. Recently, we went to the park by the lake. Everything was green, and the lake was sparkling.

Sailboats on the water, people chirping on the beach, and a true friend by my side; I started to love life again. Umut compliments my beauty. But I have no intention of embarking on a new adventure.

August 15

I'm now a waitress, and I make good money, though not as much as Elizabeth. Recently, Elizabeth gave me the wrong description of a cocktail called the "Manhattan," and I embarrassed a customer. She giggled, prepared the right one, and left. And, of course, she got the tip. No matter, there are many other customers who over-tipped me. She's jealous.

With the money I saved, I bought Nike sneakers for my brother, a perfume for my mother, and a shirt for my father. These are the first gifts I bought for them with the money I earned. I also bought myself a swimsuit.

Last Sunday, Umut and I went to the beach. The water was a bit cold. There was no sea air smelling of seaweed in this sweet lake water, but it was clean. We sunbathed a lot. He wrote beautiful poems for me and read them. Everyone thinks we went out together, but we're just friends. But tell that to Toni. It's better to fall into a cesspool than into his tongue...

September 1

There was a TOEFL course at Truman College where Umut went. He took me and enrolled me. After the two-month course, if I passed the exam, I could easily enter college. I could even work as a translator in Turkey with the certificate given after this exam. There's also a "Restaurant Management" department at this school. I didn't know there was a university for restaurant management. Umut's intention is to go there. When he finishes, he will be the manager of the biggest and most beautiful restaurants in Turkey. A manager who looks like Richard Gere!

I wish I could feel more than friendship for Umut. For now, I've hidden my feelings of love in my subconscious. I'm more comfortable this way.

September 20

My days are good at Cafe Bellini. Dr. Yilmazlar, Moşe and his wife Miranda, Peter, Adrienne, Freedler all became my friends who were very close to me. I get a lot of tips from them. I'm also on good terms with the staff at the restaurant. Even Elizabeth has started to commiserate with me sometimes.

Zeynep is moving out at the end of this month. We are looking for a student to share the house with me. Recently, a young, handsome man named Hakan has been coming to the restaurant a lot. He is an attractive man. He leaves me a lot of tips. He was in the carpet trade. I think he's doing well. Umut doesn't like him at all.

October 1

Zeynep moved out. She got married without a wedding. I hope she will be happy; she is a very nice person. We still haven't found a partner for the house. I have to pay the rent for now, even if it is too much. Umut is staying with a relative. He wanted to move in with me, but I refused. I don't want to give him false hope. In the meantime, Hakan asked me out. I said, "I'm not ready for something like that, let me think about it."

November 2

I haven't written anything for a month. I'm experiencing new excitements. I don't know if I'm making a mistake again. I'm still a young girl. It's my right to experience good feelings. I hope I have found true love this time. Hakan and I are going out, traveling, talking. I told him about myself, everything. He listens to me with interest. He has been in America for six years. He married an American woman to get a green card, then divorced her. He's had girlfriends, but he hasn't found true love yet. He has feelings for me; his feelings are real and sincere. Of course, we get along better because he is Turkish. I don't want it to be a temporary relationship this time. I can't say that I know him very well, but if we get along well, maybe I can marry him.

November 20

This month I had an unexpected event. I had a very scary time. The police from the immigration office raided the restaurant. There was a tip-off. I, along with Erkut and Roberto, two Turkish students working illegally, were caught. Luckily, Umut was not there that day. Toni got away with hiding in the garbage bin. I ran upstairs in surprise, but they saw me running and caught me there. It was the scariest day of my life, and I was destined to end up in a police station in a foreign country. There, I was trembling with fear and crying all the time. Our photos were taken, our fingerprints were taken, as if we had committed some great crime! Metin was in a very difficult situation. Who knows what punishment he will face? I told everyone not to tell my family. They would be very upset, very worried. I had no right.

Luckily, Hakan paid two thousand dollars for my bail and got me released. He told me at the police station that he was my fiancé and that we were going to get married soon. I was shocked at first; I didn't believe it was real. When he picked me up and took me to his house, he told me that his motive was serious. He even told me that we should hurry up and have an American wedding so that I could stay and work here legally. After a nightmare, a dream come true.

I told my family about it over the phone, and they were very surprised. They said that they wanted to see and get to know Hakan first, and then they wanted me to make such a decision. I did not have much time to wait. I did not want to be deported. I immediately accepted Hakan's marriage proposal, and he promised to give me a beautiful wedding in Turkey.

November 27

On Monday, November 26th, at nine o'clock in the morning, Hakan and I were in front of the judge. Actually, no young girl wants to get married in such a hurry. My heart was especially bitter because I didn't have my family with me, but what could I do, circumstances demanded it.

The day before, I couldn't resist and bought myself a white lace dress, white shoes, and a bag, unbeknownst to Hakan. After a moment's hesitation, I decided to wear them. After all, I was the bride. I did my make-up and hair carefully. When Hakan came to pick me up early in the morning, he was surprised to see me in white. "If I had known, I would have bought you a wedding dress. I thought you would wear a wedding dress for our wedding in Turkey," he said. I was actually a bit embarrassed. Even though I said, "I can take it off if you want," he said it looked great on me and asked me to keep it on.

When we arrived at a place like the courthouse for the wedding, I saw a long queue! In casual clothes, there were many men and women waiting in line with papers in their hands. I felt a little embarrassed because of my attire, so we got in line. Those who went in to get married came out five minutes later, smiling, papers in hand. After waiting in line for half an hour, it was our turn.

We went inside and stood in front of a judge who looked as if he was asleep. After looking at our papers, he asked us if we recognized each other as husband and wife. "Yes," we said. "The rings," he said. Hakan pulled out gold rings from his pocket, and we put them on each other. The judge signed and sealed the papers with sleepy eyes and said, "Congratulations, you are married." We walked out with our marriage certificate, which cost only twenty dollars. After this quickie marriage ceremony, I still couldn't believe that I was married.

That evening, after having dinner at a nice place, we went to his house, our house, as husband and wife...

December 5

When I went to Cafe Bellini two days after the wedding and announced our surprise, they were all very surprised. They didn't expect me to get married so soon. At first, they didn't look very happy. Then they congratulated me and gave me good wishes. Umut was so upset when he heard the news that he hurriedly congratulated me and left the restaurant without saying anything else. It broke my heart to see him like that.

Elizabeth's eyes were moist as she said, "You're so lucky, you've found a husband." "Come on, come on, you hit the jackpot," Toni said.

After Metin and Filiz got over their surprise, they said, "This can't be like this, let's have a party here, let's celebrate, you're like our daughter," and said that they didn't feel comfortable with me getting married in such a poor way.

On Saturday evening, I put on my white lace dress again. Hakan looked very handsome in a black suit, white shirt, and red tie. Metin Abi had prepared a long table for that night. Almost all the friends were there. Zeynep and her husband, Dr. Yılmaz and his wife Serap, Moşe and Miranda, Peter and his girlfriend, Lawyer Freed and John, and the elegant Filiz, who wore a very elegant blue dress as the hostess that night, and Brother Metin welcomed and congratulated us with applause.

When Metin made the first champagne toast in honor of Hakan and me, the entire restaurant staff joined in. Except for one person: Umut.

We ate and drank with jokes. Old Mr. Freed, who compared me to Mona Lisa, read a poem for me. A painter asked Hakan to borrow me to paint a portrait of me for his friend. We laughed, we had fun, we had our photos taken.

Even though the absence of my own family remained a pain in my heart, I was very happy to feel that I was not alone among these beautiful people.

December 20

How time flies. It's been over a year since I came to America. I feel like I have lived a life of ten years in this time. When I was packing up my things from Elvira's house to move into Hakan's house, I saw the photos I had taken with Kevin. I tore them all up and threw them away. I didn't even want him to be in my memories as a friend anymore. He heard from Elvira that I got married and wished me happiness. Elvira was also very happy that I got married. Although she wanted to meet Hakan, he didn't want to go to the bar and even forbade me to go there.

My husband didn't want me to work, so I couldn't get my job back at Cafe Bellini. I spend my time doing housework in my well-furnished house overlooking the lake. I also try to write down my experiences in my notebook, which is my companion when Hakan is away.

I wrote to my parents that I had married Hakan and that I was very happy and relaxed and sent them photos. They didn't think it was right that I was getting married alone, but they didn't say much because they didn't want me to be upset. I gave them the good news that Hakan and I would come to Turkey next month.

January 4

We entered the New Year in New York. Hakan had lived here before, so he knows the place well. He took me to a Turkish restaurant with music. We had a good time. At some point, the New Year's Eve of a year ago flashed before my eyes. A wound in my heart that had begun to close suddenly reopened; it bled a little, then went back into its place in my subconscious and hid.

The second biggest city I saw outside of Chicago was New York. It seemed too big and complicated to me. I have to send a photo of me in front of the Statue of Liberty to my parents. Chicago appeals to me more because I'm used to it.

February 15

January came and went, but we could not go to Turkey. We could not realize this plan because Hakan was busy with his work and often went to other cities for work. My family was very sad. At one point, I thought of bringing them here. Hakan said, "It would be better for us to go; you can see your family, relatives, and friends, and you can satisfy your longing for Turkey." I found him right. I want to go at the first opportunity.

February 20

Hakan and I get along well. I am kind of happy. But I get bored sitting at home all day. He never lets me go anywhere alone. I can't even go to Cafe Bellini. He's obviously jealous of Umut. I do everything he says to gain his trust. I'm sure he loves me, that's why he's jealous. I sacrifice more than my personality to make him realize that I am a faithful wife. I left my life in his hands.

March 1

One evening recently, Hakan and I went to Cafe Bellini. We had dinner with Metin Abi and Filiz Abla. Hakan decided to start a marble trade with Metin. Marbles would be brought from Turkey and sold here. We all liked this idea. We needed to do research on where we would sell the marbles. I also wanted to be useful. When I said I wanted to do research, Hakan could not object with the support of Filiz.

While Hakan was traveling, I spent a few days visiting marble coffee table shops, upholsterers, etc. The most interesting one was the marble vase I brought from the cemetery. They never bought my idea. Why?

March 15

Most of my days are spent alone at home. Clean the house, cook, do laundry, watch TV, nothing else. I started watching three TV series at once. Sometimes I read novels if I can find them. Hakan doesn't want me to talk to the Americans in the building. I honestly didn't expect him to be so conservative.

He doesn't take me on business trips either. I would love to see new places and learn new things. He doesn't tell me much about his work, even though I want to share everything with him. I would like him to tell me everything with an open heart like me.

Apart from that, he takes good care of me and his house. He buys me nice clothes, jewelry. He wants my whole world to be just him. I hope that maybe in time, as his trust in me grows, he will let me go to school or work somewhere.

April 5

Everything continues in the same way. The only places I go alone are the supermarket downstairs and the laundromat. However, I want to have a work life, a group of friends, a personality outside my marriage. I have nothing left except being Hakan's wife. Actually, I didn't come here to get married; I would have found a husband in Turkey and gotten married. What happened to my ideals? I thought I was going to have a career!

I was aware that he would not approve of my wishes. His plan to go to Turkey is constantly postponed, with various excuses. I think the best thing to do is to have a child.

April 10

Last night I told Hakan that I wanted to be a mother. I thought he would be happy. "It's too early, it's not necessary," he said. I've lost that hope too. How long am I going to put up with living like this? Why do I get bored just when I think I've found peace? Do I feel uncomfortable like Hakan says?

April 20

Hakan's business trips used to last three or four days at most. This time he's been in Los Angeles for a week. I don't know what he's doing there. It's too bad he doesn't tell me everything. I guess he calls from time to time to check up on me. I took advantage of his absence and went to Cafe Bellini. They were all very happy to see me. Even Umut was happy to see me; he said he was glad I was happy. I spent a nice and joyful day with my old friends.

April 23

When my husband returned, he questioned me. I confessed to him that I went to Cafe Bellini. He was furious. He yelled, screamed, and insulted me. I shouted that I could not live like a slave like this. "Do you want to walk the streets like a middle-class woman? You will stay at home; I will take you wherever you want," he said. I never thought he would have such an outdated mindset. I was sad; I cried.

In the evening, he came home with flowers. We had dinner together. He tried to tell me how much he loved me and protected me from the evil around me. I came to the conclusion that I had no choice but to forgive him.

May 1

At the supermarket pharmacy, I bought the materials to take a pregnancy test. With great excitement, I looked at the result and saw that it was positive. I felt joy mixed with fear. Now I will have a baby, and I will take care of it. Even though Hakan doesn't want children, I hope he won't mind if I tell him it was an accident. Who knows, maybe he will be happy to be a father.

When he came home in the evening, I didn't know how to break the news to him. I cooked a nice meal, decorated the table with candles and flowers, and told him the good news at the appropriate moment. His response was as follows: "I told you it's not the right time already. Do you know that a birth in America costs ten thousand dollars?"

I was devastated. My answer to him was, "Then I will go to Turkey and give birth there, if that's the problem. You already know how much I miss my parents. They will take care of me." I didn't want to argue any further. It was as if this news, which should have brought joy and happiness to a family, had turned into dark news. I thought he needed some time to get used to this new situation and decided to wait patiently.

May 6

Despite all my efforts, I couldn't convince him about the baby. He told me that he was going on a new business trip and that we should take care of it before he left. So he wanted me to abort the baby. I protested vehemently; there was no way I could do such a thing. When he left, he left me some money, but he didn't say where he was going. "I'll phone," he just said. I haven't heard anything from him yet.

May 10

There is still no news about Hakan. I don't know what to do, who to go to. There is no phone number or address where he went. What has happened to me? Let me wait a little longer; maybe he will call.

May 15

I've given up hope; he won't come. I guess he left me. I thought he really loved me. At least he should have felt a responsibility towards the baby in my womb. I haven't even seen a doctor yet. Should I go to the police? Maybe something happened to him? No, no, he'll be mad at me. I could lose him completely. I wish I had my mom with me. I need her so much. It's too late now. I couldn't tell them anything if I died. I didn't listen to them. It's all my own fault.

May 20

I'm about to go mad. God, what have I done to deserve this pain? I am so ashamed of myself, of everyone. I can't go to anyone and ask for help. I'm miserable waiting by the phone every day. It's as if the earth has collapsed. How tolerant, how self-sacrificing I had been to him. In return, I was abandoned with the baby in my belly. They had warned me at the time; they had said that this man was an unknown quantity, but I only see the good side of everyone, and I believed Hakan. He came to this city suddenly and mysteriously and disappeared again mysteriously.

Sometimes I believe he really loved me. Maybe he had a problem he couldn't tell me about. But he should have trusted me: Whatever it was, we could work it out together.

I have very little money left. And the bills are piling up. What am I going to do? I'm in a huge predicament.

May 25

I couldn't take it anymore. I could think of only one person I could go to: Elvira. Because I don't want the Turks to know about this situation. They would gossip a lot; everything would be heard all the way to Turkey; I would be disgraced.

Yesterday morning, I encountered a situation I couldn't understand. There was a knock on the door; I was excited, thinking it was Hakan. But it was not him. Two strange men were standing in front of me. They were dark-skinned, Arab-looking men. They asked about Hakan; I told them he was out of town; they didn't believe me. They wanted to come in and take a look; I refused. I told them I would call the security guard if they insisted. When I asked them why they were looking for Hakan, they said, "He knows." When I told them that I was his wife and they could tell me what the problem was, they didn't give me any explanation. One of them, whose name was Ahmet, said, "He should call me as soon as possible, otherwise it won't be good for him; he knows how to reach us." They left in a hurry.

I was very scared. I had already sensed that Hakan was in trouble with some of the people he did business with. No matter what, he shouldn't have left me unprotected and alone like this. I will never forgive him.

When I went to the bar last night, Elvira was very happy to see me. We hadn't seen each other for a long time because my husband wouldn't let me talk to her. When she hugged me, I couldn't hold back my tears. She realized I had a problem. "I need to talk to you, but not here," I said. She gave me the key to her house. I went and waited for her at home. When she came, her first question was, "What happened? Did your husband do something bad to you?" I told her everything in detail. I tried to explain everything to her. She felt sorry for me. She told me that I had made a big mistake staying with this man until now. Then she said, "Tomorrow we will immediately contact the police, and there is a baby on the way. Let them find him immediately because he has to pay for all your expenses and the baby's expenses," she said, immediately addressing my problem from an economic point of view. I was drowning in a maelstrom of emotions, mixed with my shattered pride, shame, and regrets. I don't want the money of a man who left me like this. And after the mysterious men who came today, I don't have the strength to go to the police and face bigger problems.

After discussing the matter at length with Elvira, I decided to abort the baby. It was the most difficult decision of my life. Since it was also Hakan's wish, there was nothing to be afraid of. Elvira told me that there is a place like a public clinic where poor people get abortions, and they can do it for two hundred dollars. Elvira will make an appointment for me tomorrow. "Tomorrow morning, pack your things and come here, and don't pay any bills," she told me. And she continued: "After the operation, I will take care of you until you recover, and after you recover, you will work in our bar. If your husband doesn't show up for a while, you have the legal right to divorce him. We'll deal with that later. Good Abby, and you can start your life again. Everything will be fine, don't worry."

In her own way, my American friend had taken care of everything. I wish I could leave everything behind and look to the future with courage, as she said. I am grateful to her for lending a helping hand, no matter how different our outlook on life.

May 28

It's all over now. Maybe it's just beginning. I am burning in a hell of my own making, like a hollow log; I feel a great emptiness inside me, in my brain, in my heart. It is as if my soul is out of this body, looking at it from the outside. It pities, resents, even hates this body. I am becoming more and more alienated from myself.

Two days ago, I destroyed the seed of a new life that had begun to blossom in me. So there is nothing left of life in me. Is this what is called fate? Wasn't there a concept of divine justice when fate was written? I once read the Turkish version of the Quran. I remember the following statement: "Humanity will survive and endure with justice." If I am not mistaken, it was Surah Hadid. I have always believed in this principle until this age. I thought that no matter what happens, divine justice will surely manifest. I see that people, especially good people, face situations they don't deserve. If I am a good person, I should be worthy of good things. I look at the world, I look around me, I look at myself, I don't see such a sense of justice. Even in the courts, sometimes it is not the one who is right, but the one with the strongest evidence who wins. So, are we not going to seek justice in this world? As even Mother Teresa said in the last days of her life after seeing the misery and suffering of innocent and sinless people in India: "Life is not fair." Life is not fair?

Where did these thoughts come from in my empty head? Isn't fate my misconceptions about people, about life? But this was the only way I knew to be right. Trusting people, loving unconditionally, being selfless... Was all this wrong? How can one live without believing in something, without trusting it? Whose fault is it that my poor baby died before it was born? I know I won't find the answers to these questions. It's best not to think about anything, nothing. I'm so tired, I need to sleep.

June 10

After a few more days of rest, I decided to work at the bar. I've been trying to get used to my new job for a week now. I don't like it, but there's nothing else to do for now. Elvira does everything she can to entertain me. She introduced me to new friends who come and go at the bar. It's a very cheerful group of young men and women. Some nights we go to concerts at the disco. Elvira tells me, "Forget everything, enjoy life."

June 22

I let myself go with the flow of life. I try to forget the bad days by feeling that many things are missing inside me. My friends and I go to very strange places that I have never been to before. These parties are held in places like basements, where people in bizarre costumes have fun in their own way. In these dimly lit places with strange decor, strange music... anything goes. They do everything I can't write here. Sometimes I find this strange atmosphere creepy.

One night recently, I went to a Gothic bar with some friends. We all dressed in black, painted our faces and eyes. Elvira gave me a blue wig. No one would recognize me like this. They put something sweet on the chest and shoulders of a half-naked girl and everyone took turns licking it. It all seems strange to me, but Elvira tells me that I should be more free in sexual matters. She says it like this: "It is a law of nature; we were programmed for sexual life when we were created, so there can be no shame or sin."

June 27

Elvira is a good-hearted girl. She has her own way of living. She is happy with her life. No matter how much I try to match her, I can't be as relaxed and cheerful as she is. At the most un-expected moments, a voice comes from the depths of my heart: "Who are you?" I ignore this voice for now. My friend Elvira, with whom I share a flat, has other things that are contrary to me. For example, she doesn't wear underwear. The other day she was lying on the carpet at home in her short shorts, talking on the phone with her boyfriend. As she moved, her privates showed through her baggy shorts; I felt disgusted. She goes to the bar like that, without panties. She's not afraid of me at all. One night she said, "I'm so cold, warm me up," and crawled into my bed.

I found out more about her; I asked her why she goes to the police station once a month. It turns out that she was caught with drugs a few years ago and was under surveillance. I have never seen her using drugs, but I still suspect her. Sometimes I think: what am I doing among these people? I don't belong here; do I have another option?

June 28

After the scene I saw last night, I realized that I couldn't stay in this house any longer. I had just come from the bazaar; I opened the door and entered the house to find Elvira naked in my bed making love with a man. When they saw me, they both continued without breaking down. I threw the packages in my hand and rushed out of the house. I felt sick. How could I ever sleep in that bed again? I have to find a way. I have to find a way out. I have to talk to Umut.

July 2

Yesterday I went to Cafe Bellini. I remembered the good times I spent there. I felt more sad. How nice Umut and the people working there were. Filiz was gone. I couldn't appreciate these good people. I followed a jinxed love. I thought that I was so infected with the jinx that I had no right to be among these good people. And before I could tell Umut anything I had planned to tell him, I left to avoid causing them more grief.

July 5

Last night I had a dream. It was one of my fondest memories of my childhood. I was six or seven years old. My mother had made me a fluffy dress with a white cat for the holiday. On the day of the holiday, she tied a white ribbon in my long hair to match my white dress. I looked like a fairy girl in my white socks and shoes. We went to visit my grandmother who lived in a nearby village. There was a field behind their house. In that field, delicate red poppies bloomed among the greenery. Ignoring the white dress, I dived into the poppy field and ran after the colorful butterflies as I always did. While I was trying to catch them, my mother was shouting behind me: "Come here, you'll get your white dress dirty!"

I relived the scene in my dream, but with one difference: as I ran merrily, the poppies turned into cobra snakes, as did the butterflies... These green and red snakes raised their flat heads towards me and tried to sting me. I woke up sweating blood in terror. Where is that innocent little Ebru now? Am I Ebru or Abby? Or am I nobody?

October 29th Republic Ball and Human Landscapes from the Turkish Community in Chicago

After reading Ebru's diary, it was as if a black liquid flowed into me and spread throughout my body. The hopeful white thoughts in my head gradually darkened. The young girl's two years of life in America had been laid out before me last night, page by page. In the morning, I woke up thinking that everything was just a nightmare. When I took the notebook out of my hiding place and picked it up again, I saw that everything I had read was true. My heart ached. I don't think the ball we are going to tonight will alleviate my grief over a human tragedy that I alone witnessed. Reluctantly, I opened the wardrobe and chose the dress I would wear tonight.

When I went downstairs around noon, I expected to see Ms. Şermin and Mr. Zeki, but they were nowhere to be seen. When I asked Umut, he told me that Zeynep had taken them on a limousine tour of the city. I guess she wanted to keep them busy with something else.

I thought of the notebook again, full of hope, disappointment, pain, and helplessness. I didn't know what to do. Should I give it to his parents? What else would it do but make you sad? There are very special memories of Ebru inside. Maybe she doesn't want anyone to know about them. When we meet in the future, when she finds out that I gave the notebook to her family, won't she be angry with me, won't she be more upset? I have to respect her private life and the memories she writes. But what if there is a clue in these writings that I didn't realize, a clue that could lead us to her? I have to talk to Zeynep about this.

In the afternoon, Zeynep dropped Mr. Zeki and Ms. Şermin at the restaurant. They were looking into my eyes as they asked me, "Is there any news?" At that moment, when I was reading Ebru's notebook, it felt as if the black water that had spread over my body was circulating on my face. I was trying not to look at their faces so they wouldn't see it. After they answered "No", they quietly went to their usual corners and sat down.

Before I left Cafe Bellini, I told Zeynep that I wanted to ask her for advice on the dress I was going to wear tonight and asked her to come upstairs with me for five minutes. She understood the situation. I gave her the notebook, maybe she could find a clue. After all, she and Ebru had lived together in the same house for a while.

At the table in the corner, Ms. Şermin was talking about the places she had visited when a surprise guest entered the door. This person was none other than Ms. Özge from the Turkish Consulate. When I saw her, I was happy that she brought good news. Ms. Özge was actually making a courtesy visit. She said that all the staff of the Consulate were interested in this matter and that they regretted the situation. After having led the ball, she added that they had decided to make an announcement on the subject at this evening's ball. She also stated that Mr. Zeki and his wife could attend the ball as special guests if they wished.

The black water inside me started to recede a little. As Ms. Özge had said, among the hundreds of Turks attending the ball, there was bound to be someone who knew or heard something about Ebru.

Mr. Zeki and Ms. Şermin said they did not want to attend the ball. They thought that if there was any news, we would convey it to them anyway.

As Metin left Cafe Bellini in his tuxedo and I in my black toilette, the husband and wife, who were sitting gloomily in their corner with Umut, saw us off, saying, "I hope you hear good news."

The official Turkish ball in Chicago is usually held once a year. This is the October 29th Republic Ball. If it does not fall on a weekend, it can be a day or two before or after. Tonight, we will celebrate the founding of our Republic with Turkish diplomats, Chicago's elite Turkish community, American, and other foreign guests in the "Moulin Rouge" hall of the Fairmont Hotel in the city center.

When we entered the hall, the cocktail party had begun. At the entrance, the Consul General and his wife, other Vice Consuls, and the President of the Turkish American Association were greeting the guests one by one, "Welcome." We took a card with our name and table number on it from the table there and mingled with the crowd in the hall. Elegantly dressed men and women, with glasses in their hands, began to make small talk with friends they had the opportunity to catch up with. The voices were humming in a mixture of Turkish and English. After some small talk with acquaintances, we went to the red-carpeted dining room.

There was a lectern in the center, right next to the protocol tables. On one side of the dais was the Turkish flag and on the other the American flag. Before the food was served, Mr. Kemal, the organizer of the event, gave a speech in English, saying, "Welcome," and after greeting the crowd, he told us that he was going to play our National Anthem from the tape and asked us all to stand up. When the voices stopped and we started singing our National Anthem in unison, I was in a state of emotion that no one else in the hall could understand. For years in Turkey, every Friday and Monday, we would open and close the school with the students by singing this anthem and looking at this flag. This flag with the moon star and this anthem were an important part of my past life. My whole teaching life flashed before my eyes like a movie. A lump was stuck in my throat. The tears I could not hold back spilled down my cheeks. I felt how much I missed my school, my beloved students, my friends, my homeland.

Afterwards, the short Consul General read a stereotypical text in English about the meaning and importance of the day. As he finished, he pointed to the young people sitting at a nearby table and said that our young people studying in America would be the hope of Turkey in the future and that we would be proud of them.

Indeed, we are happy to hear about the success of intelligent and hardworking Turkish children studying at universities here. There are also Turkish doctors, engineers, professors, businessmen, and women who are recognized for their outstanding achievements. But my main interest is in other unknown young people, other professors, in short, other Turks in America.

I listened to the table of young people and realized that some of them did not speak Turkish. These were children who had grown up here in America. Most of the families living here do not teach their children Turkish, and they brag about the fact that they don't speak Turkish, as if it were an accomplishment. These children are like the leaves of a makeshift tree with no roots, flying from one place to another without knowing.

It was the turn of Mr. Kemal, the president of the association, to speak. After congratulating us on our feast, he asked us to donate to the association and to buy lots of lottery tickets that would be sold. Until then, I had never seen any other activity of this association we were members of other than organizing women's teas, parties, and picnics. After Mr. Kemal left the podium amid applause, I thought that Ms. Özge would make the announcement I had been waiting for, but I guess the time hadn't come yet. While the food was being eaten amidst a hum of forks and spoons, a jazz band made up of old men was playing the most familiar old American tunes. "Couldn't they find another orchestra? These grandfathers don't suit our young republic," said Dr. Yılmaz, with his usual humor, as we sat at the same table. Zeynep and her husband and Moshe laughed. Sitting next to me, Zeynep couldn't help asking in a whisper, "What is written in the notebook, is there anything important?"

"Not now, you'll understand when you read it yourself," I said. I had to give some information to Metin, who was curious about what we were whispering.

The people from Kars, who make up almost half of the handful of Turkish community in Chicago, were in the majority here tonight. Why had so many people from Kars and its surroundings, a city that had been left aside in Turkey, come here? According to a rumor, someone from Kars named Osman, who came to Chicago thirty years ago by accident, first brought a large population from his village, and then one by one, everyone from Kars and its surroundings who wanted to come here. It is as if they formed a clan. Some of them work in factories, some own clothes cleaning shops and car repair workshops. There are journalists, painters, and architects among them. Wherever you go where Turks can be found, you will find someone from Kars. Most of them seemed content with their lives, having achieved a level of prosperity here that they could not enjoy in their homeland.

Meanwhile, in the ballroom, journalist and painter Yücel Dönmez was walking around with his camera in his hand, trying to capture interesting events for the news he would prepare for the newspaper he represented.

The president of the women's branch of the association, a friendly lady from Kars, came up to us, wished us a good time, and told us that there were some very nice prizes in the raffle. Meanwhile, the Consul General and his wife were enjoying the orchestra of elders.

They started the fun by dancing to the music of the "Black Tie" ball. Afterwards, other vice consuls and attachés joined the formal part of this "Black Tie" ball. After a while, there was no more room to dance on the floor. When the musicians had to take a break, those who had finished their wine on the tables rushed to the bar to drink some more and have more fun. After observing who wore what and who came with whom, they got into deep conversations. The Consul General and other diplomats and their wives were surrounded by curious people who wanted to be close to them. The Consul General's wife, who was uncomfortable with this excessive attention, at one point slipped out of the crowd of kala-fish and threw herself into a secluded place.

While we were eating our cake, which was included in the fixed menu, accompanied by American coffee, Ms. Özge appeared on the dais to take advantage of the gap. After saying "Attention Please!", unlike the others, she made her announcement in Turkish. Taking care not to disturb the cheerfulness of the gathering, she said, "Dear guests, first of all, I wish you all a good evening. I will take a few minutes of your time to fulfill a civic duty. Sir, there is a mother and father from Turkey. They came to see their daughter, or rather to find her. Because they haven't heard from her for a long time. The Erdem family has been in Chicago for three or four days looking for their daughter Ebru Erdem. If anyone has seen or heard where she is, please let our consulate or Cafe Bellini restaurant know. Because the mother and father are there every day waiting for news. Thank you in advance for your attention. Have a good time," she said.

After a short silence, everyone was talking to each other about it, truthfully or falsely. A doctor's wife from Indiana, at whose table we were sitting, said, "What happened? What happened? I don't really understand. Is someone missing?" We had to give her some detailed information on the subject, and in a few minutes, the whole room was talking about it, from those who had heard to those who hadn't, from those who spoke English to those who didn't, and then to the two invited American journalists.

Wanting to turn the mood back to fun, the organizers of the ball invited Mr. Yalçın, one of the first founders of the Turkish American Association in Chicago, to the stage. Not to make a speech. Mr. Yalçın, a former musician (he now has a curtain workshop here), was going to give us a solo drum show. This Istanbul gentleman took the stage amidst applause and played a song or two to the delight of the crowd, while elegantly dressed young girls with baskets began to wander among the tables selling lottery tickets. The beautiful Ebru should have been here now, wandering from table to table with these young girls like a pretty butterfly. Who knows where she is now with the pain she can't carry on her back? I hope something good will come out of tonight and everything will be okay. After a while, Mr. Barbaros, the Education Attaché, a former schoolmate of mine, and his wife Mrs. Jale came to us and said their goodbyes after receiving information about the missing girl; there was no one official left in the hall.

Towards the end of the night, Turkish musician Poyraz took the stage and sang his most lively Turkish songs. When the music started, the crowd, feeling relieved, started to dance the halay and then started to dance the belly dance. The ball, which had begun in a formal atmosphere, had suddenly turned into a circumcision wedding. Everyone was happy and having fun. But Moshe and Miranda, who were sitting at the same table with us, didn't look very happy. It wasn't that they weren't having fun at the ball; they had other problems.

Moshe and Miranda were the two people I felt the closest to since the first day I arrived. He was neither Mr. Moshe nor Mr. Moshe Dezara, because he was much older than us, and at the same time, he treated us like an older brother. He was everyone's Moshe brother. When he immigrated to Chicago from Turkey thirty years ago, he was one of those who started from scratch. As a result of his hard work and determination, he became a successful businessman. Now he owns a wall-to-wall carpet and sofa covering workshop and has made a fortune with his three sons. He plans to retire soon, leaving the business entirely to his children. All he wants is to travel, have fun, and be happy with his beloved Miranda.

Although he is fluent in Spanish and English, Moshe loves to speak Turkish, his mother tongue, and to make friends with Turks.

Last year, the Jewish community in Chicago chose him as the candidate of the year. He had not forgotten to invite his Turkish friends to the big party in his honor. The Turkish consul, the Spanish consul, and the Israeli consul were also there with their flags. In his trilingual speech, Moshe said that Turkey was his homeland and that every year he had gone to visit his relatives in this beautiful country that welcomed the Jews, he told me in an emotional voice, with tears in his eyes.

The Chief Rabbi made a speech praising Moshe and presented him with a plaque and a certificate for his outstanding services to the Jewish community.

As we ate our meals, Metin, Dr. Yılmaz, and the other Turkish male guests had tiny Jewish yarmulkes symbolically distributed on their heads. And, of course, the famous song "Hava Nagila" was sung, and we all danced the halay together. It was a meaningful, beautiful night.

Miranda was as elegant tonight as she had been that night. A true lady, with her always coiffed blonde hair, her elegant dress, her steady hands, her French perfume, and her restrained demeanor. Moshe had met Miranda, a Frenchwoman of Egyptian descent, on a plane trip seven years ago. They fell in love and married. It was the second marriage for both of them. No one would have thought that this couple, who had been living their second spring in the most beautiful way for seven years, would have had an unusual problem lately.

Miranda, who was a teacher in France, is very intellectual, well-mannered, and humane. When I first arrived, I received more attention and help from her than from Turkish women. She showed me the best stores to shop in. When we went shopping, we would have lunch in the most interesting places and chat with her.

She chose the restaurants we would go to together on weekends, which were characterized by various nationalities; she especially enjoyed going to Arab nightclubs. She also arranged tickets to theaters and famous musicals. Thanks to her, I had the privilege of going to the play "Zorba" starring Anthony Quinn and watching the famous actor and his marvelous performance. I still keep one of the carnations he threw to the audience at the end of the play as a memory.

Miranda and Moshe's dinner parties at their home were in every way the best reflection of French taste.

How could two people so perfect and in love have a problem? In recent months, as I began to get to the bottom of the matter, I realized that they had started to fall out for the most unthinkable reason. It didn't take long for me to realize that it had something to do with what Miranda had tried to tell me during our dinners together, and even with the content of a book she had given me to read.

Miranda was a woman who believed in reincarnation. From time to time, we used to talk and argue about the topics described in the book "Soul Mates" that she gave me. She used to say that it was no coincidence that we met our current spouses, that we were reunited because we had unfinished business with them in a previous life, and that our souls matured in each new life. I used to listen with interest to his conversations on these subjects, but one day, when Moshe came alone to Cafe Bellini, he told us that the subject had already gone too far and was having a bad effect on their marriage. Miranda went to a yoga class where she met people who influenced her to join a spiritualist group with a cult-like characteristic and joined. He had become a disciple of a leader called John, who used hypnosis to reveal people's past lives. I knew about all this, but I didn't take it seriously, until Moshe told me that Miranda had revealed to him that she had lied to him that she was going somewhere else and had gone to Egypt to do research on her past life. Moshe became concerned and disturbed by Miranda's condition, who day and night attributed everything to spirits.

On this ball evening, Miranda looked as nice as ever but languid and cheerless, while Moshe looked sad. Nevertheless, they did not forget to dance their beautiful and harmonious waltz to fit in with the atmosphere. As we were dancing with them, we came across Professor Sinan , who was dancing with a young girl named Gaye. When we approached them, we heard Gaye cursing again. When Sinan , a professor of Hittite at the University of Illinois, would come to Cafe Bellini alone, he would sit at a table, drink his wine, and listen to Turkish songs while expressing his loneliness and sorrow with tears that he could not put into words. He was a little too emotional and sensitive to live alone in America. Metin took special care of him and did his best to make him feel better. Mr. Sinan, who complained about his low salary, did not hide the fact that he was in financial difficulties because he sent some of his money to his wife and children in Germany. He did not even own a car. He used to take the train from South-side to Cafe Bellini. This train ride lasted one hour and being robbed every now and then was a bonus.

On the south side of Chicago, there are miserable black neighborhoods where even the police are forced to enter. When the train passes through that area, three or four muggers rob anyone they catch their eye. Such things are very common here. I had heard stories of such robberies from other Turks who had traveled that way. Sometimes with knives or guns, these robber-ies not only resulted in the loss of wallets, watches, and wedding rings, but the horror was unforgettable. I think it might be an extension of the big train robberies we see in American Western movies. Because during a trip, while passing through Colorado, among the historical places to see, I noticed a huge sign that read "The site of America's first and largest train robbery". The names of the heroes who committed this robbery are written one by one on this sign. This must be a part of American history.

Anyway, let's talk about our professor who is very successful in his field. Although he had been robbed three or four times on the train, he would never give up coming to Cafe Bellini to meet a handful of Turkish people, risking dangers that were unheard of even in Hittite history. On such days when he was robbed, Metin would drive him home in his car without any hesitation.

I wondered who this young girl who had been with her late-ly was, and I learned her story too. I was sure that Gaye, who swore in English and Turkish when she got drunk, had not been like this when she lived in Turkey. Although it was commonplace in the U.S., this kind of talk is something extremely strange for a young girl in Turkey to swear like this. Apparently, she first learned this language in America.

One day in the restaurant, she told me that she had met and married a black American sergeant she had met in Turkey and had come here with him to live the American dream. How could Gaye know that this dream would turn into a dark nightmare?

After trusting the sergeant, who had made a very good impression on everyone in Turkey, and after coming to Chicago, the new bride found something she had never expected. The man's ex-wife and her son were staying at the sergeant's house. They had nowhere else to go. They were very poor. Gaye never mentioned any of this to her family back in Turkey. After all, she had found this man herself and wanted to marry him, despite her family's objections.

The former husband and wife shared the same house, and their mutual friends would often come over and have strange parties. Gaye always remained a stranger among them. Of course, fights started. "You can't adapt to America," he was angry with her. His ex-wife, a big, black, black bastard, wasn't treating her very well either. He tried to make her do all the work around the house. Some days she went hungry and penniless; some days she cried alone in her room. Gaye, a Turkish girl who could only endure this situation for four months, finally summoned the courage to ask the sergeant, "What about her or me?" He replied, "I'm sorry, but I can't throw my family out on the street."

The young woman, who was too proud to return to Turkey, ran away from this strange house one day and sought refuge at the Turkish Consulate. Although the consulate officials told her that they were not interested in anyone's private life, they found a good Turkish family for her to stay with temporarily. Gaye, who had not had the chance to meet any Turkish family since her arrival, was very happy. With various difficulties, she tried to establish an order for herself. This family rightly gave her only one month to settle in. In this time, she would either find a job and a place to stay or return to her homeland.

When she was taken to the Turkish family's house, Gaye felt relieved as if she had come home. She poured her heart out to them, cried as she told them, told them as she cried. After a few days, she felt strong and decided not to return to her country but to fight here. At the end of the month, this family found Gaye a job and a place to stay. She would take care of a sick American woman in her eighties who lived alone and stay in her house.

She accepted the job desperately. During this time, her husband never called or asked for her. One day, the university student daughter of the Turkish family she was staying with took Gaye to the University of Illinois, hoping to find a part-time job at the school. Luckily, they found her a suitable part-time job, albeit as an errand girl in the school cafeteria. It was in this cafeteria that they met the Turkish professor. Here, these two people, who would never have met in Turkey, shared loneliness and an inexpressible sadness.

Gaye, a lovely girl with long black curly hair, was clearly drunk again this evening. She had had the courage to risk everything and follow a strange man she didn't know well to America, but she obviously didn't have the strength to bear the consequences of her mistake. So that's how she drank, got drunk, and cursed all the time.

"Why don't you go back to Turkey?" I asked her one day, unable to contain myself. "Everyone would make fun of me; I can't make everyone laugh at me," she said. According to her, she was a high school graduate, and with the help of Mr. Sinan, she was going to enter university and study Ottoman history.

After talking to Mr. Sinan and Gaye on the edge of the dance floor, the professor said he had something private to discuss with Metin and walked away. I tried to silence Gaye, who could hardly stand up, and took her back to her desk. Metin came back a little later and told me that the professor wanted to go to Turkey and asked him to lend him money to buy a plane ticket. Metin said that he would give him the money even if he didn't pay him back because he knew that Mr. Sinan was a very good person.

When I think of professors, I think of a few other professors I met in Chicago. It's not that there aren't successful professors who make a good living in the universities here, but I'm talking about other professors.

One day, I saw a middle-aged, dark-haired man with a mustache in the kitchen of our restaurant. He was washing dishes. I called the cook İbrahim to me and asked him who this man was and how he had been hired without our knowledge.

A Turk İbrahim knew brought him here. They asked Metin, and he said, "Give him a job." Ibrahim, alias Toni, said, "There was no other job but dishwashing, so I gave him that," and then leaned in close to my ear and whispered, "Aunt, this man, he's a professor." I didn't believe him. I entered the kitchen again and said, "Hello, welcome. I'm Filiz, Mr. Metin's wife," I said.

The man, bored, said, "Hello, Ms. Filiz. I'm Hilmi."

I said, "Mr. Hilmi, let's sit for five minutes; we'll get to know you."

Mr. Hilmi took off his dish apron and came into the living room.

I didn't know how to start. "How are you? What brings you here?"

"It's a long story. I need a job for a while. An acquaintance brought me here. Ibrahim met Mr. Metin, and I started work today."

Mr. Hilmi didn't seem to tell me much about himself.

I asked him directly what I was curious about: "Toni said you were a professor, right. Is it?"

"Yes, Mrs. Hodja. I am a professor of economics. According to Ibrahim, you were a teacher too. From where to where, we have come to this..."

I didn't want to interrogate him further; I just told him that it wasn't for him.

He washed dishes for a week. I was trying not to show her too much so she wouldn't be embarrassed. I couldn't stomach him washing dishes here, so the following week, I promoted him to waiter. In the following days, we gave him a burgundy jacket and assigned him the job of "greeter," greeting customers at the door, showing them to their seats, and giving them their meals. When we learned that he had a housing problem, we transferred him, as usual, to one of the empty rooms in our building on Bryn Mawr Street that we allocated to homeless Turks.

During the three months he worked for us, he never talked about his personal life. We didn't ask him about it either. We only learned that he had once been a professor at a university in Ankara. He remembered those days with longing. Another subject he liked to talk about was Turkey's economic and political situation. Although we listened attentively to his speeches, we could never find out what he was doing here. One day he suddenly left.

Another professor I knew was an engineer who slept in a corner of a Turkish café at night and tried to make a living by taking photographs. According to him, he had been dismissed from the university for some reason and couldn't find a job anywhere else. We tried very hard to convince him to come back to Turkey; we even promised him that we would find a torpedo. But he didn't go for a long time.

Even more interesting was a Turkish economist lady who worked as a belly dancer in Arab restaurants at night to earn money.

In addition to these, there are engineers who work as porters, dentists who sell Walkmans in parks, university graduates who sleep in junk cars, the most Turkish youth living half hungry and half full in houses where large rats roam in bad neighborhoods were some of the human landscapes I witnessed with sadness.

Recently, a Turkish woman friend of mine told me that there are many people in this situation who lie to their relatives in Turkey and, so to speak, "They crawl, but they do not return to their country." Inspired by the famous poet, I say: "I swear, living in America is not worth this misery, and this disgrace."

It was with these feelings that I celebrated our Republic tonight.

Now the ball was about to end. As Poyraz sang "*Bir Başkadır Benim Memleketim*"[6] as a closing song, homesickness was evident in everyone's voices, faces, and moist eyes. I still could not erase the image of the other Turks in America in my mind.

---

6 "My Homeland is Unlike Any Other."

The Ominous Crow and the Turks from Mexico

The next morning, before going down to the restaurant, Metin and I talked a bit about Ebru's diary. He agreed with me not to give the notebook to his family for now. If necessary, we could tell the police what was written in it, but that was the last thing to do. I wondered what kind of interpretation Zeynep would come up with after reading what was written.

I woke up early this morning for some reason. I had a feeling that the knot would be untied today. Metin was still emphasizing that it would be the right thing to do to contact the police while we were having breakfast together because Ebru's husband Hakan had to be found. He was right, but I was sure that we would get some news after the ball last night. In fact, this news could come today.

After Metin went to his work, I took my tea and went out to the back garden. It was quite chilly. After all, it was already November. As I sat thinking in the cool silence of the morning, I could smell the familiar scent of chrysanthemums blooming in pots lining the edge of the small pool. Whenever I see chrysanthemums, I think of "Ten November" comes. At school, children would decorate the picture and bust of Atatürk with these flowers. Wreaths were made from these white, yellow, purple chrysanthemums...

I started to feel cold and was about to go inside when a giant crow landed on the garden wall. Everything in America is giant, and so are crows, almost the size of chickens. It looked at me and started cawing in its ugly voice.

I recognized this ominous crow, maybe not the same one, but still a descendant of it. As for the reason why I hate this crow, it has everything to do with an incident I witnessed last spring and was very saddened by. Last spring, a female cardinal had built a nest on a branch of a tree in the corner of the garden. At first, I didn't know the name of this bird, so I called it a "red bird". Because its feathers were so bright red. It was the most attractive bird among the other colorful birds. I later learned that this attractive bird, with its crest rising like a coat of arms, was so popular in North America that it was given the title of the state bird.

This is how I understood why the proud picture of this charming red bird appears on many car license plates in Illinois. In addition to being the official bird of several states throughout history, it has been given the prestigious name of "Cardinal," inspired by the high and magnificent red cardinal's hat worn by Roman Catholic officials. Not that they don't deserve this name. After watching a pair of cardinal birds inhabiting our garden, for the first time, I witnessed with admiration the astonishingly noble behavior of the bird world.

It's like he's wearing a bright crimson cloak; the male cardinal appeared as if his face was a mask of shiny black feathers. He looked like a mysterious gentleman at a masquerade ball. The female looked more dignified with her olive and reddish feathers. There were twenty-eight kinds of birds, singing the most beautiful songs. I recognized them by their voices and melodies when they sang. I had hung a feeder in the tree for them. When it was time for the female cardinal to build her nest, I saw that the male was more protective, more generous. I watched with admiration and amazement how the male cardinal, who never left his female alone while she was busy building a nest with the feathers and grasses he had collected, offered her food and put the food from the feeder into her mouth. The female bird received the same care from her male until she fledged in the nest she had prepared and the chicks emerged. Together, the two of them carried feed to the three colorless and featherless chicks day and night, never tiring. I watched this marvel of nature with pleasure every day. One day, when I went out into the garden to watch them again, the three tiny chicks were in the nest with their beaks wide open, waiting for their parents to bring them food. Soon the devoted couple would arrive anyway. While I and the chicks were waiting like this, a large crow suddenly appeared on the garden wall. In the blink of an eye, it perched on the nest in the tree and devoured all three babies in one bite. I was almost shocked. Immediately, I picked up a stone and threw it at the traitorous crow, screaming and shouting. But it was too late; the deed was done. In the face of this horrible event, I felt like I wanted to tear my eyes out.

What would the cardinals do when they came to feed their young and found the nest empty? I didn't go out in the garden for a few days that spring so I wouldn't be sad anymore.

There was that damn crow again. It was looking at me over the wall. I shuddered with fear. This time I picked up a bigger stone and threw it at him. It flew away, shouting "gaaak" in its ugly voice. I hope it's gone!

When I walked in, I saw that the Erdem family had arrived early and were sitting at their usual table. Toni was with them, talking about something.

"Good morning, are you early this morning?"

"Good morning, Ms. Filiz." They both stood up. Ms. Şermin said, "I'm sorry we are coming early and disturbing you. You know you said; when it is announced at a Turkish ball, there is bound to be someone who has seen or knows someone. We came early in the hope that there might be some news about our daughter."

"You are right. Please sit down; have Toni bring us tea, and we can all drink it together and talk about last night," I said.

After Toni went to the kitchen, I sat down with them and tried to explain to them that the announcement had been made last night, that everyone had heard about the situation, but that no one had brought any information about it yet, and that I was hopeful that there would probably be news today, either here or at the consulate. Today we wait until the evening, and if there is no news, then the next day, as Metin suggested from the very beginning, we should report the situation to the police station. I managed to convince them that it was necessary.

As we ate our omelets and drank tea brought by Toni, we kept our eyes on the door. At this early hour of the morning, no one but knife sharpeners and dry cleaners came through the door. We had a long day ahead of us, and we had no choice but to wait. The waiters hadn't even arrived yet when three people appeared at the glassed-in outer door. Despite the "Not Open" sign on the door, it was clear that these three people were not customers. When they approached us, I saw that one of them was my relative Ertan from Wisconsin. I didn't know the two young men next to him. I asked Ms. Şermin›s permission and sat down at another table with them, and Ertan introduced the two Turkish young men next to him as Ali and Erdoğan. I wondered why they had come all the way from Wisconsin in the morning, because it was unlikely that they knew Ebru. Ertan told me that his two friends had a job at the consulate and that they had come to Chicago because there was no Turkish consulate in Wisconsin. On this occasion, he was going to visit me and ask me to help these young people if I knew anyone at the consulate.

Ertan left his wife and two children in Turkey and came to America four years ago to work and earn money. He suffered a lot in the first two years. "If I told it, it would be a novel," he always says.

He started at the lowest level in restaurants. Dishwashing, then kitchen labor, and cooking. He went through different experiences until he learned these. He was fired from some places; he left some places because of disagreements. In search of a new job, he traveled to unfamiliar villages, unfamiliar cities, alone with a few belongings in his car. He learned English and cooking at the same time. In order to learn how to cook, he worked for months without pay in various American restaurants. Most of the time, he could not send money to his family. There were times when he was homeless and slept in his car. He went through many depressions.

"If my situation had been better in Turkey, I would not have endured any of this," he says. Thinking of the family he left behind, he persevered and finally achieved what he wanted. He now owns a beautiful American-style restaurant. He also brought his wife and children. They all live a good life together. Sometimes he laments, "If I had worked this hard in Turkey, I probably would have gotten to a good place."

You cannot be lazy in a foreign country like you can in your own homeland. Others do not have time to help you. Since everyone is in a struggle, no one is in a position to look at anyone else's tears. Since Ertan had experienced these situations and knew the desperation very well, he brought them here early after a two-and-a-half-hour journey to help his two compatriots so that they would not have to go through the same ordeal.

"What are you doing at the consulate?" I asked.

"I'd better tell you everything from the beginning," Ertan said, pointing to one of the two peasant-looking young men.

"Ali is from Horoz Village near Manisa, and Erdoğan is from Evrenos Village. This is where I met my friends. I didn't know them when I was in Turkey. I traveled a lot, so I have acquaintances in many places.

Recently, I received a phone call from an Albanian friend of mine who runs a restaurant in a town near Chicago. He told me that a Turk he knew from afar had left two young Turks who didn't know anything in his restaurant and didn't want them. He called me because he knew I was Turkish. He said, 'Come and take them if you want; maybe they will be useful to you; otherwise, I will have to throw them out.' I took pity on them and decided to help them, thinking of the hardships I had suffered when I first arrived. I went and got them and brought them to Wisconsin. For now, Ali is washing dishes at my restaurant, and Erdoğan is helping me in the kitchen. They live in a house where Mexican workers stay. They are very determined children; I hope they will succeed."

"I understood so far, but you didn't tell me what you were doing at the consulate," I said.

"Now let's get to the point. You'll laugh when I tell you because it's a bit funny, but it's true," he continued. Ertan looked with a smile at the two young people sitting with a shy and bored expression.

"Let me tell you briefly. One day, a man came to Horoz Village near Manisa from the United States and told us in the coffee shop that he would take anyone who gave him three thousand dollars to America. 'I took a few people there, and they became very rich,' he said. He also guaranteed a job and made good promises. Hearing this, Ali and Erdoğan had big dreams about this attractive offer. Instead of living in poverty in the village, they decided to take advantage of this opportunity. They borrowed three thousand dollars each and gave it to the man. Since it was impossible for them to get an American visa, he was going to smuggle them into the US through the Mexican border.

"The man kept his word and, as he had tried before, he brought these two friends to the edge of a river in Mexico. The other side of the river was the United States. He told them, 'You swim across here at night. The other side is America. I will meet you there; bye-bye for now,' he said. The two poor people waited for midnight in that desolate place, afraid. Even though they knew how to swim, it was very difficult for them to dare to swim in the dark and in unfamiliar water. 'Well, we have come this far; there is no going back,' they said, taking off their shirts and pants so that they would not get wet and throwing themselves into the water. With great excitement, they managed to swim across. After they came to their senses, they realized that the pants were left on the other side, along with the passports, ID cards, and some personal belongings in their pockets. They thought about it and said, 'We are in America now; we can't go to Mexico for a pair of pants.' Trembling and shaking, they hardly got through the night. Fortunately, around noon, the man who had helped them came and found them as promised. He had tried this a few times before, so he found them as if by hand. But the next thing he knew, the two guys were in their underpants. As they explained the situation to the man, he advised them, 'We will take care of it; just keep your eyes open in America, don't do such stupid things.' This wise man advised them!

"After picking them up, he bought shorts and a T-shirt in the nearest town. After a long journey of three days, he left these two travelers of hope at an Albanian's restaurant in a village near Chicago, in search of a new job...

"There's a guy in the basement of that restaurant where they spent the week. Then the Albanian friend called me because he didn't need them or wanted to get rid of them. So I went and got them.

"The problem now is that they have no identity. I wonder if they say to the Turkish Consulate, 'We lost our passports,' will they give them new passports?"

While Ertan was narrating this incident, the two naive peasant boys were embarrassedly bowing their heads and sometimes smiling at themselves.

"I swear I don't know. How can they give a passport to a person without an identity card? You better go and ask them yourself. Maybe they will find a solution," I said.

While we were deep in conversation, Ms. Şermin and Mr. Zeki were watching us from afar, thinking we were talking about their daughter. I called them over, and they listened to the interesting story of the young people with astonishment.

In the meantime, we told Ertan about Ebru. He remembered her very well, but unfortunately, he had no information about her.

After having their coffee, our guests said goodbye and headed to the consulate.

We were alone again. In a moment of silence, we heard a "pop!" on our table. We looked up and saw a huge black spider on the fishing nets. When we looked carefully, we realized it was a plastic spider. Toni was standing a little further away, giggling again.

"God damn it, did you throw this here?" I snapped.

"I'm sorry you scared me, Auntie. I guess you forgot that tomorrow is 'Halloween' (Halloween). We were even late. Everybody made their sets weeks in advance," he said.

He was telling the truth. Doorsteps and shop windows were already decorated with carved pumpkins, ghosts, vampires, scarecrows, and other horror-inducing decorations. Toni approached our table, taking something else out of the basket. She was holding a severed hand with a bloody wrist. After winding it with the key, she placed the hand on the table. The hand was moving with finger movements. Laughing, Toni said, "Look at this; there's so much more..." I was angry at Toni for this inappropriate and untimely behavior.

"That's enough, put them away. Is now the time?"

"Metin Abi told me. I'm going to make Halloween decorations."

"Okay, go do it out front."

Mr. Zeki seemed to want to manage the situation: "Toni is right; it's been on our radar since we arrived. We see pumpkins, witches, ghosts everywhere. We even asked Umut, and he told us that it was Halloween. If this is the custom here, of course you will do it too."

Ms. Şermin obviously did not like this atmosphere of fear. "It's like they are mocking us."

Mr. Zeki replied: "What nonsense are you talking? Those who live here will inevitably follow the customs of this place. What does that have to do with us?"

On the morning of this long day that would never pass, even the funny story of the Turks coming from Mexico in their underpants could not erase the negative mood that the ominous crow had created for me and the black spider for the grieving parents.

The Garbage Story

To lighten the mood and pass the time, I started telling the distressed parents about the holidays in America, while Toni drove away with her basket to the front to make a horror scene: In America, the holiday season starts on October thirty-first with Halloween. We occasionally use English terms like this; please forgive us. One day when I was a student, we asked our language teacher: 'What is the most beautiful language in the world?' I liked his answer very much; 'Every language is the most beautiful language for its own culture,' he said. Therefore, English is the best language for American culture. Turkish is the most beautiful language for Turkish culture, of course.

Mr. Zeki interrupted me, "You are right. Recently in Turkey, there has been a snobbery of saying some words in English even though they are in Turkish. I do not approve of it at all. Since you live here, it is natural for you to perceive life here with these words."

"You're right. Let me continue if you like. As you can see, orange pumpkins are the most common motif of this festival we call Halloween. Before you came, I went and bought a big pumpkin to hollow out and make a lantern. But I couldn't resist and baked a pumpkin dessert with lots of walnuts, and we enjoyed it."

Ms. Şermin forced a smile. It is very difficult for me to turn the atmosphere created to express extreme fear into humor.

"Then in November comes Thanksgiving, which is called Thanksgiving. On December 25th, they celebrate Christmas, which is their biggest holiday, Valentine's Day in February, and Easter in April. In the basement of our restaurant, we have boxes full of accessories for each holiday. We take them out when the time comes and make our decorations. Americans experience the holidays in a very intense, enthusiastic, and colorful way. Other ethnic communities who are not of the same culture or religion cannot help but be attracted to this pleasant atmosphere, which is also supported and created for commercial reasons. After all, holidays are special occasions that unite people with good feelings, with goodness, beauty, and peace at their core. They are festivities in which everyone who calls themselves an American or who lives here melts into one pot, or seems to do so, regardless of race, religion, or culture."

Ms. Şermin, who listened to me with interest, asked, "So, do people from different countries celebrate their own holidays here?"

"Of course. Everyone also celebrates their own holidays. Religious and national holidays can be celebrated openly by every community. Just like we celebrated our Republic last night. There is a common saying here: 'This is a self-governing country.'"

I had just finished when we heard Metin's words coming next to us:

"I swear, it is a free country, but it has so many laws, so many rules to follow that it is very difficult for those who are not used to it. The more free you are in your private life, the more rules you have to live by in public life. I think Turkey is a freer place; you don't follow any rules, nobody says anything. If you don't follow the system here, you don't exist. It takes a few years to learn these systems. I know people who got tired of the strict rules of this country and went back to their country."

Turning to me, "I think Ertan is here, what's up?" he said.

"Yes, I'll tell you later; he says hi."

Metin excused himself and went up to the office room to make business calls in his usual hurry.

I was trying to explain everything I could think of to distract the husband and wife, whose facial features were drooping downward day by day as if they had been subjected to gravity, and to hasten the unbearable wait. When I mentioned strict rules, a very funny incident about Ertan came to my mind again, and I decided to tell it. The couple, who did not take their distracted eyes off the door, had to divert their attention for a while with my words and the laughter.

"Look, let me tell you an interesting and funny story that happened to Ertan while you are having your coffee.

"Ertan completed the legal procedures last year and brought his family to live with him. He moved from an apartment to a detached house so that his wife and two children would be comfortable. He had a lot of trouble at first because there were no Turkish families around. But what bothered them the most in those days was the garbage issue.

"Ertan told his wife that Wednesdays were garbage day and to put the garbage in plastic bags and put them in front of the door. She did just that. On Wednesday morning, the garbage men took the garbage from every house in the neighborhood, but not theirs. She is a wise woman. 'I wonder if we did something wrong?' she said, and looked where the garbage barrels of the neighbors were. She saw upside-down plastic bins in front of everyone's door with something written on them in English. He remembered seeing such a box in the garage, left there by the previous tenants. On Wednesday of the following week, he took out the extra garbage bags again, turned the plastic box with the writing on it upside down, and left it next to the bags. They sat in front of the window and waited for the garbage men. When the garbage men came to the street, they looked at their garbage, showed the inverted box to each other, started laughing, and left without taking the garbage again. When Ertan came home and found out about the situation, he was very angry. He immediately phoned the garbage company and ranted and raved. 'You have not registered with the garbage company yet,' was the reply he received. Ertan immediately registered as required. Now they were relieved that their garbage would be collected next week. Meanwhile, they encountered another strange situation. The front and back of their house were covered with grass. One morning, they saw that a white wooden stake with a red painted tip was stuck in the middle of the front yard. When Ertan saw this stake, he grumbled, 'Which maniac drove this stake here?' and tried to pull out the stick. Meanwhile, an American man next door was cutting the grass at his house. When he saw Ertan taking the stake out, he said, 'Oh, don't take it out; they'll come again.' He asked, 'Oh my God, who's coming?' 'The officials will come to check,' the man said. 'Who are these officials, what check?' 'So you don't know. You must be new. Officials from the municipality will come to check. You haven't mowed your lawn. This stick is a warning. The second time they come, if you cut it, they will take the stick and leave; if not, they will fine you seventy-five dollars,' the man said.

"Ertan thanked his neighbor for this information, stuck the stake back in its place, and the first thing he did was to go to the market and buy a lawn mower. He immediately mowed the lawn with his son and put the cut grass in plastic garbage bags. When Wednesday came, the family got up early in the morning and put the bags of grass in front of the door along with the accumulated garbage. They were registered anyway. There was no reason why the garbage should not be taken this time. Nevertheless, Gülay Hanım, Ertan's wife, put the plastic box with the writing on it next to the garbage, just in case. Her husband said, 'You can rest easy now; you don't have to wait at the window; they will take it anyway,' and took his son and went to work.

"As soon as Mrs. Gülay felt comfortable, she started to watch the street from behind the curtain. Finally, the garbage truck appeared. When it was their turn in front of their house, two men in gloves approached their well-organized pile of garbage soup and paused. After saying some things angrily to each other, they went back without taking the garbage. Mrs. Gülay, who was watching from the window, could not stand it any longer. She ran after the garbage men and showed them the garbage, shouting in

Turkish. They said something in English, but no one understood anything. Mrs. Gülay got very angry and phoned her husband to tell him that the garbage in front of the house had not been picked up again and to come home immediately.

"Ertan phoned the garbage company, but he could only leave a message because the answering machine went off. They had no choice but to carry the stinking garbage back to the garage.

"I wonder where we went wrong this time," the husband and wife wondered, and Ertan came up with the idea of asking the next-door neighbor. Embarrassed, he knocked on the next-door neighbor's door and explained the situation. After thinking for a while, the neighbor asked, "Did you put the herbs in plastic bags?" When he got the answer, he said, "Yes," he said, "You made a mistake; you should put the herbs in big paper bags and stick the garbage stickers (stamps) you buy from the market on each bag separately. Then they will take it,' he said.

"While he was at it, he decided to find out about the up-side-down plastic box that his wife insisted on. Sir, things that could be recycled, such as glass and plastic bottles, were to be put in it, for which a separate registration was to be made, and the garbage men were to do the turning upside down after taking out the contents. After this was cleared up, Ertan said, boredly, 'I have one more question, but I don't want to bother you anymore.' The helpful neighbor said, 'Please don't be shy; neighbors are there to help each other. You can ask anything,' and he continued: 'Like everyone else, there is a mailbox on the side of the road in front of our house; put your letters in the box after stamping them, and the postmen will pick them up from there when they come. We were happy that we didn't have to go all the way to the post office. But unfortunately, the postman didn't take our letters; they are all still inside.' The neighbor smiled and asked, "Did you raise the flag?" When Ertan said, "What flag?", the neighbor walked with Ertan to the box made of tin, which was standing on a wooden stick by the side of the road, and lifted up the red-painted stick with the red-painted tip, which was leaning on the side of the box. "When you put the letters you are going to send inside, you lift this stick; they see this sign, they take the contents, leave the mail for you, and put the stick back down. It's as simple as that.

"Ertan thanked his neighbor again and explained what he had learned to his wife at home. His wife said, 'OK, we have learned everything, but if this garbage stays for another week, we will be wiped out; we need to find a solution.' Ertan then came up with a brilliant idea: 'I'd better take care of this myself,' he said. Now it was getting stubborn. He was going to show them who was better or worse. Of course, he had Albanian stubbornness too. He woke his son up in the middle of the night. They loaded all the garbage into the car with the back open. They unloaded all the bags in a deserted empty field a few miles away. Ertan set the garbage on fire. After watching for a while, they said, "Oh, we are finally saved!" and went back home with peace of mind, but what the hell, aren't there fire trucks and police cars coming from the opposite direction?

"He took the high road until he explained the situation at the police station. He got away with a fine of five hundred dollars. From that day on, Ertan followed all the rules to the letter."

Waiting

Until noon that day, no one came to the restaurant except Ertan and his friends and then the waiters. Umut and Ray were working that day. Elizabeth had something to do, so she switched days with Ray.

Umut was very interested in Mrs. Şermin and Mr. Zeki with his usual friendliness. He said he couldn't sleep until the morning because he was worried about Ebru. Like us, he was sure that there would be news today. Last night, he said that he was asleep for a while and that he had seen Ebru in his dream. In his dream, Ebru was running on a lush green plain, her hair blowing in the wind. Then she was at the seaside, wearing a long red dress that was flying around. She was reaching out her hand to Hope, but Hope was not there. We all interpreted this dream for good. The green plain was a blessing, and the red color was an omen. The fact that she reached out her hand to Umut meant that she needed help. Ms. Şermin, Mr. Zeki, and I said, "I hope for the best," and tried to convince ourselves that we would have good news that day.

Ray, who had finished his preparations, couldn't resist dropping by. He was a thin, blond young man. I don't think it's appropriate to call him a man because he was gay. He was not afraid to openly declare that he was "gay". At first, I told Metin that it might be inconvenient for such a waiter to work in the restaurant. "Watch him in action and then give me your opinion." I was amazed to see him flitting from table to table like a butterfly, especially during crowded times. Many customers specifically asked him to serve them. In addition to his hard work, he was a very sincere and kind-hearted person. One day, when he saw Ebru upset, he knelt down in front of her, held her hands, and said, "Please, please smile your beautiful face, Abby, I ask you, please. If you have broken up with your boyfriend, it is not worth getting upset. There are so many gentlemen who like you! My boyfriend dumped me last week. I was very sad too, but I'm moving on. Come on, smile!"

Ray approached the table where we were sitting and wanted to say something comforting to Ebru's parents. After greeting them, he said these words which he asked me to translate into Turkish:

"I know Abby, and I love her very much. She is a very sweet, very sensitive girl. Because she is so young, it is her natural right to have various adventures. She knows what she's doing. I hope you will see your daughter soon. When you do, please don't be angry with her. Good luck to you. Take care of yourselves."

"Thank you," Mr. Zeki said politely.

After Ray left us, I pointed to the artificial tree in the corner: "When I first came, I thought that tree was real and watered it for a month. One day when Ray came and saw me watering it, he said it was fake. I was a little bit embarrassed, of course. 'Don't be bored; a friend of mine watered such a tree for nine months,' he told me."

They both smiled. When Umut brought our coffees, there was silence again. I couldn't think of anything to say to distract them, to make them smile a little, and to divert their attention. I was tired of talking since morning.

As we sat in silence, we noticed that the outer door opened, and a young woman and a girl of about ten came in. This could not have been what we were expecting because this woman was none other than the alcoholic Brenda. She had come for lunch with her daughter. They went to the backyard and sat down. After a while, Ray was serving them dinner, and he was walking past me, and I saw that there was a full wine glass on the tray again.

I couldn't say anything at that moment. Her husband was telling us, "Don't always give her a drink." Even though she had been in treatment for a year, when she had a crisis, she would rush to our house because it was close to us and have a few drinks. Her husband would come later and pay her back.

One day, she must have had another alcohol attack; she came to the restaurant wearing only a blouse and panties. She drank three or four glasses of wine in a hurry, one after the other. She must have started drinking at home because she was quite drunk. As the waiters tried to force her to go home, she was still begging, "Give me a drink; my husband will pay for it." Her poor husband apologized to us many times each time, saying that he loved his wife very much, that she would surely get better one day, and that he would pay the debt.

I thought she was going to have a proper meal with her daughter today, but I was wrong; the little girl's cries were heard. When I couldn't stand it and went outside, the poor little girl was crying and begging her mother not to drink. Brenda had already finished the first glass and was asking for a second. I knew this would go on until she was drunk. I leaned into Brenda's ear and told her we couldn't give her another drink. She said she had money and would pay. I shouted that I didn't need her money and that she shouldn't drink for the sake of her child. The sobbing, tearful girl thanked me. On the way back, I told Ray to pour the wine down the sink, which he was pleased to do. When they had finished eating, Brenda walked out with her daughter, looking sullen.

After witnessing this scene, Mr. Zeki and Ms. Şermin›s morale, which had improved a little, had deteriorated again, and they had fallen into a pessimism they could not express. Although they didn't say it openly, I could see it in their eyes and facial expressions.

We watched each of the lunch customers carefully as they came through the door, curious to see which one would bring us some news. Each time, we would say, "That's not it either," and experience a new disappointment.

After trying to eat our lunch together, I wanted to leave them and go upstairs, but I couldn't bring myself to leave them alone. So I started to wait with them, not knowing what we were waiting for. We were waiting, just like waiting for Godot...

In the afternoon, two acquaintances appeared. The first was Adrianne, Peter's girlfriend. She sat in a corner and ordered herself a martini. Her face was distorted. I could tell she'd come here to commiserate. I decided to go over and listen to her. She was full of it. She railed against Peter. She wanted children.

"I'm thirty-nine; my biological clock is ticking. I want to have children now, and Peter won't let me," she said, her eyes moist. But Peter had told us many times that he couldn't take on this responsibility, that he didn't plan to be a father, and that he couldn't even accept that Adrianne would be stealing his sperm if she had a baby without his permission. Adrianne was even willing to raise her child alone. She wanted Metin and me to convince Peter about this. I didn't know what to say.

"Wait for Metin; talk to him," I said. I told him I had guests and left him.

The second familiar person to arrive was none other than Zeynep. When we saw her at the door, it was as if we were relieved. She must have come with good news. As she approached us, I saw that she had a big stack of papers in her hand. After she sat down next to us, Zeynep's expression told us that she had not come with good news as we had hoped because she was asking us the same question: "Any news?"

"No, unfortunately not until now." Then he turned over the papers he had put on the table and showed them to us. Suddenly, on this flyer-shaped paper was a black and white picture of Ebru, with her name, surname, date of birth, how long she had been missing, and phone numbers for anyone who knew her or had seen her. Zeynep told us that she had been preparing these since the morning and had printed them with the photographs and information she had received from Umut. However, Umut had never told us about this.

When Ms. Şermin, who had been heartbroken for days, saw her daughter's photo on such a missing person notice, she screamed. She pounded the table with her hand and said, "I can't take it anymore! When will this ordeal end? I have no strength left. Where is this girl? Where is she?" he wailed.

Mr. Zeki was crying, his head turned towards the wall. They could not stand this tense waiting any longer. Zeynep said, "Gosh! I thought I was doing a good thing. I didn't mean to upset you; I'm so sorry." Turning to me, "Umut and I are going to paste them on walls, poles, bus stops today. We even thought we would distribute them to passersby. Maybe it will be useful. There are a lot of such incidents here, especially child abductions, so they always do this. You have to try everything, don't you think?" she added.

In short, I said, "It is."

After the mother and father calmed down a bit, Zeynep took Umut with her and went out with the missing person flyers. She left a few on the bar on her way out. Even, he pasted the missing advertisement of the Turkish girl Ebru on the window of Cafe Bellini's outer door. One detail that caught my attention was that the name "Abby" was written in parentheses next to the name Ebru.

Ebru's missing advertisement was added to the creepy Halloween decorations of the street...

The hours were ticking by. I didn't know what to do to relieve my boredom. I kept bringing food and drink to the table, trying to distract both myself and the distressed parents. In the meantime, of course, we inevitably increased our smoking.

There was not much left to talk about.

When Metin arrived, he first listened to Adrianne and promised her that he would talk to Peter about this baby. The woman who was desperate to be a mother left with one last hope.

I told Metin what had been going on since the morning, that Zeynep and Umut had gone to distribute missing persons notices.

"You are trying in vain. There is only one thing to do, and that is to immediately go to the police station and file a missing person's report. That's it," Metin cut in.

Mr. Zeki said, "I think you are right. If nothing comes out today, there is nothing else to do. I'll go to the police station tomorrow morning."

Ms. Şermin did not raise any objection this time; she remained silent. Desperation sometimes makes people do things they don't want to do.

About two hours later, Zeynep and Umut came back. They had distributed the flyers. Umut went back to work.

The restaurant was slowly filling up with customers arriving for dinner. Some of them were curiously looking at the advertisement in the window, others at the missing advertisement with Ebru's picture pasted on the side wall of the bar and talking to each other. Some of the customers had a look of surprise on their faces because they recognized her. But no one came up to us and said they knew anything about it.

After a while, we stopped looking at the door and focused our thoughts on the police station the next morning.

I got up and started walking around to relieve some of my boredom. It was seven o'clock in the evening. A woman appeared at the door. I looked carefully and realized that it was Moshe's wife Miranda. Her blonde hair had turned black. That's why I didn't recognize her at first. As soon as she saw me, she asked me if Moshe had arrived yet. He hadn't arrived yet.

I seated her at a table for two and told her that I would accompany her until Moshe arrived. She was pleased. I told her, "You changed the color of your hair. I almost didn't recognize you," I said.

"Yes. Even though I was born and raised in France, my ancestors are Egyptians. So, I dyed my hair dark, like a real Egyptian."

When she saw Ebru's parents at the table in front of us, she asked about the situation. I told her briefly what had happened and she agreed with the idea of contacting the police. In the middle of our conversation, the strangest thing happened. Suddenly Miranda's face changed. She was pointing at the candle burning in the melon glass lantern.

'Look! Do you see it?'

'See what?'

'See the light of that candle, how it flickers?'

'Yes?'

'There's no air currents here now.'

'What do you mean?'

'There's a spirit here, a spirit!'

'A spirit?'

'Yeah, I get it. It's Abby's spirit.' I got goose bumps. She went on:

'Yeah, Abby's been hanging around. She's here to see her family. Oh, my God, she's dead!'

'You're being ridiculous, Miranda!'

'No, I'm telling the truth.'

'Look. Moshe's coming, I'll get up now.'

As I walked away, the reflection in the shadow of the candle on the wall was still flickering.

Metin, Zeynep, Mr. Zeki and Mrs. Şermin looked at my yellow face and thought I was going to say something bad to them. Metin asked:

'What happened? What is Miranda telling you?'

'Nothing. She has problems with Moshe,' I said.

While we were having dinner together, despite the buzzing human voices mixed with the sounds of glasses, plates, spoons and forks, the silence at our table continued. Where there is silence there is death, where there is death there is silence. Since no one had any appetite left, Umut cleared the plates, even though they were half full of food. Then he brought us each an American coffee. We were sitting there with our cigarettes lit.

In the evening of this very long day, when I had completely lost hope that anyone would come out with news about Ebru, a tall young man in a black overcoat suddenly entered the door and answered the advertisement in the bar. when he realised that he was looking intently. Our attention was diverted in that direction. He was asking Ray something Ray pointed his finger at our table.

We all focused our gaze on the young man, a tall, thin young man in a black overcoat, coming towards us. "Good evening," he said as he approached the table. I guess the "Godot" we were waiting for had arrived.

Özgür

When I heard this deep voice saying, "Good evening," a flickering ray of hope flickered in me again, like the light of the candle Miranda had shown me. Until this moment, I hated myself for all the bad thoughts I felt, when I should always be thinking good thoughts. We were all waiting with curiosity and impatience to hear what this mysterious person would say.

He continued:

"My name is Ozgur. I am here for the missing girl Ebru."

Mr. Zeki stood up excitedly and said: "I am Ebru's father and this is her mother. Mr. Metin and Ms. Filiz are the owners of this restaurant. Ms. Zeynep is also helping us," he said.

Metin took a chair from the next table,

"Have a seat, we are listening to you," he said. Shermin

The lady rushed out in a hurry:

"Have you seen her? Where is she? Why didn't you bring her here?"

"If you want, I'll tell you everything from the beginning," Özgür said and sat down with slow movements.

Mr. Zeki said to his wife.

"Calm down, ma'am, of course he will tell..." he said. And Özgür, in his deep, deep voice, paused. pausing, he began to tell us:

"I came here for the announcement made at the Republic

Ball last night. I was there. I decided to tell you what I know in case I can help you. I don't want to excite you; I don't know where she is now, but I believe I have clues that will lead you to her."

Ms. Şermin said, "Are you her friend, my son?"

"Şermin, let the boy tell it from the beginning, don't keep interrupting him," Mr. Zeki snapped.

Özgür continued: "No, I'm not really her friend. I saw her only once, by a strange coincidence."

This time Metin became impatient:

"Where did you see her, when did you see her?"

"I don't know how to say it, somewhere you would never think of. In a church."

We all said, "In a church?"

At the same time, we all thought that this young man was wrong, that he must have mistaken Ebru for someone else.

"Yes, about a month ago, I saw her in a church. I am very sure that the girl I saw was the wanted Ebru. If you allow me, I will tell you everything I know in detail." We all fell silent. The frowning young man in a black overcoat took a few sips of water from the glass in front of him and started to tell us, gazing into the distance:

"About a month ago, I don't remember the exact date, I went to a bar with friends. When I stepped out of the bar to find a taxi and reached the corner of the street, it was well past midnight. It was almost three o'clock. After waiting for about fifteen minutes, I was able to find a taxi. I got in the car, said 'Hello' to the driver, and told him where I wanted to go. The driver said 'Okay' and started driving. After a while, he turned to me and noticed my accent, asking where I was originally from. I told him I was Turkish and that I was studying here. After he mentioned that he was Taiwanese, he said, 'You are the second Turk I know.' The effects of alcohol had not yet left my body, keeping me in a state between sleep and nausea. To be honest, the idea of chatting with the taxi driver didn't seem good at all. I was thinking about getting home as soon as possible and throwing myself onto the bed. 'His saying he knows a Turkish person had slightly activated my dazed attention mechanism. I continued to talk. 'Oh really, who is this first person you know? Maybe I know them,' I said. He told me that this person was a Turkish girl named Abby, and that they had met at a church he attended, describing her as very religious and a good girl. Later, he suggested that it would be a good idea for me to meet her, so he proposed that I go to that church one Sunday. Without thinking, I said, 'Sure.' While handing me his business card, he asked for my phone number. For some reason, I gave my phone number to this Taiwanese taxi driver named Dindo."

"As I threw myself onto the bed that evening, I was thinking what a strange name Dindo was. I had forgotten about the Turkish girl. The next day, I didn't think about this meeting at all, but when I came home in the evening, there was a message waiting for me on the answering machine. It was Dr. Benjamin calling. He was a friend of Dindo. He said he was calling to invite me to church and that they would be pleased to see me there this Sunday if I was available. Apparently, he was one of the respected members of the church. I didn't take the message seriously because I wasn't planning to go.

"The next morning, Dr. Benjamin called again. After a meaningless conversation, I couldn't resist his insistence and agreed to go to church. He would pick me up in front of my school next Sunday.

"On Sunday, I was waiting in front of the school at the time we discussed. A blue car approached me. A man in a suit got out, who looked East Asian. There was also a woman waiting in the car. The man approaching me introduced himself as Dr. Benjamin. After the introduction, he invited me to the car. He had a reassuring demeanor and way of speaking, but I was still hesitant. However, at this point, I realized I could no longer turn back and got into the car.

"The woman in the car was his girlfriend. She was sitting in the front seat with a few books that I understood were religious on her lap, smiling at me. I smiled back.

"On the way to church, Dr. Benjamin talked a bit about himself. Like Dindo, he had come here from Taiwan. He was doing studies related to medicine here. Before coming to America, he had been a Buddhist. Like every newcomer, he had also gone through tough days here."

While listening to him, the Turkish girl I was told about came to my mind. Who knows, maybe the reason I accepted to go to church with a somewhat suppressed feeling was her. I started to wonder about her. What could be the reason that drew her to the church? Perhaps, like Dr. Benjamin, she had stumbled upon a door that opened in a deadlock. Because sometimes, crises lead people to an unknown quest for purity, a search for belonging.

"Anyway, let's not prolong the conversation, we finally arrived at the church. While I was thinking of those magnificent churches that remained in my imagination from Istanbul, I was faced with an ordinary building that looked prefabricated. It wasn't a building that captivates you with its simplicity either. It was just a place. Its religiosity was determined by a cross figure at the door. Inside, as I had guessed, it was filled with East Asians. Alongside them were Americans and two Turks whose had not meet yet.

"While I was waiting to meet Abby right away, I was seated in a row by Dr. Benjamin. He told me, 'You will participate in the service first.' Meanwhile, I was looking around, thinking where this girl was. When I asked the doctor, I learned that she would join the service from the upper floor. We would meet after the service. "First, the music started. In the middle of the hall, there was an orchestra made up of young East Asians. Then, in a place like a platform, four people took turns talking about world problems and how religion, that is, Christianity, could provide solutions to everything. After the speeches ended, everyone turned to the person next to them to summarize the talks. After prayers in a language I didn't understand, the orchestra started playing again and everyone continued the hymn recitation standing up.

"Finally, the ritual was over. I was ready to meet the Turkish girl. Actually, I was eager to get out of there as soon as possible, but after waiting so long, I had to see this girl. Finally, Abby came down with the Bible teacher from what looked like a balcony. I could tell she was a slim, beautiful girl, but she looked very tired. "Hi, I'm Özgür," I said. "Nice to meet you, I'm Ebru," she said. Her face was pale and expressionless. I didn't know what to say. "What are you doing here?" I asked. "I pray," she said. She said she was with very good people and that she was happy here. She was asking me how I found the service. I was more interested in getting her talking. "Where are your family, where are you from?" I asked. "They are in Izmir," she answered briefly. "Do your family know you are here?" I asked, and she said, "They don't need to know," sounding uncomfortable with being questioned. I tried to explain to her that we could meet outside and talk, but she said, "I can't talk to anyone right now; I need to purify myself." I asked her to be more specific, and she responded with a question that surprised me: "Did you feel the Child Jesus in your heart during the service?" I didn't know what to say. At that moment, the Bible teacher, who was also a nurse, approached us. She was telling us that Ebru understood the Bible very well. Although Ebru was standing next to us, she seemed to be far away. I realized that I couldn't communicate with her. I left with a heavy heart. I never saw her again. Dr. Benjamin was not there.

I never went to that church again, despite Benjamin's constant phone calls and even promises to contribute to my university fees. As for the Turkish girl, I thought that it was useless for me or any other Turk to try to help her because she had already lost her soul in my opinion, sorry to characterize it that way; it was too late. Maybe I was wrong; I don't know.

Özgür seemed to have put an end to his speech. As for us, just when we thought we had caught him, we were left with our necks bowed, as if we were looking after a bird that had flown away again.

Mr. Zeki, who was heartbroken by these stories, with a last hope, said, "Is that all you know? Look at this photo; is it the same person?"

"Yes, I've already seen the missing person's notice on the door; that's her."

Ms. Şermin was frozen after what she had listened to, not speaking at all.

The text was discarded: "Then give us the name and address of this church, and we will go and find it."

"Now I was going to tell you about him," said Özgür, "I had planned to go and find her before I came here and bring her to you. In fact, I was going to phone you immediately, but I didn't do that because I wasn't sure if it was the same person. When I saw her picture on the door, I had no doubts. I was telling her; in the morning, there was a class at school. In the afternoon, I got up and went to that church.

I went. I asked for Ebru. 'She hasn't been back for two weeks; she went back to her hometown,' they said. I looked for Dr. Benjamin, but he was nowhere to be found. Then I saw the nurse, the Bible teacher who taught Ebru, and she recognized me. She was very happy that I had come back; she was sure that I would come back. When I explained to her why I had come, she became curious. 'Our classes were going very well. Dr. Benjamin and I didn't understand her sudden departure. So, she didn't go back to her country,' and she said it would be better if I talked to Dr. Benjamin. Because she had been staying at his house before she left; she had nowhere else to stay. I immediately asked for Dr. Benjamin's address. She didn't give me his phone number, but she wrote down this address." Özgür took a piece of paper out of his pocket and read it:

"1702 N. Sheridan, Suite 309 (Lake Tower Condominium), Chicago."

"Well, didn't you go there?" I asked.

"No, I ran out of time; I came here right away," replied Özgür.

Ms. Şermin pulled herself together a little, "Maybe she's still there. Let's go and look right away. Oh, my son! What was she doing in churches?"

This time Zeynep said she had an idea: "I'm going to call unknown numbers and find the phone number and talk to the doorman; he will know if Ebru is there."

She did as she was told. She found the doorman, or rather the security guard. Unfortunately, the doorman said he didn't know anyone named Ebru or Abby, and that Dr. Benjamin's phone number couldn't be given out because of the rules. He wasn't there at the moment anyway.

He said he had to go free and asked for permission.

"I hope I've been helpful. I'm really curious too. I'll come back tomorrow if you need me. We'll talk to Dr. Benjamin. I am sure we are on the right track," he said.

We thanked him. Mr. Zeki said that the information he provided was very important, "God bless you, my son. Thank you for doing your research and coming all the way here," he said in a shaky voice.

Özgür said, "Good evening," and walked out the door, disappearing down the dark street in his black overcoat.

Ms. Şermin started to cry.

"What is my daughter doing in churches? Where will we find her now?"

There was nothing left to do after that. To avoid witnessing more of these heart-wrenching scenes, Metin thought it appropriate to say:

"Now everyone go to bed. Get a good rest. Tomorrow's a good day. We will go early in the morning and find that apartment building in Sheridan and Dr. Benjamin. God willing, we will reach Ebru. Good night to all of you."

Jane Doe

I slept very uncomfortably last night. I woke up every now and then, frightened and startled, as if some evil spirits were bothering me.

Metin believed this house was haunted. He said that a German husband and wife used to be murdered in this house. Since Metin started living in this building, he felt the presence of these spirits. There are many such haunted house rumors in Chicago. A famous restaurant that is said to be haunted by ghosts was visited by tourists on Halloween. Americans produce countless ghost movies and stories about spirits, either because they love these subjects or because they want them to be true.

When Metin was staying alone in this building, he went down to the kitchen in the middle of the night to get something to eat and saw something white like a ghost passing by. He told himself not to be afraid: "If I don't fear them, they will fear me." According to him, these spirits loved him; in fact, they did not want anyone else in the house but him. When Metin's brother came from Turkey, they never wanted him. The poor boy always felt sick. One night, Metin suddenly woke up, and without realizing it, due to the influence of these invisible beings, he was sleeping in his brother's bed. He went into the room where he was lying and was about to lift him up and throw him out when he tripped over something, and when he felt like falling, he came to his senses. When he realized what he was about to do, he returned to his room, frightened.

I can't say these spirits liked me much either. Because I often felt heavy in my sleep. Perhaps because it was an old building, I would also hear creaky noises at night. Later on, they either got used to me or had to accept me, and I didn't feel much discomfort. All this could have been a coincidence or our imagination.

Today is Halloween, October thirty-first. One of the reasons why I spent last night in nightmares could be this artificially created atmosphere of fear. Considering the tense and tragic situation we have been living in the last few days; I think it is natural for me to be in such a troubled state of mind.

When I woke up in the morning, I didn't even want to interpret the bad dreams I had. I had a book of "Dream Interpretations" I had brought from Turkey. "A sane woman like you believes in these?" my friends would joke. But when they had a dream that impressed them, they would immediately get on the phone and tell me about the dream and shyly ask me to find out what it meant from the book. Even some of their American colleagues at work started asking for dream interpretation over the phone. In fact, most of what was written in the book was nonsense. Strangely enough, human beings have always been interested in interpreting the unknown, no matter how illogical it may seem.

Speaking of interpreting the unknown, I asked Zeynep about her interpretation of Ebru's diary.

"I think Ebru went to look for Hakan without telling anyone, to make him pay for what he had put her through. It was a plausible possibility, but since no one knew where Hakan was, it seemed impossible to reach Ebru for the time being.

Metin was still asleep. I got dressed and went downstairs. As I drank my coffee, I watched the morning on Halloween Street. The dark clouds gathering in clusters in the air completed this Halloween decor. Since workplaces and schools were not on vacation today, people passing by were trying to get somewhere with quick steps.

As usual this morning, when I was in a metaphysical mood in the face of situations that I could not solve with my logic, as I am these days, I was watching at least two out of every ten passersby walking along the road talking to themselves. Some of them were even gesticulating while talking. I had come across such people in our restaurant a few times. I remembered a lonely middle-aged woman who talked loudly to herself and laughed. Whenever she came in, the waiters were always amused. Whatever the psychological and sociological reasons, I decided that this was a very common phenomenon in America.

In the afternoon, the real Halloween festivities will begin. Many people, will be to the streets in their outlandish costumes. Everyone will try to scare each other. Crazy parties will take place in homes, workplaces, and schools. Children will dress up as fairy tale and cartoon heroes such as Snow White, Peter Pan, and Superman. They will go door to door collecting candy and chocolates with bags in their hands. At night, the adults will go to masquerade balls. Today, we will follow Ebru's trail in search of a Far Easterner who became a Christian by taking the name Dr. Benjamin.

Metin appeared at the kitchen door wearing a coat. "Come on, get your jacket, and let's go as soon as possible," he said.

"I will, but did you get the address of that house?" I reminded him.

"Got it. I already know that building. It's near Bryn Mawr Street. I'll find it right away."

I said, "What do you think, is she there?"

"I don't think so, but if she's not there, we'll probably find out something. And even if we don't find out anything, you know we'll go straight to the police department from there. It's a mistake that we haven't been there until now," he said.

"I'll make a phone call to Ms. Şermin. Have them wait for us in front of the hotel," I said.

When we arrived in front of the hotel, we found the husband

and wife ready and waiting for us. Mrs. Şermin was wearing a black jacket and a long patterned scarf to protect herself from the wind. Mr. Zeki was wearing a brown jacket. They no longer took care of their clothes as they did when they first arrived. It was obvious from their yellowed and sunken faces that they had not slept much last night.

The poor woman on the road prayed, "I hope my daughter is there. End our suffering today, Lord." Mr. Zeki was trying his patience to the limit, not wanting to make any comments, probably because he was afraid of being disappointed again. As a man, he had to be strong.

In twenty minutes, we were on Sheridan Street. Following the numbers, we found the Park Tower, a skyscraper rising by the lake. On the left side of the wide staircase at the entrance, the American flag was flying at the end of a high pole. After parking the car in the guest parking lot on the side of the building, we climbed the stairs and entered through the revolving door. It resembled a hotel lobby decorated with carpets, flowers, and armchairs. At the desk across from us stood a swarthy attendant in a burgundy-colored uniform. After asking us if we were visitors, he told us that we could only keep the car in the parking lot for fifteen minutes, and if we stayed longer, we would have to pay ten dollars. So anyone who came to visit the residents of this building had to pay.

The security guard asked us who we were visiting. He said he would phone that person and ask if he would accept. Otherwise, we wouldn't be allowed in. That's the rule here.

Metin looked at the paper in his hand, "Dr. Benjamin, apartment 309," he said, then added, "please hurry; it's very important." We had to catch the doctor early before he left his apartment.

I asked impatiently as the attendant searched for a phone number on the computer:

"Excuse me, do you know a lady named Ebru who was staying in the same apartment?"

The man looked up at us and then paused for a moment.

"Are you asking about Abby?" he said. "Yes," I said, and then I asked Ms. Şermin to take out her photograph. The middle-aged swarthy man, who looked at the photograph carefully, raised his eyebrows from under his burgundy-colored cap; "Ah, yes. This is that Turkish girl! Did you come for her?" he asked.

Ms. Şermin and Mr. Zeki were listening attentively to the conversation, trying to make sense of the man's facial expression.

Metin said, "Yes, is she here? Her parents came from Turkey for her."

The officer said, "So you are Turkish. I am also from Pakistan; my name is Valli. I love Turks very much," and turned to Mr. Zeki and Ms. Şermin, greeting them with "Welcome."

Mr. Zeki understood what was being said. He turned to the Pakistani and said, "Ebru, here?"

"I haven't seen her in a few weeks. She was with him. I'll phone him now," Valli said. Valli spoke with a smiling face, and it was clear that nothing bad was on his mind. Ms. Şermin did not understand a word of what was being said; "Was she here? What did he say? Tell me about it," she was saying. "So if we had come two weeks ago, we were going to find her. What a setback!"

Metin said, "Don't blame yourself. How would you know? Now let's have a talk with this Dr. Benjamin guy. He needs to know where Ebru is going."

As Valli dialed Dr. Benjamin's phone number, she was telling him that Abby was a very nice girl.

Metin to Valli, "Tell him Abby's parents are here; tell him to come downstairs immediately; it's very important," he said.

Valli dialed the number. "Good morning, Dr. Benjamin. This is Valli at the front desk. You have some visitors. Abby's parents are here. They want to talk to you about her. They say it's very important. Can you come downstairs?"

After waiting for a while, Valli said, "OK," and hung up the phone. Turning to us, "Wait in those seats. He'll be down in a minute," he said.

Sitting in the waiting area, Metin said, "This is not the person we spoke to last night. The guard has changed. Valli knows the girl."

Mr. Zeki had some hope. "I wonder if Valli knows other things about Ebru. How about we ask him?"

"Hold on, let's see this doctor first. There is no need to panic. Valli is busy with other people right now," Metin said.

Ten minutes later, a middle-aged Taiwanese doctor in a tracksuit, at the signal of Valli, told us he was coming towards us. When he approached us, he introduced himself. Metin stood up and introduced each of us one by one, then told the man to sit down and we would have some questions for him.

The man smiled at all of us, said he was pleased to meet us, and sat down.

Metin asked the most important question first, of course: Where was Ebru now?

Dr. Benjamin, in a state of shock, said, "Isn't she in Turkey?" At that moment, all our hopes were crushed again. Even Mr. Zeki and Ms. Şermin understood what he was saying.

After Metin explained the situation in more detail, Dr. Benjamin seemed more and more worried. We asked him to tell us everything he knew about Ebru. He started at the end:

"Abby left me a note about two weeks ago. She said, 'Thank you for your help. I'm going home in a hurry, and I'm sorry I didn't get to say goodbye in person. Goodbye,' she wrote. It was a surprise for me that she left so suddenly, but I was glad that she went back to her family."

Mr. Zeki and Ms. Şermin wanted me to ask a lot of questions one after the other. We said we wanted to see that notepad, but unfortunately, he had thrown it away. Ms. Şermin asked me to ask why Ebru was staying in this house. Then Dr. Benjamin started-ed to tell everything from the beginning.

About two months ago, an American girlfriend of Ebru's brought her to the church, told her that she needed help, and left her with some of the clergy there. After listening to Ebru, they introduced her to Dr. Benjamin. Because he was the one who was looking after the student youth in need. There were other university students like Ebru who were receiving help. The church did not discriminate, no matter what religion they belonged to, and provided financial and moral assistance to such young people in difficult situations. Then he started to tell me the details about

Ebru: "When I knew her, Abby was in a depression. She was a lost soul who had lost her self-respect and self-love. She could not forgive herself for the mistakes she had made. Every day we taught her God is great and forgiving, that He can forgive her through prayer, and that if she believed in her heart, she could be forgiven of her sins. So she could forgive herself and be forgiven. She would save her soul through Jesus. We made a lot of progress in the first month."

Ms. Şermin interrupted him.

"But my daughter is a Muslim. Ask them why they made her a Christian," she said. And we did, and his answer was like this:

"We do not pressure anyone on religion. Our door is open to everyone. If she has chosen this path of her own free will, we respect that and do what we can to help. If Abby had stayed a little longer, I think she would gain self-confidence and start life anew. She would be enrolled in the college of her choice, and her school expenses would be covered by our organization. She left without waiting. Of course, it is her right to choose. If she decided to return to her hometown, we respect her decision. But now you are saying that she is not there; I am very surprised and worried."

Mr. Zeki said he had a question. He insisted that he wanted to know why Ebru was staying in this man's house. The Taiwanese answered:

"She had no place to stay and no money. She had encountered very ugly incidents at a girlfriend's house where she had stayed before. She told us that she was ashamed of everyone, that she couldn't look at the faces of her old acquaintances, especially the Turks, and that she was responsible for a short and unhappy marriage, and that she couldn't even find the strength to meet her family before she recovered. I have two separate rooms in my apartment. I suggested that she stay temporarily, and she accepted. As soon as she started college, we were going to arrange a place for her with the other students who lived close to the school."

This time, Metin interjected as if to settle the score: "Well, Dr. Benjamin, didn't it ever occur to you that this girl has a family, and you should let them know?"

"Of course, I tried that too. She certainly didn't want that. She is a grown girl; she was free to do what she wanted. I couldn't put too much pressure on her."

"And was she happy in your house?" I asked.

"I told you, she was depressed. She was usually in the cellar after coming back from work; she would go to her room and pray. She was. I would leave her alone with herself. We didn't see each other much at home, sometimes at dinner. She didn't talk much. I didn't ask her personal questions so as not to disturb her. She had no complaints about staying here. Her reckoning was with herself. We would only talk about religious matters. Sometimes she would get very quiet, and her silence frightened me. Just when I thought things were slowly getting better, she suddenly left."

Ms. Şermin asked me to ask if Ebru had any of her personal belongings at his house. When she left, she left a few pieces of clothing and religious books. Dr. Benjamin took them to the church to be given to the poor.

Neither the strength of our brains nor the courage of our hearts were enough to connect the broken links of this unfortunate chain of events we were trying to trace. We were stuck at some point.

At that moment, Metin thought of something. Hoping to get one last clue, he asked, "Do you know the girlfriend who brought Abby to the church? How can we find her?"

"No, I don't know her. She brought Abby to church one day when I wasn't there and left her. I would have recognized her if she were a church-goer. She must have gotten information from somewhere else and brought Abby to the church to help her. I'll ask the staff anyway, and if I find out anything, give me your phone number and I'll call you. Or if you find Abby, please let me know; working so hard on her, her disappearance makes me nervous.

"I'm terribly disappointed. I'm very sorry. If there is anything I can do, I will do my best. Don't hesitate to call me. God help you."

A question mark popped out from every corner of my brain.

What was the real reason why this man and Ebru were living together?

If Ebru was happy in this house, if she was really being helped in her struggle to reclaim herself, to make peace with herself, why had she suddenly left this house? Why had she not visited the church for two weeks? Why did she write "I am returning to my homeland" in the note she left? And most importantly, where did she go from here? None of us could express these questions at that moment, but I was sure that the same things were going through all of our minds.

Breaking the silence, I asked Dr. Benjamin one last question, looking into his eyes: "You don't have any information or any guesses as to where she might have gone?"

"I'm afraid not," he said, closing the last door. There was no point in wasting any more time there. As we were about to thank the Taiwanese and leave, Metin turned to the man and said:

"We are going to the police department from here. I think they will definitely call you and investigate you, be prepared," he said, putting an end to the conversation. We thanked Valli and left with our necks bowed.

In the car on the way to the nearest police station, everyone in the car was trying to reason things out in their heads; they were trying to fill the empty spaces or not fill them.

The scarecrows in the gardens of the houses we saw on the roads we passed, the ghosts caught in the trees, and the pumpkins grinning at us in front of the doors and windows seemed to mock us.

Ms. Şermin, who was sitting next to me in the back of the car, held my hand every now and then, saying,

"Oh, Ms. Filiz, I am so scared, so scared! I hope nothing has happened to her. God, why did you put us through all these troubles? What did we do wrong? My daughter is like an angel; I couldn't understand why she was so depressed. I wish she had told us everything and gone back home. What was she doing with these strange people? Oh, it's all my fault; I shouldn't have sent her here."

"Don't give up hope, Ms. Şermin, the police here work well. When you give them the necessary information, they will find Hakan immediately, maybe he is with her. Even if she is somewhere else, I am sure they will find her soon. I hope this will end your troubles." I couldn't find anything else to say. I really wanted to believe what I was saying.

We finally arrived in front of the police department. Metin said it would be better for me and Ms. Şermin to wait in the car for now. Mr. Zeki had the same idea.

As he and Metin were climbing the stairs of the not very big stone building with a flag hanging on it, Mr. Zeki's timid and uneasy mood was evident. Maybe he was blaming himself for being in such a difficult situation in a foreign country where he did not speak the language, or he was blaming his lack of English for not understanding what was being said. Perhaps he was unable to think of anything right now.

Waiting, waiting again... Five or ten minutes passed; during this time, Ms. Şermin kept asking me questions, but I couldn't give her satisfactory answers. I had Ebru's diary in mind. We had to tell the police about it.

Another ten minutes passed. Ms. Şermin›s nerves were on edge.

"Ms. Filiz, I can't wait any longer, please let us go inside. I am very curious."

"Ms. Şermin, the police will not find your daughter right now. Forms will be filled out, necessary information will be given, a missing person report will be filed. Photographs will be shown, and investigations will be made within the framework of the information provided. Everything has a sequence."

"You mentioned photographs, and that reminded me. They are all in my bag; Zeki didn't take any pictures with her."

Ms. Şermin had found a way for us to get in. I couldn't resist any longer.

After explaining to the guard at the door why we had come and showing our ID cards, we went into a hall inside. There wasn't much to see except a row of chairs, a telephone, and a coffee machine in a corner booth. This must have been the waiting room. Opposite two rooms with blinds on the windows. Other parts of the police station were not visible from here. The young black police officer, wearing a silver ID badge on the breast pocket of his navy blue uniform, told us to sit on the chairs there and wait; he then went into one of the rooms. After a few minutes, he came out again and told us we could come in. We hesitantly entered through the door indicated. An elderly police commissioner sitting at a large desk in front of us said "Hello" and told us to sit down. At a smaller table to the side, Mr. Zeki and Metin were writing something on the papers given to them. When they saw us, they looked up as if to say, "Why did you come?" I felt the need to give an explanation,

"We brought the photos," I said.

The text read and translated some questions aloud, and Mr. Zeki answered them. Date of birth, height, weight, hair color, eye color, when he came to the USA, when he got married, information about his spouse, when he was last seen, and by whom, and many other questions were answered, and then Mr. Zeki signed the paper.

The soft-faced police commissioner, who said his name was Steve, was dressed in civilian clothes. He only wore a badge around his neck like a necklace. He must be a detective, I thought. After chatting with us for a while, he took the paper that Mr. Zeki and Metin had filled out. He told them to sit on the chairs in front of the table. As he entered the answers into the computer, he began to ask more detailed questions. In chronological order from the day Ebru first arrived, he listed which schools she had attended, where she had stayed, and who she had been with.

He covered a lot of information about her husband and his work. Metin and I had read Ebru's diary, so we told everything we knew. Metin did not forget to mention the Church and Dr. Benjamin.

All this took about an hour. Then the commissioner asked for the photographs. Ms. Şermin handed over the photos with trembling hands. In one of the photos, Ebru was standing between the tables at Cafe Bellini. Umut must have taken this picture. There was also a beautiful portrait of her taken in Turkey, always in her mother's purse, next to a giraffe at the zoo; Kevin must have taken this one too. In the other two photos, Hakan and Ebru were alone together in one, something like a wedding picture, and the other was a picture of happiness taken in front of the fireplace in their home.

I think Ebru sent these photos to her family from America.

The commissioner looked carefully at the photographs and asked for a detail we never expected. Were there any obvious marks on Ebru's body or face, like moles or scars? No, there were no such obvious marks.

The old man spread the pictures on the table and did not speak for a minute or two. His smiling face became serious. He seemed to pick up the phone in front of him and say to someone he called Tom, "Bring me the file with this number," and said something else in terms we didn't understand. I locked eyes with Metin, and our looks were asking each other, "What's going on?" Meanwhile, Commissioner Steve was looking for something else on his computer.

A few minutes later, the young uniformed policeman came into the room with a file in his hand and put it on the table.

When I looked sideways, I saw the word "JANE DOE" written on the file. "Jane Doe!" I said slowly to Metin, because he, like me, knew very well what Jane Doe meant. Jane Doe was the name given to unidentified women, dead or alive, in America. If it was a man, it was called "John Doe".

The silence, the eerie silence grew and grew. And again, the unholy thought came back to me. Where there is silence, there is death, and where there is death, there is silence.

Mr. Zeki broke the silence,

"What in God's name is going on, for God's sake, why don't you tell us?" Metin answered:

"Nothing is happening, we are waiting."

Silence again. Nothing could be heard but the rustling of papers being shuffled by the police commissioner. The experienced policeman, who occasionally glanced at our information, finally looked up at me: "Could you please take the lady outside?" he said. I sensed something bad was going to happen. I turned to Ms. Şermin, who was trying to catch her breath,

"He's telling us to wait outside," I said.

"No, I want to stay here too. I have the right to know what happened," said Ms. Şermin. Realizing that she didn't want to leave, the policeman looked at Metin and me,

"I'm going to give them some bad news, but I have to show the father some photos to be 100 percent sure for identification. The mother might feel bad," he said.

Metin and I froze as we realized that what we feared had happened to us. What could we say to the parents who had come to this point with a hope they did not want to lose! This was going to be the hardest, most painful translation we had ever done in our lives.

The husband and wife were trying to read our expressions

with puzzled and fearful eyes, waiting impatiently for the words to come out of our mouths. Metin paused for a moment, then gathered his courage and turned to Mr. Zeki:

"The policeman says that he has a file containing, how should I put it, photographs of an unidentified young girl. He wants to show them to you to see if there is a resemblance. Don't be afraid; it might not be her."

Mr. Zeki, with a pale face, "Are you talking about photographs of a corpse? I don't understand?" Ms. Şermin screamed:

"What! Oh my God, what are you saying? Is my daughter dead? This can't be, there must be something wrong." She stood up and continued speaking:

"Show me that picture; I recognize our daughter." Mr. Zeki also stood up and held his wife.

"Şermin, get out! I'll take a look. I'm sure it's not her. Ms. Filiz, please take Şermin away."

I took Ms. Şermin›s arm and dragged her out of the room. The grieving woman was hysterical, still shouting and screaming:

"They're lying. What was written on that file, you read it. You said a name called Jane. My daughter's name is Jane? If it was Ebru, it would still be a possibility. But no matter what, get out of here before I find out everything."

"Ms. Şermin, I understand your situation very well. As a mother, you have the right to know everything, but there is nothing certain. Please calm down. Let us wait in the car. Be a little patient," I said.

"What patience do I have left? I've been patient for three months. I've had enough. I can't take it anymore."

She couldn't hold back her tears. I could hardly get her into the car. After that, I was more worried. Where do such things find me? I always wanted to witness happy events.

We were waiting for Mr. Metin and Mr. Zeki with our eyes on the door. This waiting was the worst, the most unbearable. What was going on inside? We had not translated one of the sentences the commissioner had told us. What they didn't know yet was that these were photographs of a corpse, the body of a young girl, which had been pulled out of the lake thirteen days ago, according to estimates. The time was very close to when Ebru disappeared. So did the information provided, which is why the police decided to make an identification. Since they called her Jane Doe, this body had not been identified until now. I wonder how poor Mr. Zeki is

looking at those photographs now? What if it really was Ebru? What would happen next? If it wasn't her, the knot was still unresolved. Where was Ebru? My head was in chaos. The distraught mother was not in a position to make these judgments now because she was delirious:

"Ebru! Come, my daughter, save us from this torment!"

I don't know whether we waited in the car for fifteen minutes or half an hour. It seemed as long as years to us. As I listened to Mrs. Şermin›s sobs, my heart was breaking into pieces.

Finally, Metin and Mr. Zeki appeared on the stairs. Metin took Mr. Zeki's arm, and the man who was walking with difficulty seemed to shrink and shrink. When I saw that his face was ashen when they approached, I understood everything. So Jane Doe was Ebru herself. I thought about what she had gone through here in the past two years. The chain reaction of one misfortune after another had ended her life with such a tragic final link.

Ms. Şermin, through the open car window,

"What happened? What happened?"

Mr. Zeki, who was holding on to the door of the car with one hand, let out the sobs he was trying to hold back.

Seeing her husband like this, Ms. Şermin understood everything, but she said nothing because she could not accept such a catastrophe. She was in shock at that moment. Metin put Mr. Zeki in the front seat next to him.

After glancing at the papers in his hand, he put them to the side and started the car. No one was talking. Again, that otherworldly silence had descended upon us. It was such a holy silence that no one could ask, "What are we doing now? Where are we going?"

Halloween Continues

After driving around in the Halloween decorations for a while, the mother, who was trying to come to her senses, suddenly broke the religious silence:

"Zeki, tell me, what happened to our daughter? Mr. Metin, at least you tell me, what happened to Ebru?"

When no one responded, she continued in a loud voice:

"Is she dead? I ask you!"

The father, in tears, turned back and nodded his head "yes". Then Ms. Şermin let out a horrible scream. I got goosebumps.

We cried together.

When we got to North Clark Street, I realized we were heading home. Metin stopped the car in front of the door that led to our apartment, not the restaurant. He told me to take them upstairs. So, we did. We barely got these two wrecked people up the stairs.

They cried for a long time at home. They sang laments. We gave them water and cologne, hugged them, and cried with them. We found nothing to comfort them.

None of us could put things in a logical order, make connections, and fully understand what was happening.

For a while, Metin and I went into the other room, leaving them alone with their grief. Husband and wife had to live and share this pain in their own way.

I asked when I was alone with Metin:

"For God's sake, tell me, what is this all about?"

"According to the police commissioner, a woman's body was found in Lake Michigan thirteen days ago. The autopsy determined that she had drowned and had been in the water for two days. Her age was listed as twenty to twenty-three. I've seen the photos too. All the descriptions match. The girl in the photo looked quite different from Ebru because she had been in the water for two days. Her hair was tangled, but as you said, the innocent Mona Lisa smile that appeared even on her bruised and lifeless face was proof that she was Ebru. I wish I hadn't seen it. I can't get it out of my mind."

"Poor Ebru... And where did they find the body?"

"Quite a ways out of town, on the road to Indiana, on a sailboat on the shore of the lake. Then the police searched the area. There was no identification or anything special on the girl other than the pants and shirt she was wearing. They couldn't find her bag either."

"Why would she have gone so far? She couldn't have gone there alone; there must have been people with her. So why don't those people come forward?"

"Unknown. They haven't even determined whether it was a suicide or a murder. It's a very mysterious case. The case is not closed; it is still being investigated."

At that moment, I realized that I had not asked the most important question.

"Metin, where is the girl's dead body?"

"I swear, I asked about that too; the body stayed in a hospital morgue for a few days. When no one came to claim it, they gave it to the funeral service. Oh, I just remembered; there was the name of a cemetery on the papers I was given. Gosh, I forgot the papers in the car. I think it was Graceland Cemetery."

"You know, the cemetery north of Clark Street? I think that's what it's called."

"It's probably."

"What do we do now?"

"Mr. Zeki wanted me to at least see my daughter's grave at the police department."

"When they see the grave, maybe they will accept the truth; otherwise, it is not possible for them to believe."

"Maybe they want to take the body to Turkey; it is very difficult to go to Turkey from here."

"I know, we'll figure it out," Metin said. They say life is the sum of opposites. Everyone talks about living in the U.S. What about dying in America!

I thought of the late Mr. İsmail. How he had organized his death and those left behind before he died. But not everyone is lucky or unlucky enough to know their death in advance like Mr. İsmail.

When the doctors diagnosed him with cancer and told him he had only a few months to live, he immediately started making plans. First, preparations for his wife and two children who would stay in Chicago. Then he made plans by visiting all his friends and acquaintances or by phone; he told them that he was going to Turkey to die, said goodbye, and said farewell. In his homeland, he prepared the material and spiritual conditions for his funeral in accordance with religious rituals and his journey between two worlds with peace of mind. Mr. İsmail was the husband of Ms. Hülya, who now often came to Cafe Bellini to have dinner with her lawyer. The transfer of a body from here to Turkey costs at least ten thousand dollars. Last year, the father of a friend of mine came from Turkey to visit his daughter. At the insistence of his daughter, he decided to see a doctor while he was in America. When the doctor told him that he needed to be hospitalized immediately and have an operation on his heart, his daughter and son-in-law gave everything they had and had the father operated on. But something unexpected happened. The day after the bypass surgery, the father suddenly died. The man who was doing well when he came back from Turkey was gone when he was supposed to be even healthier. Should the daughter worry about how to explain the situation to her mother in Turkey, or how to send the body back home? They managed to pay for the hospitalization with some help from the poverty fund and emergency funds, but the funeral had to be embalmed, put in a special coffin, and taken to Turkey in a special way on a plane; it was very difficult to cover these costs. The only thing to do was to collect donations from Turkish citizens living here. Indeed, this was done, and he was sent off on his eternal journey. Putting these thoughts aside for now, I asked Metin:

"So, what do we do now?"

"We're taking them to the cemetery. Look for Jane Doe; we need to find out. I'm always up to something weird like this."

"They have no one else, so how can they know that they will meet death in the wilderness?"

"I'm sorry; of course, we will do our best; it's our duty."

The crying and shouting in the living room grew louder and louder. It was with great distress and difficulty that we were able to tell them that we were going to the cemetery. It was not easy to get the bewildered parents into the car.

It began to drizzle as we drove north on Clark Street. On the roads, groups of Halloweeners were already milling about, dressed in their ghastly costumes. The lifeless decor suddenly came to life. Looking out the car window, I saw something no one else had seen, and I shuddered. One of Ebru's missing flyers, blown away by the wind, was lying on the side of the street, and the Halloweeners were stepping on it, unknowingly.

It took us less than twenty minutes to arrive at the cemetery, which we always drive past and which has a huge sign on the entrance gate reading "Graceland Cemetery". The grieving mother and father fell silent again.

When we arrived at the entrance gate, we ignored the stone building on the left and drove in on the asphalt road. The stone sculptures, sarcophagi, and obelisks, which were also visible as we crossed the street, showed that this was a mausoleum.

As we drove slowly, we saw the names, surnames, birth, and death dates of the deceased written on the pedestals of these monuments.

With sarcophagi made of marble, granite, bronze, or iron, statues of angels, pointed obelisks, cross-shaped and book-shaped figures, pyramids, vases in the form of jars and jugs on columns, which we thought contained the ashes of the dead, and mausoleums in the shape of houses, it was like a nineteenth-century art historical museum.

These monuments, each obviously built by famous architects and designers, some of them with the name of the architect written on them, were a sign that this was a tomb of the rich. The grave of the poor Turkish girl Ebru could not possibly be among them.

Looking out of the car window at these monuments, the mother and father seemed as if they were living vaguely in a different world.

"It can't be here; I think we're wrong; we've come to the wrong place if you want, Metin," I said.

"I'm of the same opinion. I wish we had asked someone at the door," he said.

I said, "I'd better get out and go into that building that looks like an office and ask someone, and you drive and wait outside the gate."

Metin, "Let's do that," he said and stopped the car for me to get out. I was getting ready to get out when all hell broke loose. He had never heard our conversation.

Ms. Şermin, who had been sitting quietly until that moment, suddenly opened the car door and jumped out. She wandered among the graves and started wailing and shouting. She was very miserable with her scarf slipping off her head, her hair getting wet from the light rain, and her face wet. Mr. Zeki followed her and tried to hold his wife. Ms. Şermin was talking without listening to anyone:

"What is my daughter doing here, among these infidels!"

Having lost herself in this strange place, Ms. Şermin wandered among the sarcophagi, columns, and statues while continuing to lament:

"Ebru! Ebru! My daughter, where are you? What have we done to deserve this pain? Come out now, come out! Oh, there she is. I found you! Zeki, look where they put our daughter!"

When we came to Mr. Zeki and Ms. Şermin, we were horrified by what we saw. We froze like stone statues in that cemetery.

The tomb in front of which Ms. Şermin stands is a large glass box with steel framed sides, set on a marble pedestal, and a statue of a young girl with long hair, made of summer stone, lying inside... A name is inscribed underneath: Jane Fellows died in 1883 at the age of sixteen.

Ms. Şermin was kneeling in front of this monument, continuing her lament:

"My daughter, they put you here! In a glass case! I guess they couldn't bury you because you were so beautiful..."

I couldn't take it anymore. I grabbed the unconscious woman by the shoulder,

"Mrs. Şermin, please calm down. Stay composed. We are in the wrong place. Look what it says; this is someone who died a century ago," I said.

"Just look at the name. Isn't this the name they gave to my daughter?" she replied. Mr. Zeki, trying to gather himself, helped his wife up. We took them to the car. Metin, who was waiting inside the car, looked at me as if to ask,

"What's going on?" I couldn't say anything.

Mr. Zeki was silently crying. I told them to go to the outer gate by car and that I would stop by the office to get information. As the car drove away, I took a shortcut through the graves to reach the office building, passing in front of a pyramid-shaped tomb guarded by an angel and a sphinx. As I passed by, I noticed a crucified Jesus, a statue of a boy holding a holy book sitting on a stone chair caught my attention. Whatever those were, I suddenly startled when I came across a giant statue draped in a black metal cloak, covering its mouth with one arm, with only two large dark eyes visible. On the bronze background behind it, it read: "The Statue of Death." I paused for a moment, staring at the statue. I realized I was breathing death. People don't want to think about their own death, but in such an environment, is it possible not to feel the cold wind of death? I shivered and headed towards the stone building. The door was open. There was no one in the entrance area. Inside the hall, on one side were rows of chairs and a podium-like table, while on the other side were lined office desks.

A woman sitting alone at one of the tables said to me when she saw me,

"Hello, can I help you?"

"Yes," I said. Before I could finish my sentence, she picked up two brochures from the table and handed them to me.

"Look, these lists have the names and numbers of all the famous people buried here. Also, if you check the map, you can easily find the person you're looking for. If you came in a group, we can also arrange a car tour," said the middle-aged, unpleasant woman.

She was reciting these sentences in a lifeless, robotic manner. She probably thought we were tourists here to see the graves of the celebrities.

"No, we didn't come for a grave tour. We're looking for the grave of a friend who died thirteen days ago," I said, pointing to the car outside.

"Her family is waiting in the car. This person is referred to as 'Jane Doe.' It's a complicated situation.

"Upon hearing this, the surprised woman said, "I'm sorry, but she can't be here. You've come to the wrong place." As I thanked her and left, I glanced at the paper the woman had handed me. This cemetery covered a hundred acres of land. The list of important people buried here was impressive! Almost all the great figures who made Chicago what it is in the 1800s were gathered here: G. Pullman, the Marshalls, and even the famous Detective Pinkerton were buried here. I just didn't come across Al Capone's name. The paper stated that the valuable architect who signed the monuments in this cemetery also had his own grave here. As I exited the gate of this immense cemetery, I looked back one last time at this monument field and thought about how the silent citizens of Chicago, who turned a swamp into a metropolis, now lived here as a part of history. On the other hand, another voice inside me was involuntarily asking what else these thousands of people in the cemetery were, other than the bones that had merged with the earth six feet below, or the ashes that had been kept in closed vases for centuries, and I couldn't find an answer to this phenomenon. When I saw our car, which looked like a hearse, I realized that I was trying to distract myself with other thoughts to distance myself a little from Şermin Hanım's unbearable grief. With no other option, I helplessly got back into the car.

"They're not here," I said briefly.

Meanwhile, Metin, who was examining the paper given by the police again, said, "It will be Grace Cemetery. We were surprised by the similarity of the name. We came without even looking at the proper address, thinking I knew the place. There's another address written here." Zeki Bey seemed to be speaking in his sleep:

"Then let's go there."

When I sat next to Şermin Hanım, her vacant gaze and silent demeanor made me even more anxious. The place we were going to was at least half an hour away. Halfway, Metin suggested stopping somewhere to eat, but he received no response at first.

Then Mr. Zeki spoke in a very slow voice, "We don't have anything to eat, but you might be hungry," he said.

Actually, we were in no mood to eat either. Hoping to change the mood a bit, Metin stopped in front of a café so that we could at least have a drink. We calmly got out of the car, and as we sat down at an empty table inside, the now familiar Halloween decorations were once again in front of us. The hollowed-out, empty-mouthed grinning pumpkin on the counter and the witch puppet with a pointed cone and black broomstick were starting to get on our nerves.

Metin brought us all a hot cup of tea and put a plate of scones in the center. We were drinking our tea in silence when a costumed group entered. There were all of them, from skeletons to devils. One of them who was Dracula opened his mouth and showed us his long vampire fangs, thinking it was too much. We were caught in the hail while running away from the rain.

We put the sleepwalking parents back in the car and drove off into another fearful unknown, not even wanting to think about what we might encounter. It was the worst journey of my life. We pitied these people too much to say, "How did we get into this?"

When we arrived at the cemetery on Algonquin Street, we saw a completely different scene. It was a flat field of green grass. It didn't look as bleak as before; there was no monument. Names and dates were inscribed on stone plaques arranged in neat rows. Small wreaths of fresh flowers at the bedside of many, live flowers in vases, colorful windmills whirling in the wind gave the place a refreshing air. There was a flower greenhouse next door. Probably that's why the grass hadn't turned yellow and the flowers hadn't wilted.

As we moved silently and respectfully towards the tall glass buildings visible in front of us, Mrs. Şermin was reciting the Fatiha with both hands outstretched. Just then, what should we see but a hollowed-out pumpkin grinning at the head of a grave! These Americans are really crazy, I thought. Who would think of celebrating Halloween of a dead person like this!

Ignoring them, we entered the one slightly in front of the two adjoining buildings. There was no one in sight. It was empty and deserted. After looking around for a while, one of the doors opened. When a thin, old man asked, "Can I help you?" Metin handed him the official death certificate. The man read the paper, "Wait a minute," he said, and went back to his room.

Again, we were in the waiting period of an equation with many unknowns.

The old man must have gone back to his office to find out where Jane Doe was buried, based on the information written on the paper, we all commented inwardly.

How could we have guessed at that moment that we had not yet reached the last link in the chain of misfortunes?

Five minutes later, a thin man with white hair appeared with some papers in his hand. Metin asked,

"Were you able to locate him?"

"Yes," was all he said.

"Where is she?" I asked, this time impatiently. He handed the papers in his hand to Metin and asked him to go to the building next door and show these papers to the person there. We all went quietly to the building next door, which was a tall building decorated with marble. We entered through the big glass door.

To the right was a chapel. It must have been for a religious ceremony for the funeral. There were statues of Jesus and the Virgin Mary and large candles on a table. At the front was a stage-like place where the coffin was to be placed, with a small dais below and a row of sandalies lined up in front of it.

There was no one here. There was a long corridor on the left, and after a little while, we came to a door. The door stood half ajar. Metin knocked on the door, and a slow voice came from inside, "Come in," he said.

We went in. There was a desk in the room and a cupboard where I guessed the files were kept. There was also a computer on the table. A man with a yellow complexion, graying hair, who looked to be about sixty years old, who seemed to be busy at the computer, asked us, like everyone else, "How can I help you?" he said.

Metin handed all the papers in his hand and tried to explain in a confused way that we had come to visit the grave of a young girl named Ebru Erdem, and that the person identified as Jane

Doe on the papers was the same person. People here don't talk much for some reason. The man told us to sit on the chairs opposite for a few minutes.

First, he looked at the documents, then he searched for something on the computer. He asked about the family of the deceased. After writing down the names of the parents and some other things, he slowly got up and told us to follow him. We went into another corridor, the pale man wandering like the shadow of death, and we followed him.

Finally, he stopped in front of a large door and started to open it with the key he took out of his pocket. We were getting bored, thinking that the paperwork was not finished yet.

The door opened to reveal a large round room. Why had this man brought us here? After all, he was just going to show us a grave.

When we went inside and looked around, we saw that all of the cabinets were covered with shelves. Some of these cupboards were glass, built-in cupboards. On all these shelves, in the cupboard compartments, there were rows and rows of vase-like containers. Some of the cells on the wall were decorated with photographs, artificial flowers, tiny flags, and miniature statues and shrines made of white marble. On the shelves were wooden, even gold and silver framed name plates. Some of the vases were made of gold, silver, and precious stones such as sapphires; others were also made of marble. There were also earthenware, such as pots.

As the four of us looked around awkwardly, the man with the pale complexion said, "You are probably in a place like this for the first time. You look surprised."

Metin, getting bored, said, "Sir, I think there's a mistake. If you read the papers I gave you carefully, we came here to see the grave of Jane Doe, Ebru Erdem. As you can see, her family is in a very bad situation. Wouldn't it be better if you took us to the grave as soon as possible, without dragging this out any longer?"

Mr. Zeki and Ms. Şermin did not understand a word of what

was being said; they were silent like ghosts. They didn't even have the strength to ask questions.

The man with the yellow complexion had an extremely cold demeanor when he said, "I see. And I'll tell you, Jane Doe's remains - I will of course deliver them. But first, let his father sign this paper." Metin handed the paper and pen to Mr. Zeki for him to sign and pointed to the signature line. Mr. Zeki did as he was told as if he was living in a dream world. I was at the end of my patience.

"I guess we have nothing left to do now but go to the grave," I said. The pale man sounded a little angry, "Madam, that girl has no grave. I will deliver her ashes to you."

I was terrified once again. I realized I was biting my lip, and the only word that came out of my mouth was "Eyvah!" in Turkish.

Metin got angry and shouted,

"Who told you to burn her body to ashes? What right do you have?"

With a yellow face that was getting more and more distorted, he said,

"The dead body of this young girl was sent here from the hospital for burial. It is an unclaimed, unidentified body. We kept it in the morgue here for three days. No one came forward to claim it. According to the procedure, we couldn't keep it any longer. It was cremated in the crematorium next door. We temporarily keep the ashes for a while, and if no one claims it, we scatter the ashes in the cemetery. You are lucky; we hadn't done that yet."

Mr. Zeki had gotten into Ms. Şermin›s arms for support, but they could hardly stand. They thought we were going to leave here and go to the cemetery. But when I said, "Oh no!" they realized that something was wrong again. Two pairs of exhausted eyes were looking at me. Metin continued to hold the man to account:

"Why didn't you bury her somewhere but burned her? This is a child of a Muslim family; there is no such thing in our religion."

The pale one felt the need to explain in more detail: "How should we know what religion you are? And what are you saying? The funeral and cemetery costs at least three thousand dollars. Who's going to pay that? They buy their place here and pay in installments. Or they buy the marble drawers you see on the outside of this wall to put their ashes in.

"When orphaned corpses arrive in this way, they are first bled, then burned in an oven, and the ashes are kept in a container, in accordance with the rules. We have a very good organization and experts in this field.

"In case you don't know, every year the percentage of people who want cremation increases by twenty percent. Because it is cheaper. Look at these plastic containers, for example, twenty dollars. If you have money, you can choose gold, silver, and marble vessels. There are also earthenware ones. Anyway, I'll deliver your trust."

The man in yellow moved towards the shelves. While I was watching him to see which vase he would choose, Ebru suddenly appeared in front of me. It was as if her dream was in front of me. One rainy day, when she came to Cafe Bellini with a marble urn from the cemetery, I saw her exactly as I saw her in front of me. With her hair wet and that innocent smile on her face...

Reaching for the shelves, the man's weak hand picked up neither marble, nor earth, nor a wooden vase. All the man had in his hand was a small cardboard box. A label was stuck on the box; the label read "Jane Doe", the date of death, and a number.

One shock after another, like the aftershocks of a great earthquake, continued to shake us. Metin and I looked at each other. What were we going to say to these poor people? "Here is your daughter in this cardboard box?" What were we going to say? We looked at the faces of Ms. Şermin and Mr. Zeki; we were experiencing one of the most difficult moments of our lives.

Metin could hardly muster all his courage,

"Mr. Zeki, I don't know what to say. I don't have the strength anymore. We are receiving the body now. They cremate the unclaimed dead here. Their ashes were in this box. I'm sorry, I didn't know how to tell you," he said.

The father, thoroughly distraught, began to tremble before he could hear the end of the sentence. He could hardly stand on his feet. Hearing the same words, Ms. Şermin suddenly collapsed. The pale man and I embraced Ms. Şermin and carried her to the armchair outside. Metin took Mr. Zeki's arm and led him outside, holding the cardboard box containing Ebru's ashes in one hand.

The ashes of the unfortunate Ebru were not even placed in a marble urn like the one she held in her hand when she was alive.

Poppy Field

Thirteen days ago, on that ominous rainy night, Ebru had left her home in Sheridan, closed all the doors of her life one by one, and traveled to Cafe Bellini on a bus with other people who had lost themselves, and then disappeared into the darkness after making a choice.

After walking for a while, she found hersself by the lake, in the park where she and Umut sometimes came. The rain had stopped. There was only a slight cool breeze. Couples making love in cars parked against the lake were vaguely visible. She sat on a wet and cold rock. The white foamy waves of the dark waters had calmed down. Everything in front of her now looked like a black-and-white photograph. But she wanted to experience other colors and shades. She couldn't.

What she valued more than life itself was love and affection. There could be very few people on earth who could understand the innocence of this person who surrendered herself to her loved ones without preconditions.

With every event that happened to her, something of herself, of her own self, was lost, and she eventually consumed herself. Her brain and she did not calculate that her soul was not strong enough to handle these difficulties.

She was a stranger to everything, even to herself. What had happened to the principles, those beautiful values she believed in as she wrote in her notebook? I thought that if you gave love, you would receive love. I thought that humanity would endure and last with justice. What foolishness it was to believe that if you were good to yourself, everyone would be good to you. There was nothing left to believe in anymore, not even in herself. After losing all his values, all that remained was a body she hated. She had to cut her vital ties with that too.

As her eyes lingered on the still waters of the lake, she did not see two dark figures get out of a car parked next to her in the twilight and approach him.

One of the men called out: "Hey, baby! What are you doing all alone?" She didn't get any answer. The other one with a beer bottle said, "Let's have fun together, you're cold, come into the car."

After waiting for a while, when the young girl again did not make a sound, they took her by the arm on both sides and dragged her towards the car.

"Are you sick? Let's give you a ride home, tell me where your home is?" No sound again. They put her in the back seat of the car. The one in the back next to her, the one in the front said, "Turn on the heater, let her warm up a little bit, let her come to her senses."

The driver started the engine, turned on the heat. Before he turned up the volume on the radio, a rap music was playing.

In the car with no clear destination, the two friends asked Ebru one question after another along the way, but they could not get an answer to any of their questions. She didn't speak; she was silent. The two men, who were getting drunker and drunker as they drank beer, said,

"I wonder if we are with a looney?" and laughed and had fun with the music.

After traveling a long way, they came to a deserted place. This was at the other end of the same lake. I have no imagination to guess what happened there. Or I don't even want to think about it.

The young girl, who had lost consciousness for a while, turned away from these unknown men and looked over a rock into the waters of the night. There she saw the poppy field where she had played as a child. In her white dress and with a white ribbon tied in her long hair, she was running through the red poppies, trying to catch the colorful butterflies.

Realizing that the girl had disappeared into the waters, the two men, frightened, left the place in a hurry and promised each other to keep the secret.

Two days later, the authorities were notified of the body of a young woman washed ashore after it was spotted by several people out on a sailboat on the lake.

Based on my intuition and guesses, I connected the disconnected links of Ebru's life chain with events I witnessed and events I did not. Why had Ebru suddenly run away from Elvira's house? Were there other things she didn't write in her notebook? She thought she had found the peace of mind she was looking for in the church and with Dr. Benjamin - why had she suddenly given up? Why had she told Ozgur about the Child Jesus in church? Did she feel remorse for the baby she had destroyed? Why had she deemed herself unworthy of Umut's pure love? I leave the judgment on these matters to my readers. But I believe in one thing; in the poppy field where Ebru found the peace she was looking for, she is still chasing butterflies...

Note: One can think of this as a hope: Maybe those ashes do not belong to Ebru, since no DNA test has been done. Who knows, she may be living quietly somewhere, erasing her bad memories.

Sixteen Years Later

Sixteen years have passed. One day, I felt like visiting the old Cafe Bellini. I quickly found the two-story building number two thousand nine hundred and thirteen on North Clark Street. The new name of the restaurant is "Duke of Ferth."

I entered with an indescribable feeling of entering a historical place. Everything had changed except the white French chairs from our time. The person who bought the building from us was a Scotsman. Reflecting his culture and personality, this place looked like a Scottish pub.

We sat on the bench in the mirrored corner where I used to like to sit. Music was playing softly. It was neither Julio Iglesias, İbrahim Tatlıses, nor Sezen Aksu. It was Scottish music with bagpipes. On the wall behind the bar, a huge antlered stag's head stared mournfully with its dead eyes. On the other walls were paintings of lush green Scotland, pictures of hunting with horses and dogs, photos of Scottish soldiers in plaid skirts, and old family photos in black and white... Old clocks, old books, and many other antiques lined the shelves.

A slim young girl, Ebru's age, with blonde hair and blue eyes, smilingly said, "Hello," and approached our table. As she handed us menus, she was explaining the specialty of the day. I told her that we were the former owners of this building and that I wanted to see the back sections. "With pleasure," she said. In the second hall, there was no trace of our sea decor. There were old-style long tables and chairs reminiscent of the Middle Ages. Everything had changed, but the walls, ceiling, windows, and garden were the same.

Sixteen years ago, the voices, laughter, crying, sadness, and anger of people from various parts of the world, with whom our lives intersected in the same time period and in the same place, must have permeated these walls. Who knows who and what lived here in the years that followed? If only these walls could speak...

When I sat down again, I ordered a Scottish beer and the fish that the waitress raved about. There was no one else in the restaurant because we had arrived early, at noon. As we ate, all my memories of this place and the people in these memories emerged from the most hidden corners of my brain. My brain kept no secrets like these walls.

I don't know what happened to Metin's fairies in this building, but my ghosts filled the place. They all came to life one by one.

At a small table near the bar, Peter and Adrianne are sitting, talking animatedly. Elizabeth, with her pink face, is waiting at the head of them to take Peter's order for a new cognac. Next to them, Mark and James are drinking wine.

At a large table by the wall, Dr. Yılmaz, Serap, Kemal Bey, and his wife Karen are eating shish kebab. Dr. Yılmaz gestures as he describes his latest surgery and reminds his wife that he sent flowers to the funeral of a patient who died young last week. Serap and Karen look around and burst into raucous laughter.

On the other side, immaculately dressed, white-haired Moshe and his elegant wife Miranda are drinking their coffee.

Mr. Sinan, the Hittite Professor, and Gaye are also here. While the professor is absent-mindedly listening to Turkish music, Gaye is still cursing life.

In the second hall, the old lawyer Bernie and his wife Joan, the real estate tycoon Lou, and his wife Debby, and other real estate agents are talking seriously about business. With a sad smile, Ebru serves them.

Umut walks around with one eye on Ebru and one eye on the mirror, holding a tray.

The happy Swedish couple, the Arab girl and her boyfriend, continue their seemingly endlessly cheerful conversation in the corners. The grumpy Sherveen sits alone, sullen, in the garden.

Zeynep sits at the center table with a troubled Turkish family, listening to their problems.

Ms. Özge brought the spouses of the newly arrived consulate officials and gave them information about Chicago.

Everybody's here now. Ray flies like a butterfly, carrying drinks to the customers. Cemil Abi secretly drinks beer while he works. Soon his American wife will show up.

Cook Ibrahim (Toni) looks around the hall through the small kitchen window in his white chef's hat. He needs to find out who came and what they did for the next day's gossip.

Suddenly they all disappeared from my sight. I could only see Ebru's mother, Ms. Şermin, and her father, Mr. Zeki, crying in a corner. I closed my eyes tightly, and when I opened them again, they had disappeared just like my other ghosts...

And where are these people now? What happened to them? Six months after the Ebru incident, Metin sold this building. He left the running of the restaurant to Toni and Elizabeth. Like two tightropes don't walk on the same tightrope, the two shrewd money-makers eventually went bankrupt, one week one week and the other the next, robbing the cash register themselves. Unable to pay even the rent, they lost the restaurant with all their belongings through foreclosure. Toni, Ibrahim, the cook, returned to Turkey. They didn't hang him there, but they made him do two years of military service. Then we heard that he returned to his village, got married, and had children. Now he has found a new source of income by sending people from Turkey to America with money.

One day, years ago, I ran into Elizabeth in Downtown, near the immigration building. She was wearing a fur coat. She asked about Toni. She was mad at him for stealing her money. I asked her what she did for a living. She married newly arrived Poles for green cards for ten thousand dollars.

Peter refused Adrianne's request for a child. After a short time, he went bankrupt and returned to Greece. Adrianne gave birth to twins with a man she found in a bar.

Lawyer Freed died at the age of eighty-six without having had his fill of the world. His wife Joan went to Israel.

Lou, a real estate tycoon, continued to buy buildings in Chicago and elsewhere. His beautiful young wife left him after she owned most of the properties.

Dr. Yılmaz and Mr. Kemal separated from their wives. One of them bought their wives an expensive car and the other a new diamond ring, but to no avail. The ladies did not return to their ex-husbands.

Moshe and Miranda left in love. Miranda started to work as a teacher somewhere, but it didn't last long. Later, when Moshe learned that she was miserable, he moved her into an apartment in Florida because he still loved her. In recent years, I have heard that Miranda is in a nursing home. Moshe is now living a happy retirement life with his newfound friends.

We heard that Ray, the gay waiter, had fallen ill a few years later and was hospitalized. We suspected that he had contracted that fatal disease.

Professor Sinan returned to Germany with his wife and children. I never found out what happened to Gaye.

Ms. Özge retired from the Turkish Consulate. She still works successfully in various associations to promote Turkey in Chicago.

Zeynep is one of those who left her husband. She reunited with him. While dealing with her new job and children, she continues to help the Turkish community in any way she can.

Umut left Cafe Bellini shortly after Ebru's death, unable to bear the pain. Years later, one day I met him at the consulate. He had married an American stripper. They had a daughter. They named her Ebru. He started working as a real estate agent. He remembered he owed me a hundred dollars. I told him to forget it. He was trying to look happy.

Ebru's friend Aslı was very sad when she heard what happened to Ebru. Believing that she was partly responsible for this tragic outcome, she felt remorse but did not show it to anyone. After graduating from university in Boston and getting her master's degree, she returned to Turkey. She got a good job. In a short time, she married the son of one of Izmir's well-known and wealthy families.

Another person who felt more remorse than Aslı was Ebru's husband, Hakan. The day after we contacted the police, Hakan Yıldırım was located. The young man, who was trying to get rich through swindling, had been arrested and imprisoned in Los Angeles for fraud he had committed in a carpet business with Arabs around the time he had to leave Ebru because he was wanted. He didn't let anyone know that he was in jail. Hakan, who got out after serving two years in prison, believed that he was to blame for Ebru's death and carried the painful memories of his beautiful wife in his own prison.

As for Ms. Şermin and Mr. Zeki, after losing their daughter in an unbelievable way, they returned home after making the most painful journey of their lives. They buried Ebru's remains in a cemetery in her homeland. Before they left, Metin took her ashes out of the cardboard box and put them in a marble box. According to what I heard, the grieving family did not recover for a long time and were never the same. Ebru's brother became an engineer, got married, and even had a daughter, but they didn't name her Ebru to avoid a similar fate.

During this time, there have been many changes and developments among the Turks in Chicago. In the last ten years, Turkish-American traffic has intensified considerably. THY flights even started. The number of incoming students increased rapidly. Graduate students, those doing research, those looking for a job, those looking for adventure have multiplied.

Instead of a handful of Turks trying to undermine each other, there is now a more conscious Turkish community that knows what it wants. The quality of the growing Turkish population in

America has gradually improved. Slowly, albeit belatedly, the Turkish presence has begun to be felt in every field. Especially in Chicago, the contributions of our valuable Turkish doctors, TACA, and our volunteer friends who have been very active in various associations have been great. We can even say that we now have senatorial candidates. These developments are really pleasing. Oh, if only there was not the other side of the American coin!

I would like to talk a little bit about our diplomats who came and went during this period. Some of these people sent by the Republic of Turkey saved money, some of them educated their children, some of them took care of their health problems, and some of them actually worked within the limited time they stayed here.

In these sixteen years, this city has seen many important and famous Turkish visitors. In addition to a now deceased president, we have welcomed many ministers, members of parliament, mayors, and large delegations. Some of these official visitors stayed for months and received treatment for health problems. Some of them stayed in the most luxurious hotels and shopped in the most expensive stores to increase their knowledge and manners. Some of them gave speeches in abundance.

It was the artists and scientists who added color, excitement, and meaning to our lives. Famous writers, musicians, comedians, athletes, and actors have left their mark.

Turkish schools and courses with a religious identity were also opened and started operating in Chicago. Sects proliferated. Turkish-owned businesses and restaurants have increased in recent years. Turks started doing business with each other and supporting each other. I think most of the newcomers no longer feel as lonely and desperate as the pioneers who first arrived.

Chicagoans, who have made history with their determination, must not have been able to digest losing the title of having the tallest building in the world to Malaysia, and while they were preparing new projects to become number one in this regard again, my husband Metin, who has the same spirit, has become the most successful Turkish businessman in Chicago in the meantime. I believe he deserves the title.

As for me, Filiz, I continue to write in my Chicago diary, reminding expatriates that this bright city, which has brought down the stars in the sky, also has dark streets full of life mines, while I live a quiet, happy life in my house outside the city, alone with nature.

THE END

www.ingramcontent.com/pod-product-compliance
Lightning Source LLC
Chambersburg PA
CBHW010443170726
48283CB00011B/3329